A RIVIERA RETREAT

JENNIFER BOHNET

Boldwood

First published in Great Britain in 2020 by Boldwood Books Ltd.

Copyright © Jennifer Bohnet, 2020

Cover Design by Debbie Clement Design

Cover Photography: Shutterstock

A CIP catalogue record for this book is available from the British Library.

Paperback ISBN 978-1-83889-187-9

Ebook ISBN 978-1-83889-189-3

Kindle ISBN 978-1-83889-188-6

Audio CD ISBN 978-1-83889-246-3

MP3 CD ISBN 978-1-83889-690-4

Digital audio download ISBN 978-1-83889-186-2

Boldwood Books Ltd
23 Bowerdean Street
London SW6 3TN
www.boldwoodbooks.com

To Richard with love

PROLOGUE

A restless Amy Martin wandered alone through Belle Vue Villa one Sunday afternoon in late March, lost deep in her memories and regrets. Today, the fifth anniversary of the opening of 'Bell Vue Retreat', was bittersweet in so many ways. She opened the kitchen door and stood on the terrace looking out over the garden towards the Mediterranean Sea glinting in the afternoon sunshine in the distance. Situated high up in the hills behind Cannes, Belle Vue Villa, one of the smaller belle époque villas along the coast, had enviable views overlooking the sea and over to the Esterel Mountains.

Standing there, Amy sniffed the air and looked around her appreciatively. The perfume from the several mimosa trees in the garden wafted past her, courtesy of the gentle onshore breeze. Amy thought, not for the first time, how life could surprise you with its endless unexpected twists and turns. Some bad. Some good.

The death of Aunt Tasha, her mother Fleur's older sister, had been so sad, but leaving her Belle Vue had been a wonderful surprise – and something of a lifesaver. The two siblings had remained close throughout their lives, but whilst Fleur had stayed near to home when she married, Tasha had followed the love of her life to France and embraced everything that country had to offer. Amy remembered countless family summers spent in Belle Vue Villa, listening to the two sisters reminiscing about their eccentric childhood in the wilds of Somerset.

Fleur had been devastated by her sister's early death, telling Amy she'd always known that the villa was to be left to her because a childless Tasha had adored her. 'It's just that none of us expected it to happen so soon,' she'd cried.

Walking alone into the hauntingly silent villa the day the notaire had handed her the keys, knowing it was now hers, Amy had failed to stop the tears flowing. Tears of sorrow but also of guilt. She'd seen so little of Tasha in the last few years. They'd talked regularly and Fleur had kept her up to date with Tasha's news and later her illness, but Amy had rarely visited. Pressure of work had been her prime excuse, although sadly not the full truth. The guilt that had flooded her body after that last hospital visit to see Tasha had been painful. The fact that Belle Vue had enabled her to escape her old life and create a new one for herself gave her an overwhelming feeling of gratitude. Knowing it was the direct result of Aunt Tasha dying though was the hardest thing to bear and accept. A true bittersweet inheritance.

Tasha had run Belle Vue Villa as a successful auberge after Francois, her husband, had died and Amy knew that the villa would have to continue to earn its keep for her in the future. Rather than having holidaymakers turn up willy-nilly looking for a bed, Amy decided to focus on offering short retreats for writers and painters throughout the year. That way she'd always know how busy she'd be – with the added bonus of not having to worry about unexpected or unwanted strangers knocking on the door at all times of the day or night.

Lots of Tasha's guests had left comments in the visitor's book over the years, saying how special the house felt; how serene the atmosphere around the place was; several had said the villa was definitely a little French paradise. Amy had vowed to herself that she would do her utmost to keep the lovely ambiance that Tasha had masterfully created in and around the villa, while she endeavoured to put her own stamp on the place.

Five years on, Amy knew she could feel proud of what she'd achieved at Belle Vue. The auberge was now a popular venue as a retreat for artists and writers and it was her guests who left compliments in the visitor's book and were returning time and time again. One particular writer had returned four times last year, saying she wrote more in a week when staying there than she wrote in a month at home. Amy knew Tasha would be proud and thrilled for her at the way the retreat had found its place in a niche market and taken off so well.

Turning back into the kitchen, Amy picked up the photo of her aunt that stood on the dresser and gently touched it. She owed Tasha so much. Thoughtfully, she replaced the photo. But how to show that gratitude? Tasha had always drummed into her the notion 'it's easy to take, but you must always, always give back too'. Amy knew that if Tasha had still been alive, she'd have wholeheartedly endorsed the current 'do a random act of kindness for a stranger' memes that seemed to appear every day on social media.

Amy smiled, remembering how Tasha had thoroughly embraced social media, joining groups, signing up for causes and having hundreds of friends on Facebook. Amy also knew her grateful act of 'paying it back' was long overdue, but despite thinking about it for weeks, months, not a single idea had surfaced. Nothing she thought of seemed grateful enough.

She glanced at the kitchen clock. A little early, but she'd open the bottle of wine she'd bought especially for today and leave it to breathe for a while. Opening a bottle of wine and silently toasting Tasha while watching the DVD of the film *Enchanted April* was a ritual that always finished off this particular day for Amy. Tasha had introduced her to the film and together they had watched it countless times.

As the credits rolled at the end of the film, Amy switched off the DVD, poured the last of the wine into her glass and opened her laptop, her head spinning not only from the wine she'd drunk but also with the perfect idea of how to give something back. To finally thank the universe for her good fortune.

Like the film she'd just watched, where an advertisement drew four women together, all strangers to each other, for a holiday in an Italian castle in the 1920s, her random act of kindness would begin with an advertisement too. Not in a newspaper but on twenty-first century social media.

Are you a woman who longs to spend time in retreat? Or simply in need of a holiday?

Answer the following question: Who wrote the book *Enchanted April*, and in less than one hundred words say which character you identify with most and why you need to win a holiday (June 6–16) at a retreat in the countryside behind the French Riviera. Travel expenses not included but low-cost flights are available to Nice. Transport to and from the airport will be arranged. Please note the date of the holiday on offer is NOT changeable or transferable.

Competition closes midnight the 31st of this month.

Three lucky winners will be notified by email within one week of the competition closing.

* * *

A week later on the first of the following month, Amy opened the file she'd saved all the entries in and began sorting through the replies. All sixty-five of them. Quite a respectable number, considering the details had been on Facebook for such a short time. Some entries she discarded immediately – either the answer to the question was incorrect or the writer was clearly blagging in the hope of winning a holiday. One entry even brazenly stated 'no idea of the answers, but I need a holiday so would be very grateful to win.'

Amy printed out the rest of the entries, numbering the pages individually from one to fifty-seven as the printer threw them out into the tray. Then she tore up some paper into small pieces before numbering those too, from one to fifty-seven and placing them all in a deep cake tin with a lid and shaking it violently for several seconds. Carefully, she took the lid off, closed her eyes tightly and plucked out three random pieces of paper. When she opened her eyes and looked, she'd picked out numbers 13, 27 and 41.

Flicking through the printouts, she identified the corresponding numbers:

Number 13 was a Vicky Lewis from London.

Number 27 was a Chelsea Newman from Bristol.

Number 41 was a Matilda Richardson, also from Bristol

Opening her laptop, Amy emailed the three women to tell them the good news. Paying back her good fortune had officially started.

1

Vicky Pinehill, née Lewis, had the house to herself for the evening. Something that was happening several times a week now the children were older and out and about living their own lives. It had been strange at first to find herself with the odd hour not spoken for – the time hers to do with as she wished. With both Tom and Suzie out working now, time to call her own had increased. Time that Anthony had already suggested she used to get more involved with the constituency, take on more of the paperwork for him – in effect become even more of a full-time politician's wife. Of course, Vicky supported Anthony in every way she could, but she didn't relish the thought of taking on more responsibility in his political life. Politics was his life, not hers.

Although it had to be said that Anthony himself didn't seem that happy these days either. His initial euphoria the day he'd won his seat and promised 'to do his best for everyone' had gradually disappeared. Killed, Vicky suspected, by the mountain of bureaucracy he was faced with on a day to day basis. If she did take on more of the office side of things, it would free him up to concentrate fully on the things that were important to him. And leave her life still in the rut she was beginning to feel desperate to escape from.

Vicky sighed. After all the years of being a mum and a wife, surely it was her turn now? She wanted, she realised, to be Vicky Lewis again. To find the girl she'd once been. To pick up the pieces of the life she'd abandoned when she became pregnant and married Anthony. She'd enjoyed her short foray into the world of books and publishing after university, but she didn't particularly want to go back into that world. At least not from the same angle. She'd always longed to write and she'd had this idea for a novel for ages now. Had even started to scribble sentences and scenes down in a notebook she kept hidden in her bag but there always seemed to be something more important to attend to when she had time to spare.

She searched the wooden cabinet underneath the television where they kept their collection of DVDs. A Facebook advertisement she'd seen a few days ago for a competition to win a retreat type holiday in the South of France had reminded her of one of her all time favourite films, *Enchanted April*. While Anthony was in Westminster this evening for a crucial vote and both the children were out, she was going to pour herself a glass of wine and lose herself in a gentle story set in a world she suspected sadly no longer existed. Bliss.

Two hours later as the closing credits faded away, Vicky sighed. Italy in the 1920s must have been wonderful. Replacing the DVD back in its case, she picked up her laptop and logged on to Facebook. Looking at the competition questions again, she briefly wondered whether it was genuine or just a con to bombard people with dodgy internet holiday sites.

The question who wrote the book was easy – Elizabeth

von Arnim – rumoured to have been the lover of H. G. Wells at one time.

Which character did she identify with the most? Lady Caroline Dester was too young. Lottie Wilkins? A bit perhaps, but she didn't have children. Mrs Fisher was too old, so it would have to be Rose who spent a lot of her time with children and did good works.

Vicky smiled to herself. Apart from two mornings a week in the local charity shop, she didn't do good works per se, she left that to Anthony, but she'd done her child rearing duties – anyway, she had a soft spot for Miranda Richardson, the actress who played Rose, ever since her days of Queenie in *Blackadder*.

But as for the reason why she should win a holiday, that was difficult. The question made her feel selfish and self-indulgent. There were far more deserving people out there; people who couldn't afford to go away; people who needed to get away. She simply wanted some time on her own to gather her thoughts and make a plan of what she wanted to do. Not necessarily for the rest of her life, but for the next few years at least.

A holiday in a retreat would give her the ideal opportunity to think things through, have time to concentrate on her writing and to decide whether or not she could actually write a novel. Shame it wasn't in Italy like the film, but the South of France was a good substitute. And those particular days at the beginning of summer were perfect. Tom and Suzie would be busy at work and Parliament would still be sitting, so Anthony wouldn't have much free time to miss her. It wouldn't hurt the three of them to look after themselves for once. Maybe she'd ask Anthony's mother to come and stay.

The fact that the competition questions were based around a favourite film must surely mean she'd be on the same wavelength as other people should she win? Which was unlikely as she'd never won anything in her life – oh wait. Once, on holiday, she'd hooked a plastic duck at a fairground to win a goldfish in a plastic bag, but her mother had vetoed accepting it as it would only die before they could get it home and into a proper bowl. She remembered howling all the way back to their holiday chalet.

Oh, blow it. She'd send an entry off in her maiden name, Vicky Lewis. The chances of her actually winning were what? Probably as high as the odds of her winning the lottery. But, and it wasn't a big but Vicky realised, when she didn't win, she'd find a cheap B&B somewhere on the coast and do an Agatha Christie for those ten days at the beginning of June.

2

Hiding away from the world every evening in her small flat after the mammoth fallout that had occurred in her life, Chelsea Newman spent a lot of hours on her laptop. She flipped through endless Facebook pages, read all the fake news and entered mindless giveaways and competitions. None of which helped her to forget how stupid and gullible she'd been, behaving like a teenager rather than a twenty-three year old woman with her own business. At least her father hadn't heard about the disaster that was her personal life yet, and she prayed every night that he never would. She could imagine his sorrow, mixed with disdain at her actions, if there were to be repercussions for the business. Especially after the way he'd supported Elsie and her.

She and Elsie, best friends since catering college, had been keen to set up their own bijou cordon-bleu catering business. When the bank had taken one look at their business plan and refused them the necessary loan, her father had made them an offer they couldn't refuse, despite Chelsea wanting to do things independently.

A successful and shrewd businessman, Simon Newman offered to bankroll them and give them six months interest free credit to help them get the business underway. Chelsea accepted only after she'd extracted a promise from him that he wouldn't interfere with the way she and Elsie ran it. So far, he'd stuck to his word.

They'd done very little advertising, relying on their cooking to be their best advertisement for spreading the word. Just two years later, and they'd found their niche in the growing demand for weekday lunchtime functions and the occasional evening cocktail party. They employed one full-timer, Tina, who helped in the kitchen and two casual part-timers to help serve the food at functions. They were paying back the loan and Chelsea was planning to move out of her rented flat at the end of summer and buy one of the apartments in the new development on the edge of town.

To celebrate the anniversary of the business Simon had taken her out for an expensive evening – theatre followed by dinner – telling her how proud he was of her success. Neither of them mentioned her mother. Elsie had, of course, been invited but couldn't come the only evening Simon was available.

Meeting Kit three months ago had been the icing on the cake for her. Tall, blond and too handsome for his own good, she kept pinching herself at her good luck in meeting him. Chelsea couldn't believe that he liked her as much as she adored him. Of course, with him working and travelling a lot as a publishing representative, they didn't see each other as often as Chelsea would like. Kit did text or phone every evening though and that kept her going from one date to the next.

Her own life was in a happy place but she was becoming increasingly worried about Elsie. On the surface she was still the same, but Chelsea had sensed that something was troubling her – something that Elsie had refused to talk about when Chelsea had tackled her. She'd simply shrugged and insisted there wasn't anything wrong. Chelsea knew that she was going to have to insist soon that they sat down together and get Elsie to explain what was troubling her She hoped and prayed it wasn't a case of Elsie wanting out. The success of the business was down to her as much as to Chelsea – and she doubted that she could manage it on her own.

Absently scrolling on down through Facebook, Chelsea saw another competition ad – this time for a free holiday in the South of France. She clicked on the details. She'd never heard of either the book or the film called *Enchanted April*, but five minutes on the internet and Google had given her the author's name, a list of characters and a summary of the plot. Which sounded decidedly old-fashioned, in her opinion. The only character she could possibly identify with would be Lady Caroline Dester – simply because she appeared to be the youngest.

As for why she needed the holiday – that bit was easy. She simply wrote, 'I've messed up my life spectacularly and need to get away, regroup and lick my wounds.' A quick read through and she pressed the enter button. Highly unlikely she'd win, but dreaming about a holiday in the South of France was better than wallowing in the despair she was currently feeling.

If anyone had asked her how life was a week ago, Chelsea would have replied with an enthusiastic, 'It's super, great.' And it had been. Then, without warning, it had fallen apart.

It had been a Friday lunchtime and she and Elsie had taken a late booking to do a champagne buffet lunch for twenty in one of the prestigious office blocks down on the waterside near the town centre. Apparently it was to be a surprise for the sales team after the best month ever, the plummy voiced woman placing the booking had explained.

'I do hope you're free. You've been highly recommended and if you're as good as rumours suggest, you could become our regular caterers. We entertain a lot.'

'It's very short notice and we do have another buffet luncheon already booked in for this Friday,' Chelsea had said, hating the thought of turning a prospective regular customer away. 'But we can certainly supply an array of finger food and champagne. Our basic price for twenty people is—'

'Cost is not important but quality is,' the woman had cut her off. 'I want the best. Be at the office with everything set up, ready to serve, by twelve thirty.'

Chelsea went to say a polite goodbye and had realised the line was dead. What was the woman on? Barely forty-eight-hours' notice and rude with it. Maybe she was just having a bad day. If she was as rude face to face on Friday, then catering for her would definitely be a one off; they didn't need clients like her.

Friday morning, Chelsea and Elsie had arrived early at the offices and a friendly receptionist had shown them into the function room. Elsie, Chelsea was pleased to see, seemed to be like her old self, happily telling Chelsea about a party she'd been to the evening before where she'd met this man, Angus, whom she really liked and was seeing at the weekend. By 12.25, the food was laid out and bottles of the already chilled champagne were in their ice buckets. Thankfully there had been no sign of the rude woman so far.

At 12.30, the receptionist had poked her head around the door. 'Everyone's on their way.'

Minutes later, the room was crowded with people and

Chelsea and Elsie were busy pouring drinks and handing food around.

Chelsea handed a glass of champagne to a woman, who thanked her before turning to the man at her side. 'Where's the boss and golden boy then? Isn't it his sales figures we're supposed to be celebrating?'

The man had shrugged. 'Office door is locked. Imagine they'll be congratulating each other in the usual way. Don't know why he puts up with it.'

The woman had almost choked on her drink. 'Come off it. It's one of the reasons they're married. She's a right nymphomaniac. And he's more than happy to oblige, especially after being away all week.' Picking up a bite-size onion and fish tartlet, the woman had moved away.

'Nymphomaniac? They can't be talking about the rude woman, can they?' Chelsea had whispered to Elsie as she carefully uncorked another bottle of champagne.

Seconds later and the hub of chatter that filled the room went down a decibel as a blonde woman walked in purposefully.

'Hi, everyone. Chris will be along in a moment. He has no idea that he's the inspiration behind this week's celebration,' she said, glancing across to Chelsea and Elsie and the table where the food was laid out. She had made her way over to them. 'It all looks delicious,' she said. 'I'm Marcia and I'll have a glass of champagne please – which of you ladies is Chelsea?'

'That would be me,' Chelsea had said, smiling and handing her a glass. 'Enjoy.'

'I intend to. Ah, Chris, you're here. I thought you deserved a surprise this week,' Marcia had said, turning to face her husband as he appeared at her side. 'I know you've already helped yourself to the caterer, but feel free to help yourself to some champagne and food. Oh, not hungry? I wonder why?'

She had turned to look at a pale Chelsea, who was clutching the table for support and staring at the man she knew as Kit.

'I rarely mix business with pleasure, but I've made an exception on this occasion,' Marcia had added. 'Two things. One: stay away from my husband. And two: don't bother to send me an invoice for today's lunch as I have no intention of paying you. You can sue me if you want, but I doubt that you will.' And with that, Marcia had jerked her head in Kit's direction and swept out.

Chelsea had watched, frozen into silence as Kit, without a backward glance, had hurried after his wife, before she'd collapsed as the enormity of what had just happened hit her.

3

Slipping on a patch of ice on the pavement outside the library the last week in January and breaking her ankle meant that a disgruntled Matilda Richardson was confined to her flat with time on her hands. Even the view across the Downs, with its glimpse of the magnificent Clifton Suspension Bridge that had enticed her and William to buy the flat in the first place, failed to lift her spirits. But it was the dependence on others that irked her the most.

She knew she wasn't good at hiding her irritation at her neighbour, Sheila's good natured bossiness and the taking over of her day to day life for weeks on end. She was grateful to Sheila, truly she was. Life with a broken ankle would have been a lot harder without her, but Matilda's independent streak always made it difficult for her to ask for help from anyone. Josh, her son, being the exception, but as he was away working with the environmental group Sea Shepherd for another month or two, she simply had to submit to Sheila's kindness – even if she did feel guilty about accepting everything she did for her.

It wasn't as if she and Sheila had been close friends before the accident. Friendly acquaintances, yes. Since William's death, they'd enjoyed the occasional coffee together in the café in the mall when they happened to meet up. But friends who talked about more than the weather or the state of the country under this useless government, no, they weren't friends like that.

Matilda had had few close female friends since school. The idea of going on a girls' night out had never appealed and she'd definitely prefer to go without the proverbial borrowed cup of sugar if she ran out rather than knock on a neighbour's door. Consequently, she'd had no best friend to call on in her hour of need, but Sheila had stepped up to the mark. Matilda resolved to find her a nice gift once she was back on her feet and life took on its normal routine again. Normal routine. Matilda sighed. The trouble was her normal routine, even pre-broken ankle, had become somewhat dull and uninspiring.

Throughout their married life, she and William had never felt the need for a large social circle, mainly preferring their own company, and that of Josh, when he was home. But being a widow was proving to be a lonely state and it was only now, unexpectedly confined to the flat with time on her hands and nothing to do except read and watch DVDs, that Matilda began to wonder about the rest of her life. At twenty-eight, Josh, her only son, was showing no signs of settling down and having a family, so grandmother duties were unlikely to feature in her near future.

A knock on the unlocked door interrupted her thoughts and Sheila bustled in for the second time that day.

'Coffee time. I brought us each a slice of the coffee and walnut cake I made last night. I hope you like it,' and she set the tray down on the table in front of Matilda.

'Thank you,' Matilda said, smothering a groan and accepting a plate. 'I'm going to be the size of a house if you keep feeding me cake every day.'

'Nonsense, there's nothing of you. Especially compared to me,' Sheila sighed, looking down at her own ample body.

'When this is healed,' Matilda said, pointing to the black box around her ankle that had replaced the plaster cast, 'maybe you'd like to come walking with me?' Not being able to go on her usual daily march across the Downs was, she knew, adding to her current frustration.

'I'd enjoy that,' Sheila said hesitantly. 'You know that DVD you lent me last week? *Enchanted April*?'

Matilda nodded. 'You said you really enjoyed it.'

'Oh, I did. Love gentle period dramas like that. There was a competition on Facebook yesterday. Did you see it?'

'No.'

'The questions were all to do with that story.' Sheila paused. 'So I've entered.'

'Good for you. What's the prize?'

'A ten day holiday in June, to a retreat in the south of France.'

'Sounds wonderful. I hope you win – you deserve a holiday after all you've done for me,' Matilda said.

'It's not for me – I couldn't possibly go anywhere like that. No, I've entered in your name.'

Matilda looked at Sheila, stunned. 'What?'

'It would be a nice place for you to finish convalescing. The chances of you winning are quite low, I should imagine, but I thought I'd better tell you just in case.'

'What were the questions?'

'Author name, which character you identify with and why you need a holiday. For that last one, I said you lived alone, had broken your ankle and really needed time to recuperate and that *Enchanted April* was your favourite film.'

Matilda didn't have to ask which character Sheila had linked her to. It would be the haughty and difficult Mrs Fisher, without a doubt.

She sighed. 'Like you say, winning is extremely unlikely, but thank you for thinking of me. Is there any coffee left in the jug?'

Extremely unlikely it may have been, but the day Matilda was finally discharged by her doctor and told to take it easy for a couple more weeks, Sheila ran into the flat waving a piece of paper.

'You've won, you've won! You're going on retreat to the South of France.'

DAY ONE OF THE HOLIDAY – JUNE 6

4

Amy parked the car in the multistorey and, making her way out, crossed the main road and went down the flight of metal steps that took her into the street that led into Cannes via the covered market. The last couple of months had been busy enough with some regular guests, but today was the day the competition winners were arriving.

Amy smiled as she entered the crowded market. She loved this place. Loved shopping here, her wicker basket over her arm slowly filling with local produce. Loved all the variety of food on offer. Loved... everything about it. After five years, the stallholders all knew her. She always tried to buy from the smaller stalls, the ones with the old ladies behind trestle tables, with the produce of their pottages, rather than the big commercial stalls. Pierre, the gardener she'd inherited with Belle Vue Villa, grew a lot of their vegetables – potatoes, onions, courgettes, peppers and all the summery salad stuff, but at this time of year, she always bought the asparagus, roquette, courgette flowers, rosé garlic and the freshest juiciest raspberries imaginable from madame in the centre of the market. Then there was the cheese stall with its brie and the creamiest buffalo mozzarella she'd ever tasted.

Wandering around, Amy brought her thoughts back to the things she needed and stopped in front of the boulangerie stand, buying three baguettes, a sourdough round loaf and some olive bread. Everything on her list ticked off, she made her way to the coffee shop in the street near the top end of the market. Time for an expresso and a favourite palmier biscuit before heading home.

Sitting there people watching, Amy's thoughts drifted to the three strangers who were the winners of the competition she'd impulsively advertised. Was it a little crazy, this idea of hers inspired by the characters in her favourite film? Were the three prizewinners she'd picked out genuinely in need of a peaceful break like she hoped? Would they be women who would understand the ethos behind her wanting to do someone a random kindness? Maybe she should have asked her regular retreat guests to nominate someone deserving of a holiday.

And what if the three winners she'd picked didn't get on? Then the next ten days would seem like ten weeks. The little she was able to glean from the competition entries and the follow up emails told her that the three of them were unlikely to have much in common. Vicky and Chelsea's email replies to her own 'you've won a holiday' email had both been phrased in excited language and thanked her effusively. Amy thought Matilda's reply had been slightly reserved, but the phrase 'looking forward to it immensely' reassured her that she was pleased to accept the prize.

Amy sipped her coffee and prayed this holiday would work out well for all of them – herself included. She'd really wanted to do something to say thank you and pay back her good fortune and she knew Tasha would approve of what she was doing. Whatever. It was too late to stop it now. This afternoon she was driving to the airport to collect them all. Vicky Lewis was arriving on the London flight at 3.30. Matilda Richardson and Chelsea Newman were flying from Bristol and would land at 4.15. The plan was to greet Vicky and take her for a coffee while they waited for the other two, before all travelling back to the villa together.

Fingers crossed there were no strikes or flight delays today which could complicate the best laid plans.

* * *

A couple of hours later, Amy was waiting in the Arrivals Hall at Nice airport, holding up her first placard with 'Vicky Lewis' written on it. Watching anxiously as people started to come through from the luggage area, she sent up a silent prayer that everyone would get on and that Belle Vue Villa would work its magic.

Amy liked Vicky the moment she walked through into Arrivals. They were about the same age and she sensed a kindred spirit.

'Hi, Vicky. I'm Amy,' she said, holding out her hand.

'Hello, Amy – the giver of free holidays. I can't tell you how happy I am to be here,' Vicky said, smiling as they shook hands.

'I'm happy you're here too,' Amy replied, returning the smile. 'Good flight? I thought we'd have a coffee together while we wait for the others. Are you okay with your wheelie suitcase? Or would you rather take it to the car?'

'Have we got long to wait?'

'No. About half an hour,' Amy answered.

'Coffee then, please. My case is quite manoeuvrable.'

Choosing seats in the coffee shop where they had a good

view of the ETA board in the hall, Amy told Vicky a little about the retreat and the surrounding area before glancing at the laptop bag strapped to Vicky's case.

'Your email said you wanted time for yourself to think about the future and to try and write,' she said. 'I hope this time at Belle Vue will help you with both of those.'

Vicky sighed. 'I hope so too. I couldn't believe I'd won when you emailed me the news. I feel guilty about accepting, if I'm honest, but time out just for me couldn't have come at a better moment. Now the children are grown, I'd like to do something for me rather than get sucked into other things with all the free time I now supposedly have.' She glanced at Amy. 'My husband, Anthony, is keen for me to take on more in his constituency than I really want to. He doesn't under-stand why I'm so reluctant. Oh blast!' Vicky looked at Amy. 'Please don't tell the others my husband is a politician. People tend to treat me differently when they hear whom I'm married to. At least I can still manage to have the occasional private moment using my maiden name.'

'Your secret is safe with me,' Amy said, hoping Vicky didn't suspect she'd immediately started wondering who her husband was. Or whether he was in the Cabinet. 'I know how husbands have a habit of assuming and taking decisions they have no right to take, given half the chance.' Before Vicky could say anything, Amy continued quickly, 'Not that I have a husband any more. I left him around the time my Aunt Tasha left me Belle Vue.'

'Thank you,' Vicky said, clearly relieved, but not liking to pursue the matter of Amy's ex-husband 'Did you say the others are coming on the Bristol flight? It's just landing, according to the board.'

'Better get back to meeting and greeting then,' Amy said, standing up and reaching for her name placards.

'I'll come with you,' Vicky said, jumping up and following Amy.

Matilda and Chelsea came through into the arrivals hall together. Matilda leaning on a stick and Chelsea with both her backpack and Matilda's case loaded on a trolley. Amy, seeing Matilda's stick, sighed, hoping that moving around the house and grounds wouldn't be a problem for her. There were a few flights of steps dotted around the place. At least she'd allocated Matilda the 'Fitzgerald' room on the ground floor which had French doors opening directly onto the terrace at the side of the house.

Amy introduced Vicky and herself to Matilda and Chelsea before they left the airport concourse to make their way to the car, Chelsea sniffed. 'What's that lovely smell?'

'It's the eucalyptus trees,' Amy said, pointing to the tall trees that lined the car parks and the circumference of the airport offering shade. 'I forget the particular variety, but the heat of the sun releases the oil aroma from the leaves.'

'The sky is so blue,' Vicky said. 'So different to the London I left this morning. And it's so warm.'

Once everything was stowed in the car and with Vicky and Chelsea insisting Matilda took the front passenger seat so she could stretch her leg out, Amy began the drive back to Belle Vue. While she concentrated on the road, she hoped the other three would chat amongst themselves and slowly get to know each other, but they were all too busy looking at the Mediterranean on one side and the villas and other sundry buildings on the other.

Half an hour later, Amy turned into the driveway and they all got their first glimpse of Belle Vue Villa, their home for the next ten days.

Chelsea uttered a spontaneous, 'Wow.'

'What a beautiful place,' Vicky said, gazing at the

Provençal mas with its mellow stonework, the terracotta roofs on different levels and the rampant purple bougainvillea over the front and side of the house.

'You have a delightful home,' Matilda added. 'I think we are about to spend time in paradise.'

'Oh, who's this?' Chelsea asked, bending down to stroke an energetic bundle of white fur.

'This is Lola. I inherited her along with the villa,' Amy answered. 'She's supposed to be a pure Bolognese, but I suspect there's a rogue gene in there somewhere.'

'Whatever she is, she's gorgeous,' Chelsea said. 'Love her curls.'

'Come on, I'll show you to your rooms,' Amy said. 'All the rooms are named after famous people who had a connection with the South of France. Matisse, Fitzgerald, Hemingway, Piaf et cetera. And you, Lola, can stay outside,' Amy added sternly. 'She's not allowed in the bedrooms, but she has been known to sneak in occasionally.'

Ten minutes later and Amy had shown them all to their different rooms, pointed out the trays with tea and coffee and, after telling them aperitifs on the main terrace at the front of the house would be at 7.15 with dinner at 7.45, she left them to unpack.

* * *

Matilda sank onto the Lloyd Loom chair thoughtfully placed to take in the view and sighed with pleasure. Such a lovely room, and the view through the French doors leading onto the terrace was a meeting of intense blue sky over the green of the garden and the azure blue of the Mediterranean nudging the coastline on the horizon.

When Sheila had told her she'd won the holiday, she'd tried to persuade her to take it for herself.

'I can't. It's in your name and the rules clearly state it isn't transferable.'

In the end, Matilda had stopped arguing and replied to Amy's email, accepting the prize. Now she was here, she was looking forward to relaxing, enjoying the break and hopefully making new friends. Chelsea had been so helpful and kind when they'd met in the departure lounge at Bristol Airport and realised they were both competition winners on the way to Belle Vue Villa. Vicky seemed a friendly woman and as for Amy herself, well, as the giver of the holiday, she was clearly a generous and thoughtful woman. And so graceful in her movements.

Matilda picked up a book from the low table conveniently placed at the side of the chair. F. Scott Fitzgerald's *Tales of the Jazz Age*. One of his books she hadn't read. She knew Fitzgerald had spent a lot of time on the Riviera during the twenties and thirties when the Jazz Age was at its height – maybe there would be some tales set down here?

Hopefully her ankle would be strong enough before the end of the holiday for her to walk unaided around Antibes in Fitzgerald's footsteps. She'd dutifully spent the last few months doing the exercises the physiotherapist had given her and trying to use her stick less and less, which had proved difficult. Her ankle was definitely better, but she was terrified of falling again and the stick had become like a third leg – one that gave her confidence and a sense of security.

Right now, she fancied a reviving cup of tea. One of the Earl Grey teabags she'd spotted on the tray would do nicely.

Waiting for the kettle to boil, she found her iPad and sent Josh a quick email.

I've arrived safely. Villa is wonderful. Hope all is well with you.
Love Mum x

Taking her tea, she opened the French doors and stepped out onto the terrace. A small wrought-iron table and two chairs had been placed to one side of the doors. Perfect. The garden in front of her was a beautiful mixture of lawn and flower beds containing a variety of wonderful white and scarlet roses. A hedge of pink oleander stretched down the right hand side where she could see a man carefully hoeing away at the weeds.

A garden was the main thing she missed when they'd sold the old family home that William had inherited from his parents and downsized into the flat. With Josh leaving home and William wanting to shorten his daily commute to work, it had made sense, but Matilda had wept a secret tear or two over the decision. She'd loved pottering around the garden of an evening, William at her side as they caught up with each other's day. William had promised that once he'd retired they would move to France, find a cottage with a garden and the two of them would grow old together, living the country life they'd always dreamed of living.

A heart attack had decreed otherwise, killing William one Sunday morning as they'd strolled through Clifton village towards their favourite restaurant for lunch. And just like that everything had changed.

For the past sixteen months, Matilda had lived alone in the flat, coming to terms with her loss and trying to find consolation in the numerous pots she'd jammed together on her small balcony – and failing miserably. Every time she watered and tended to the pots, in her heart she was wishing herself somewhere else – in a cottage with a proper garden. When she'd mentioned her feelings to Josh on one of his visits, he'd advised her to take her time deciding what to do, and not to do anything too drastic too quickly.

Winning the holiday here, courtesy of Sheila and Amy's kindness, had started her dreaming again of moving to France. Thoughts she'd squashed as being an impossible dream for her to do alone. But something was beginning to niggle away in her brain, telling her she wasn't that old, that she still had years of life left in front of her. William had left her financially more than comfortable and she knew that, more than anything, he would want her to be happy.

Matilda finished her tea. Maybe being in France for ten days would help her decide what to do with her future. Tomorrow morning she'd enjoy taking a wander and exploring the gardens as she started to really think about the rest of her life. Right now, though, she was going to sit here and simply admire the view before unpacking and getting ready for aperitifs and dinner on the terrace. For the first time in months, she was feeling hungry. Must be the sea air, she decided.

In the 'Edith Piaf' room next door, Vicky had taken one look at the en-suite marble bathroom, the deep claw-footed bath with its gold taps, an array of fragrant toiletries on a shelf, and started to run a bath. Her unpacking could wait. At Anthony's insistence, it was showers all the way at home and as much as she loved being pounded by the hot water of a power jet shower, she did sometimes long to immerse herself in litres of perfumed water for a rejuvenating soak.

Vicky glanced at the book on the bedside table – *The Life of Edith Piaf*. She smiled. When Amy had told them the rooms at Belle Vue were named after people who had a connection with the South of France, she'd hoped for the Fitzgerald room. Instead, Amy had given her this particular room. How could Amy have known? Vicky's mother was a great Piaf fan. She'd even travelled to Paris back in the sixties to go to the funeral with thousands of adoring fans. When Vicky had asked, 'What was so special about her?' her mum had shaken her head, 'I'm not sure. She didn't have an easy life, but her voice and songs spoke to millions. Still do.'

Ten minutes later, happily soaking in the scented water with her eyes closed, her mother's favourite Piaf song, 'Non, je ne regrette rien', floated unbidden into Vicky's conscience.

I have no regrets, the song went. How many people could honestly say that? The life Vicky was currently living certainly wasn't the one she'd envisaged as a teenager. Back then she'd planned to go to university, obtain a good degree and then travel the world, possibly as a travel writer, earn enough money to buy her own home and be independent, marry in her early thirties and settle down to family life with two children. In her mind, it had all been mapped out.

Only family life with two children had come to fruition. Meeting Anthony when she was eighteen, falling pregnant with Tom within weeks of starting her first job, had derailed the rest of her life plans. She certainly didn't regret having the children. Or marrying Anthony. She'd loved him from the beginning and she still did. Only she hadn't reckoned on him changing course from IT consultancy and becoming a politician. Of course, they'd discussed it, but with hindsight Vicky realised neither of them had really anticipated the changes it would bring into their lives. The biggest for Vicky being the loss of privacy.

As far as other regrets went, although she didn't regret any of the past twenty-odd years, she knew that if she wasn't careful, didn't do something with her own life from here on in... well, that she would regret. But standing up to Anthony was hard. Not because he was unkind or difficult but simply because she felt guilty for wanting to do other things. Winning this holiday had caused the first major row they'd had for years.

She had been on Facebook looking at the holiday details and starting to make a list of all the things she'd need. List making was in her DNA and for a long time Vicky had tried to fight the habit, but in the end, realising how satisfying it was ticking things off as they were accomplished, she gave in. As she'd made a note to check her passport, find a suitable case in the attic and look out some summer clothes, Anthony had walked in and looked at the computer screen.

'Facebook? Surely you've got better things to do than waste time with that? I could certainly do with some more help in the office.'

Vicky had bitten her tongue to stop herself protesting that she'd only been on there five minutes, saying instead, 'Guess what? I've won a holiday to the South of France.'

'When for? I can't see me getting away until the recess,' Anthony had replied. 'And even then, anything longer than a week will be difficult.'

Vicky had taken a deep breath. 'It's only for one person.'

'You mean you're going on your own?'

Vicky had nodded. 'It'll be some me time and give me a chance to work out what I'm going to do for the next few years. I was thinking of asking your mum to come and stay?'

Anthony had stared at her, ignoring the question about his mother. 'It is a legitimate competition, isn't it? It's not some sort of backhander from someone hoping you can influence me in some way?'

Vicky had gazed at him, exasperated, wondering when he'd become so selfish. 'There are three winners and I'm one of them. I do not know the person who has organised the competition or any of the other people. Okay?'

'You'll have to give me the details and I'll register it with the Members' Interests committee. I don't want any backlash over my wife accepting freebies.' Anthony had looked at her. 'And you should know that I'd really rather you didn't accept this holiday.'

'And you should know, I need this holiday. I want some me time,' Vicky had said. 'Ten days where someone else does the work not me. Days to relax, read a book, go for a walk, think about the future, all without an agenda or having to watch the clock.'

'D'you think I don't often long for that too?'

Vicky had shaken her head. 'It's not the same,' she'd said. 'You're doing what you love to do in life. For years, all I've done is kept house, cooked, cared for the children and supported you whenever you've needed me to. I need space to find the real Vicky Lewis again.'

'You're talking about empty-nest syndrome.'

'No, I'm not. I just feel that the real me has been swallowed up by other people's lives and now I have to rediscover me and my own dreams. You know I've always wanted to write, well, going on this retreat will give me the time and space to see if I can.'

'You've never said any of this before.'

'Well, I'm saying it now. I just want to be me as well as your wife, a daughter and a mother. Vicky Lewis deserves another crack at living her own life.'

Anthony had sighed as he ran his fingers through his hair. 'I had no idea you felt like this. I thought you were happy?'

'But you never thought to actually ask me if I was happy,' Vicky had snapped. 'Anyway, I was and still am, basically. But you've become more and more involved with politics, the children are starting to live independent lives, I need to find something for me.'

Later that same evening in bed, Anthony had pulled her close, sighing. 'I'm sorry I was such a grump earlier. You're right. You need some time to do whatever makes you happy. Enjoy your retreat – I'll take you to the airport by the way. Maybe we can snatch a long weekend away, just the two of us, when you get back? I've always fancied a naughty weekend in Brighton.'

Vicky had slept in his arms that night, feeling more hopeful that the two of them could work things out. That maybe things weren't starting to fall apart after twenty-three years of marriage.

And now she was here in this glorious villa looking forward to the next ten days. Amy was really lovely and Matilda and Chelsea seemed nice. It would be fun getting to know everyone, making new friends. Vicky stretched a leg out and turned on the hot water tap with her toe. This was truly blissful. Vicky Lewis was on her way back to her lost world.

Chelsea, at the other end of the house in the 'Elizabeth David' room, dropped her backpack on the floor and flung herself down on the bed and lay staring up at the ceiling. She and her guilty conscience were in the South of France. She felt dreadful about leaving Elsie to cope, but Elsie had insisted, saying business was quiet for a week or two and she was quite capable of managing on her own. 'Unless you don't trust me?' she'd said, stunning Chelsea into silence with the animosity in her voice.

She'd call her later and apologise again for her part in

'Kit-gate'. Hopefully it was becoming old news now – surely overtaken by another nine-days' wonder scandal – and the business would survive the calamity of that Friday booking.

Kit-gate. How stupid had she been? Why and how had she allowed herself to become something she despised – a mistress to a sleazy, cheating, married man. She was so angry with herself over the whole thing, not least because it could destroy their reputation in the food business despite all their hard work over the past couple of years. Elsie insisted she shouldn't blame herself but, truly, who else could she blame? The signs had all been there from the moment Kit had locked eyes with her. Kit who was as false as his name.

Away a lot during the week, never around at weekends, could never stay overnight. She'd been just plain dumb. If she were honest, believing she and Kit were an item had suited her. The last thing she wanted was too cloying or demanding a relationship – she enjoyed her freedom, her independence and the prospect of buying her own place. But as much as she told herself she hadn't known he was married, she also knew she hadn't dug beneath the surface of his life very deeply. She'd taken the things Kit had told her at face value.

Chelsea could only pray that Marcia would be satisfied with the humiliating public showdown she'd staged and not punish Chelsea or the business further by telling associates not to use them. It had been a very public and expensive humiliation all round. Chelsea felt she'd had no alternative but to promise Elsie she'd pick up the costs of that fateful lunch. She winced at the memory of just how much the two cases of very upmarket champagne alone had cost her before totting up the price of the actual nibbles.

Kit-gate had taught her a couple of things though. One: she'd never, ever take anything a man said for granted again, and two: she'd learnt again that life could fall apart quicker than twisting the cork out of an expensive bottle of champagne.

Chelsea took a deep breath and swung her legs off the bed. She'd promised Elsie she'd enjoy this break away from the fallout, recharge her batteries, and get ready to concentrate on work when she got home, maybe even think up some new recipes – after all, this was France, a country renowned for its culinary expertise. But above all she intended to try and enjoy this unexpected holiday.

Standing up to fetch her backpack, she saw a book on the bedside table. *Lunch with Elizabeth David* – a novel. Elizabeth David, an icon among chefs long before Chelsea was born, had nevertheless inspired her own dreams, making her long to be a good cook. She had a couple of novels on her Kindle for bedtime reading, but they could wait. This one looked far more interesting than those.

Glancing out through the French doors, Chelsea saw the sun glinting on a large swimming pool and she caught her breath. Of course, a pool was de rigueur down here, but this one looked so inviting. As a teenager, swimming had been her life. She'd spent so much time at the local baths, her mum had laughingly told her if she wasn't careful she'd grow a tail like a mermaid. Both her mum and dad had proudly driven her the length and breadth of England when she was chosen to represent the swimming club in galas at county level. She'd even been tipped as a possible for an Olympic team. But that was before the accident.

It was a long time since she'd swum, either competitively or for pleasure, but that pool was so inviting. Grabbing her backpack and turning it upside down, spilling the contents on the bed, Chelsea grabbed a swimming costume. She'd thrown a couple in with her clothes at the last moment, along with her goggles.

Twenty lengths later and Chelsea felt better than she had for weeks. Swimming had always energised her and cleared her head, like going for a walk or a run did for other people. Unconsciously, decisions were being made as she did her fast crawl up and down the pool. She'd concentrate on growing the business, buying her own place and avoid any relationships with men. Kit-gate would soon be nothing more than a memory. An expensive blip in the scheme of things. And she'd start swimming again regularly.

She'd swim ten more lengths and then go for a shower before meeting up with the others on the terrace for aperitifs. Having eschewed food since that horrible Friday, existing mainly on black coffee and toast most days, Chelsea suddenly felt her tummy rumble in anticipation.

5

Once she'd settled everyone into their rooms, Amy went to her own for a shower and a change of clothes. She'd worn what she termed her 'meet and greet' outfit of smart white capri pants with her short-sleeved red-striped Breton top and her wedge espadrilles to go down to Nice. It was only early June, but the temperature was already nudging thirty celsius. The air conditioning in the car had been on, but Amy still felt hot and sticky from the drive.

Amy's bedroom, the 'Isadora Duncan', was the biggest bedroom in the villa and Amy had taken care turning it into a relaxing personal space, as well as where she did her paperwork for the retreat. In one corner, hidden from view by a beautiful ornate baroque-style room divider screen, was a desk, comfortable chair and a small three drawer wooden filing cabinet. The three partitions of the screen in antique white, made from wood and canvas, blended in perfectly with the coffee and cream decor of the room. An exercise bar was placed in front of a large gilt mirror that was fixed to the wall by the door that led to the en suite. An eye-catching antique kissing chair upholstered in scarlet velvet placed at the foot of the bed was the real statement piece in the room. On the wall behind the bed, Amy had hung the large portrait of Isadora Duncan she'd discovered in an antique shop in Nice. Amy loved how the painter had captured the essence of how an unconventional Isadora moved her body in dance, so free and flexible, with no preconceived shapes.

While she showered and towelled herself dry afterwards, Amy found herself thinking about the three women she'd collected from the airport. She remembered realising as she read their competition answers, they all had a genuine reason for wanting the holiday. A need to get away from normal life for a while. Vicky hoping to find herself again after years of being a mother and supportive wife. Chelsea because something in her life had gone drastically wrong and Matilda, who on the face of it was simply recuperating from a broken ankle, but Amy sensed there was something under the surface worrying her.

Each woman was different, but all seemed nice and easy to get along with. At least Amy hoped they were. Personality clashes were definitely not needed. Fingers crossed, the three generations would come together happily and settle down for a fun and enjoyable holiday. A holiday that would help each of them sort out their lives when they returned home.

Amy smiled wryly to herself. The only way she'd been able to sort out her own life had been by running away from home five years ago, thanks to Tasha. For her, though, running away had been the right decision. Updating and turning Belle Vue into a retreat had kept her busy for the first year and once she'd opened to guests, business had built up steadily.

Pulling on a pair of shorts and a loose top, she glanced at

her watch. Time to check on Olivia, her friend and cook for the villa, and to prepare the nibbles for aperitifs.

'Everything smells as wonderful as ever,' Amy said, going into the kitchen. 'Everything okay?'

Olivia looked up from the mozzarella and tomato salad starter she was preparing and smiled at Amy before answering her in rapid French.

'Bien sûr. Comme d'habitude?'

'Oui,' Amy said. 'I'll set the terrace table and then sort the aperitifs if you don't want me to do anything.'

Olivia had been Tasha's cook and Amy had fond memories of the meals she'd cooked for the family during summer holidays over the years. Tasha's Will had stipulated that Olivia and Pierre, the gardener, were an important part of Belle Vue and were to keep their jobs. She knew that Amy would find them invaluable. And that was so true.

In the early days, the three of them had grown close as they grieved for Tasha and Amy had involved them in her plans for the house. Olivia, like her brother Pierre, had been born and bred in the village and their maternal Italian grandparents lived across the nearby Italian border. Olivia was the same age as Tasha and over the past couple of years had partially filled the void left behind by Amy's godmother. Olivia's daughter had married a local farmer and two years ago, much to Olivia's delight, had made her a grandmother. When Amy had arrived to live permanently in France, Olivia had welcomed her into her own family and Amy had enjoyed many a Sunday meal at their table with their noisy extended family. These days, whenever Amy had guests, Olivia cooked the evening meals at the villa, which meant every afternoon, her pasta-loving body could be seen making its way slowly up the drive.

Pierre, a widower in his late fifties, had been a gardener

all his working life. He was one of the gentlest and kindest men Amy had ever known. His knowledge of plants was legendary. She'd learnt so much about the garden from him.

The brother and sister were more than Amy's friends – they were her French family. Olivia in particular was her sounding-board as far as the villa went – and in her personal life too.

Amy had placed the nibbles on the table and was lighting the citronella candles in their terracotta pots placed strategically around the terrace, when Vicky appeared. A Vicky who already looked relaxed and happy wearing a light kaftan-style top over a long flowing cotton skirt.

'I've just had the most amazing therapeutic bath,' she said, accepting a glass of chilled rosé from Amy. 'Sheer bliss. May I have one every day? Or am I going to cause a water shortage?'

Amy laughed. 'Have as many baths as you like. Our water here is spring-fed, but there is no danger of us running out.'

'You have no idea how happy that makes me,' Vicky said, raising her glass. 'Cheers.'

Matilda was the next to arrive. Without her stick, Amy noticed.

'Not late, am I? I have to confess to falling asleep in that wonderfully comfortable chair in my room.'

'No, you're not late' Amy said. 'Glass of rosé or would you prefer something else?'

Matilda shook her head. 'Rosé will be lovely. I always think of rosé as a wine that one should only drink in the heat of summer and preferably in the South of France. Both conditions of which are met here. Santé.'

Vicky, standing looking out over the garden, sighed. 'It's so beautiful here. I've only just arrived and I feel I never want to leave.'

'You're not the first to feel like that,' Amy said. 'Ah, Chelsea. Glass of wine?'

'Umm, could I have something to nibble first please? Otherwise I think the wine will go straight to my head, it's so long since I've eaten properly.'

'Sure, help yourself,' Amy said. 'I always find swimming makes me hungry too. But do leave enough room for the lamb Olivia has roasted.'

While they enjoyed the nibbles and rosé, Amy started to explain a little about the retreat and her plans for the week.

'I'm used to running retreats and courses here where everyone who comes usually has a shared interest with the people in the group. Having the three of you here, all strangers and probably with nothing in common, is a first for me. I'm hoping you all get on,' and Amy smiled at them before taking a sip of her wine and continuing.

'The eight rooms with names are the bedrooms – mine's on the first floor and is the "Isadora Duncan". Do please feel free to explore the rest of the house,' Amy said. 'Breakfast is a help yourself affair in the kitchen and you can eat in there, wander out here or eat on your own terrace. Pierre, the gardener, brings the fresh croissants and pains au chocolat up every morning from the village at about 7.30. I get lunch – usually bread, cheese, salad and charcuterie from the market, which is my limit, I'm no cook. If you're going out independently for the day, just let me know. Olivia will come in to cook dinner every day unless we decide to eat out one evening.'

'Sounds wonderful,' Vicky said. 'Having food bought, cooked and placed in front of me without me having to organise it. I'm not a very good cook either,' she confessed, looking at Amy.

'I'm happy to arrange a couple of days out if you're interested?' Amy said. 'A group visit to Monaco? Antibes? Both are easily accessible from here. And, of course, Cannes is just down the road.'

'I'd love to go to Monaco,' Chelsea said. 'And if you could introduce me to a millionaire that would be cool.'

'I don't think I know any,' Amy laughed. 'But we can certainly have a look around.'

'I had a holiday with my husband and son in Antibes years ago,' Matilda said. 'If my ankle is strong enough, I'd enjoy another visit.'

'Right. I'll organise a day out to Monaco, followed by one to Antibes. I thought tomorrow could be a quiet day, let you settle in.'

Olivia appeared just then and placed their starters on the table before wishing everyone 'Bon appetit'.

Over dinner, the four of them got to know a little bit more about each other. Matilda, having told them she had one son and had been a widow for nearly two years, said. 'You and your husband, Vicky – what do you both do?'

'Me – I've been a stay-at-home mum for years, but that is about to change. I want to write a novel.' Vicky gave Amy a quick glance before adding, 'As for my husband, he's a civil servant.'

Amy looked at her and smiled. Well, that was one way of describing a politician without lying.

'I run a small catering firm with my best friend, Elsie,' Chelsea said. 'And before anyone asks, I'm single but currently off men. Unless I meet a millionaire in Monaco, of course.' She laughed. 'No, seriously, the next time I meet someone I like, I'm going to interrogate him about his background as if I'm a member of MI5 before I even agree to have a coffee with him.'

Everyone looked at her, waiting for her to expand on her words, but Chelsea shook her head.

'Sorry. Still too raw.'

'You're young,' Matilda said. 'When you've recovered from your bad experience, I'm sure you'll meet someone you can trust – probably when you least expect to. At least that's the way it was for me,' and Matilda fell silent.

Amy realised the silence following Matilda's words as everybody waited for her to explain was in danger of spoiling the happy atmosphere that had surrounded them all during the meal.

'I agree,' Amy said. 'Life likes to throw the occasional curveball at us, but sometimes I've found catching them is the best way forward.'

'What did you do, Amy, before you came here?' Chelsea asked curiously.

'Me? I was a ballet dancer.'

'Is that why your bedroom has the name Isadora Duncan?' Matilda asked.

Amy nodded. 'I have a bit of a thing about her. She was unconventional and my idol as I was growing up. Ah, here comes Olivia with dessert and champagne to toast the beginning of your holiday.'

Once the champagne had been poured, they all raised their glasses as Amy gave the toast.

'Here's to a happy holiday for you all at Belle Vue Villa. Santé.'

As she sipped her own glass of ice-cold bubbles, Amy glanced across at Matilda. She appeared to have something in common with the older woman. But whereas Matilda's bad experience with a man in the past seemed to have been over-taken by a more positive one, Amy knew hers still had the power to affect her life, denying her the one thing she longed for. No man had yet appeared to reassure her and make her feel better about life. To encourage her to love again. In fact, like Chelsea, she too was currently off men and sometimes doubted she'd ever trust a man again, full stop.

DAY TWO OF THE HOLIDAY – JUNE 7

6

Vicky woke to silence the next morning and for a moment she struggled to work out where she was. Normally, her day began at six thirty, when she awoke to a cacophony of traffic noise and the sounds of various neighbours leaving for work. Here, apart from the odd pigeon cooing from high up in one of the garden trees, the silence was absolute – not even the cicadas were up yet – and was wonderful to listen to.

Lying there, Vicky was relieved to recall that breakfast was a help yourself affair. Her body might have been conditioned over the years to waking her up early, but she was definitely not a social being first thing in the morning. It wasn't just a caffeine hit she needed, it was time on her own to wake up properly. The nightmare of the school run years was thankfully over, but Anthony still liked her to join him for breakfast.

Was Anthony missing her this morning? She'd texted him to say she'd arrived safely and that the villa was lovely, but he hadn't replied properly. Just sent one of those thumbs up signs. Well, there was nothing really to say, was there? He'd already told her to enjoy herself and he wouldn't waste time saying the same thing again. Not because he didn't care but because, as far as he was concerned, he'd said it once and he wasn't one for repeating himself. He'd always been straight-forward like that. Unlike many of his fellow politicians, he would always try to give you an honest answer. It had got him into trouble with the party more than once, when they'd wanted him to toe the official line.

Telling the others last night that he was a civil servant hadn't exactly been a lie, but she hadn't wanted to tell them the truth. At home, once people knew whose wife she was they could never resist having a dig at 'this inept government' or, equally embarrassing, asking her to lobby Anthony for some cause on their behalf. She doubted anyone here would do either of those things, but still, she wanted to be just herself, Vicky Lewis, for the next nine days. This holiday was about being selfish for once and seeing whether she could actually start to write a novel – and kickstart a life of her own alongside Anthony's.

Vicky stretched luxuriously. Having such a comfortable double bed all to herself was wonderful. Five more minutes and she'd shower and go and find some caffeine and maybe a croissant.

Half an hour later, she was sitting on her terrace, a mug of coffee from the jug under the very professional looking machine in the kitchen and a pain au chocolat on a plate placed on the small wrought-iron table in front of her. She didn't think she was the first to be up, the coffee jug was only half full, but she hadn't seen anyone on her way to and from the kitchen.

Sitting there enjoying the calm and the early morning sunshine, she thought about the plans for the week Amy had mentioned and came to a decision. The excursions would be enough entertainment for her, she wouldn't need to go anywhere else. She'd spend the mornings on the other days working on her laptop, have a swim before lunch, and then write again for a couple of hours in the afternoon.

Right, she had a plan. She was always happier when she had a plan and with luck this particular one should produce a sufficient amount of writing by the end of the holiday. Writing that might, or might not, be good enough to give her a new career. Vicky sighed.

She'd been reading a couple of 'How to' books and a writing magazine, all of which had been at pains to point out how the market was changing, how difficult it was these days to get an agent, not to mention a deal with a publishing house. But she was determined to have a go. If she didn't even try to write something during this holiday, she'd be forever wondering whether she'd let herself down.

* * *

For the first time since Kit-gate, Chelsea had fallen asleep the instant her head hit the pillow the night before. Woken at 6.30 by the 5.30 alarm on her phone because she'd forgotten to deactivate it or set the clock to French time, she turned over and went straight back to sleep for another five minutes, which turned into two hours.

Fully awake this time, she pulled on her swimming things and, grabbing a towel from the bathroom, she made for the pool and dived in. Thirty lengths later, she turned on her back and floated. This felt so good. The sky above her was already deepening into the azure blue she'd heard so much about, without a cloud in sight. She watched as a formation of half a dozen ducks flew overhead, idly wondering where they were headed. A nearby pond? Or the coast? Above them, the vapour trails of three or four planes criss-crossed in streaks across the sky.

Gently floating down the pool, Chelsea reached the shallow steps and got out. Wrapping her towel around herself, she walked back to her room, showered and dressed before making a coffee using one of the coffee bags from the bedroom tray. She pushed away the thought of the fresh croissants that would be available in the kitchen.

Standing sipping her coffee and looking out over the garden, Chelsea thought about the day ahead. What to do? Sit by the pool this morning sunbathing and reading? Maybe another swim? Then, after lunch, wander down to the village or even go into Cannes. Chelsea thought about the contents of her backpack, wishing now she'd given more thought to the clothes she'd flung in. Especially with visits to Monaco and Antibes on the agenda. She'd brought jeans and tops, one maxi dress, a skirt and her faithful denim jacket. Her maxi dress was the only garment that could be vaguely described as smart. If Elsie was here, finding something suitable to wear wouldn't be a problem.

Chelsea smiled to herself. The phrase 'travel light' didn't exist in Elsie's vocabulary. She would have brought the largest suitcase she could drag behind her, filled with enough clothes to last her at least a month, never mind ten days, just in case.

She'd texted Elsie late last night to tell her she'd arrived and how gorgeous the villa was, but there was no reply from her this morning. She'd try and ring her later today and check that things were all right. Whether the part-time girls were coping, whether there had been any repercussions over her stupidity. Elsie had told her she was to enjoy her time away and to try and forget the whole incident by the time she returned home. Which was, of course, impossible. It wasn't something she'd forget for a long time. From their comments last night, she guessed that both Matilda and Amy had had some sort of man problem in the past. Not that it could possibly have been half as publicly humiliating as her recent experience; Chelsea shivered just thinking about it again.

She imagined Amy and Vicky were both in their late thirties or early forties, which would make them at least fifteen years older than her. A lot could happen in the next fifteen years. Be good to think she and Elsie would be running a successful business by then and she'd be married with a family like Vicky. But definitely not married to a boring civil servant. She wanted somebody with a bit more go about them than that. A musician maybe. Vicky seemed quite vivacious and full of life, you'd have thought her partner would be the same, but a civil servant!

Feeling the heat of the sun intensify as she stood there, Chelsea decided against going out. She'd give Elsie a quick ring now and then spend this first day of the holiday lazing around the pool, sunbathing and swimming. After all, wasn't that what holidays were supposed to be about?

She frowned when she rang Elsie's number and the phone went straight to voicemail. Unlike Elsie not to answer. She'd try again later.

In the meantime, she'd indulge herself and go and get a couple of freshly baked French croissants from the kitchen for her first breakfast in France. In the past, swimming had always made her hungry and today had been no exception.

* * *

Matilda, having methodically changed her watch to French time, knew that first morning when she woke at 6.30 that it was too early to go to the kitchen in search of food. So she made herself a cup of tea and took it back to bed and started to read the first short story in the Fitzgerald book. Two hours later, she showered, before making her way to the kitchen in search of caffeine and something to eat.

The kitchen, with its warm terracotta floor tiles, cream cupboards, granite work surface and yellow and blue tiles forming a colourful splash-back above the counters and behind the large range, was light and airy. A large refectory table stood in the middle of the room, a wicker bread basket containing a couple of croissants, pains au chocolat and a single almond slice, stood in the centre of it. Two long baguettes lay alongside. A dish of butter, pots of fig jam, honey and marmalade were clustered together with plates, mugs and cutlery. Lola, curled up in a basket alongside the range, thumped her tail in welcome but stayed where she was.

Pouring herself a coffee and helping herself to a pain au chocolat, Matilda sat at the table. Where was everybody? Was she the last to come for breakfast? She'd hoped to see one or two of the others there and share a companionable half hour or so discussing how they were all going to spend their day.

She'd almost finished her pain au chocolat, a delicious rare treat, when Chelsea arrived.

'Morning, Matilda. Am I too late for a croissant or two?'

'Still several in the basket – including a flaky almond one,' Matilda said. 'There's coffee in the jug too.'

Chelsea shook her head. 'I'm just hungry. Need some carbs before I go for another swim. You got any plans for today?' she asked, taking a plate and putting a plain buttery croissant and the almond one on it.

'As it's our first day, I thought I'd explore the garden, sit by the pool, read. You know, generally take it easy. You?'

Chelsea, having just taken a large mouthful of croissant,

the flakes of which were coating her lips, couldn't answer for several seconds, then she said, 'The same really, but I plan on having several swims too. Gosh, these are good,' she said, before taking another large mouthful.

'I'll see you down by the pool after my walk then,' Matilda said.

'Okay. Ciao.' And Chelsea was gone, but not before taking another croissant. 'Elevenses,' she said with a grin.

'Ciao,' Matilda echoed, smiling. She liked Chelsea. Felt they could be friends despite the age difference. The girl had clearly gone through a bad relationship recently, but Matilda sensed lurking under the surface was a real 'girl next door' who anyone would be proud to call a friend.

Chelsea had seen her struggling to manage both her stick and case at the airport and had instantly dashed over to help. Discovering they were both travelling to Belle Vue had been a delightful surprise. They'd chatted and got to know each other a little on the flight over. They both lived in Bristol – Chelsea across town in the less affluent district of Kingswood, compared to Matilda's posh end of Clifton. Neither of them could believe they'd won the holiday.

Matilda finished her coffee and was eyeing the units under the work surface speculatively, wondering which of them housed the dishwasher, when Amy appeared.

'Good morning. I hope you slept well? Join me for another coffee?' she said, going to the machine. 'Have you seen the others?'

'Thank you,' and Matilda pushed her cup over. 'You've just missed Chelsea. She came for croissants, said she needed the carbs for her swim. I haven't seen Vicky.'

'I think Vicky's already working on her laptop,' Amy said. 'D'you have any plans for today?'

'I thought I'd have a wander around the gardens, if that's

all right with you,' Matilda said. 'I need to loosen up my ankle with some gentle exercise. Then I'll sit by the pool and read until lunch.'

'This is your home while you're here. You're free to wander wherever you want. Maybe some hydrotherapy would be helpful for your ankle if you don't want to swim. Just sit on the edge and exercise your legs in the water. Did you bring a costume? If not, I keep a supply of spare ones for guests.'

'Thanks. I did bring one, but to be honest I'm not that much of a swimmer.' Matilda looked at Amy. 'Which day are you planning for the Monaco outing?'

'Not sure yet,' Amy said. 'Why?'

'I'm thinking I'll maybe give it a miss. I'm not sure my ankle will cope with too much walking. I remember a long hill and flights of steps leading up to the Palace. I wouldn't want to hold you all up.'

'You won't,' Amy said. 'Wait and see how the ankle feels on the day we decide to go. You can always have a coffee at one of the pavement cafés and watch the boats.'

'True. Right, I'm off to get my stick and explore your beautiful garden.' As Lola stretched and walked towards her, Matilda bent down and scratched her head. 'You coming to show me the way?'

Amy laughed. 'That dog has her own itinerary. One that mainly includes finding Pierre wherever he is in the garden and being fed biscuits.'

7

After Matilda had left, Amy tidied the kitchen, happy that everyone appeared to be settling in. Hopefully, barriers would start to break down during the day and dinner this evening would be a more relaxed affair as they all started to bond and become friends.

Once the kitchen was tidy, Amy made her way to her bedroom, intent on doing her normal exercise routine at the barre in her room before catching up on some paperwork. She might not be a professional ballet dancer these days but she still adored dancing and was determined to stay as supple as possible for as long as possible.

She was checking through bookings for the retreat in August when her phone rang.

'Hi, Mum,' Amy said, pressing the speaker button. 'How you doing?'

'Fine. Dad and I were planning to come over sometime this summer. Any dates to avoid when you're full?'

Amy quickly skimmed through the bookings chart. 'First week in July is currently free. After that, there's only one weekend free in late August. Shall I pencil you in for the July week?'

'Please.'

'Done – already looking forward to it.'

'So how are the competition winners?' Fleur asked.

'All three are really nice,' Amy said, knowing her mum had been sceptical at the wisdom of giving three people a free holiday.

'Good. Glad it's working out. Heard anything recently from…?' Fleur said, leaving the question hovering in the air.

'No. Why should I? All communications go to you. He doesn't know where I am. Besides, it's in the past. Over,' Amy sighed. She knew Fleur couldn't help bringing up the subject of her ex-husband every time she phoned, but she wished she wouldn't.

'Darling, you know that's not true. It's unfinished business,' Fleur said gently. 'You need proper closure so you can move on with your life.'

'I have moved on – or doesn't moving to France count?'

'You know what I mean. You're still young, I hate to think of you on your own forever. Apart from running away to France, you've done nothing about anything. I'm surprised he hasn't really put the pressure on yet, remembering how forceful he could be. It's not good, the way you've ignored things. It's been five years now. You need to get closure.'

'I know how long it's been, Mum,' Amy said. She also knew how much Fleur herself had been hurt when things had gone wrong for her. 'I promise by the end of this summer I'll have looked into sorting out all the legal stuff. All the paperwork is here – including a letter from the notaire who has agreed to act for me. I just haven't had the energy to kickstart things.' Or the inclination if she were honest. It was easier to let things drift.

'Good. You owe it to yourself to sort things. We'll talk about it more in July when we see you.'

After a few more minutes' general chat, Amy said goodbye and put her phone down on the desk. She loved her mum dearly and deep down knew she was right about getting closure on the past, but ignoring it and hoping it would all miraculously sort itself out had been the easier option. It wasn't as if she'd met anyone new and needed to have the past all tidied up and pushed away into the recess of her mind. Somehow, she couldn't see herself ever forgetting how hurt she'd been at what had happened.

Amy took a deep breath. She'd concentrate on Belle Vue for the summer months and then, come September, she'd start to organise things to bring an end to the biggest mistake of her life. For the next week or so, though, she was going to enjoy having the three competition winners here and giving them a good holiday. She'd enjoy taking them to Monaco later this week – it had always been a favourite place of hers and was full of happy memories. It had been too long since she'd spent time there.

* * *

The gardens surrounding Belle Vue were absolutely beautiful and extensive, Matilda discovered as she wandered along various paths deep in thought, little Lola bouncing in front of her leading the way.

Matilda, who'd owned several dogs in the past and missed not having one in her current life, slipped back without noticing into her old habit of talking things through with her canine companion. Saying things out loud to a dog couldn't be misconstrued as talking to yourself. Everybody did it. And somehow stating the problem out loud made it easier to think about.

'So, Lola, what d'you think I should do then?' Matilda said. 'Admit to Josh that I'm glad he stopped me selling up quickly after William died, but I feel the time is now right. A small cottage with a garden somewhere in the countryside – maybe on the outskirts of a village. Even here in France. Or do I give it another six months and see if I feel more settled?'

The little dog stopped and looked back at her briefly before charging off down a path to the right.

Deep in thought, Matilda failed to notice Lola bound up to a man pulling weeds out of a flower border and jumped when a voice said, 'Bonjour, Lola, ma petite. Et bonjour à vous, Madame.'

She looked around in surprise and saw Pierre, the gardener, regarding her quizzically. He'd clearly heard her talking to herself. Had he understood her words though?

'Bonjour,' Matilda said, greeting Pierre with a smile. He was as slim as Olivia was plump, but the eyes that were studying her were the same intense blue and his smile a genuine one.

'The garden is beautiful,' Matilda said, hoping she'd used the right French words. 'You must work very hard.'

'The work is hard, yes, but the results are my reward,' Pierre replied in English.

'You speak English very well,' Matilda said, relieved she didn't have to struggle to try and remember her basic French.

'I live there many years ago. I work in a big garden there when I learn to garden. Kew Gardens. You know it?'

Matilda nodded. 'Of course. I haven't been for some time, but years ago, William, my late husband, and I visited frequently. And we went to Chelsea Garden Show every year too.' She stopped. She hadn't gone this year, or last year. Simply hadn't been able to face it.

'You have a garden in England?' Pierre asked.

'Not any more,' Matilda said. 'I miss it. I have pots, but it's not the same.'

'Then you definitely need to move again and have a garden. It is good for the soul,' Pierre said. 'While you stay here, you must enjoy this garden.'

He had heard and understood her mutterings then, but somehow Matilda didn't mind as much as she thought she would.

'You know, I think you're right. I'll have to talk to my son and convince him it's the right time.'

Pierre looked at her before picking up his hoe again. 'If his mother is happy – the son will be happy. Enjoy your day,' he said, turning away to concentrate on the weeds again.

'You too,' Matilda said.

Walking on, she smiled to herself. Funny how easy it was to take a stranger's advice and feel that somehow he understood her need.

* * *

Chelsea finished her breakfast croissants, changed into her swimming costume, picked up her phone, her book and grabbed a towel before closing her bedroom door and making her way to the pool.

A quick text to Elsie to make sure everything at home was all right and then she'd read.

Elsie's reply five minutes later was reassuring:

✉ All good. Stop fussing. Some new enquiries for next month. Hope u r having good time. xxx

Chelsea breathed a sigh of relief. It did look as if everyone who had told her Kit-gate would die away was right. She should stop worrying. Another couple of months, it would all be forgotten and she'd be able to show her face again without feeling people were whispering about her behind her back. And the business didn't look as if it was affected if there were new potential clients making enquiries.

Sitting on the recliner, she rubbed sunscreen on her face and body. Hopefully she'd manage to acquire a nice gentle, healthy tan over the next week. Screwing the cap back on the sunscreen bottle, she adjusted the angle of the recliner before lying back with a happy smile. It was so peaceful here, the only noises the sound of the cicadas out of sight somewhere in the trees and the gentle movement of the water against the sides of the pool as the pump moved it endlessly through the filter.

She picked up her book and tried to concentrate, but for some reason she found it difficult to get into the story. It wasn't at all the kind of novel she'd expected and she put it down, closed her eyes and simply lay there soaking up the sun, thinking about how different life would be when she got home.

As the heat intensified, she got up and opened one of the large parasols, before picking up her goggles and deciding to cool off in the pool. Rather than do her usual energetic swim, she grabbed one of the noodle foam sticks floating around in the shallow end and, pushing it in front of her, slowly kicked down the length of the pool.

Turning to swim back, she realised Matilda was sitting on the edge, her feet in the water, watching her.

'Hi. You coming in for a swim?'

'Not right now. I thought I'd join you sitting in the sun,'

Matilda said. 'I've brought a couple of cold drinks if you'd like one?'

'Thanks,' Chelsea said, climbing out of the pool.

'This place really is a mini paradise, isn't it?' Matilda said. 'I know I'm finding it easier here to think about dreams for the future and how I'd like it to be.'

Chelsea glanced at her. 'You still have dreams for the future?'

Matilda nodded. 'Of course. Why are you surprised?'

'I thought you'd have your life sorted being so...'

'Old and the wrong side of sixty?' Matilda said gently. 'It's even more important now to try and get things right.' She took a sip of her drink. 'You said something on our first evening about being off men and feeling raw. You really should stop feeling like that. You need to put it behind you and get on with your life.'

Chelsea nodded. 'I know. I've come to terms with the fact that it was my own stupid fault, but I haven't quite reached the stage where I can forgive myself. Also I'm—' At that moment, her phone pinged with an incoming text. 'Excuse me a moment,' and she picked up the phone. And froze on seeing the caller ID, before reading the message.

✉ Texting because I have the feeling you won't pick up when you see it is me. I need you to explain what the hell has been going on. RING ME. Love Dad.

So much for thinking Kit-gate was fading into the past. Chelsea's heart sank. Now her dad had heard, the proverbial had well and truly hit the fan.

* * *

From where she was sitting on the little terrace outside her room, Vicky could see Matilda and Chelsea chatting down by the pool. Chelsea, although a few years older, reminded Vicky of Suzie in many ways. Smart, full of energy and a zest for life that might have been derailed recently, but Vicky doubted that Chelsea would stay down for long. She wondered about going down to join them but decided against interrupting them. She thought briefly about going for a swim, but she'd never been much of a swimmer. She'd have to do some exercise though while she was here, otherwise, with the wonderful food that Olivia clearly intended to feed them, she'd be a blob by the end of the holiday.

Vicky stood up. A walk around the garden and then maybe she'd join the other two for a bit before settling down to some writing. She'd hate them to think she was stand-offish.

The garden, she discovered, was full of hidden pathways and secret little nooks and crannies to hide away in. Vicky caught her breath in delight as she found the most perfect little wooden summer house in the shade of a large linden tree. Octagonal in shape, its tongue-and-groove construction had been painted the palest yellow, while the roof was an aqua blue, crowned on its peak with an owl-shaped weathervane.

Tentatively, Vicky lifted the door latch and smiled as the unlocked door opened. Inside, the walls had been painted the same yellow as outside, white muslin curtains were tied back at the windows and a large creamy tapestry rug lay in the middle of the terracotta tiled floor. In front of one of the windows, a wooden table with a multicoloured glass art nouveau lamp stood, its droplets twinkling as the sunlight caught them.

Three wicker chairs were scattered around and, something Vicky had always coveted, a chaise longue had been placed at the back. Gently lowering herself on to it, Vicky discovered it had been expertly positioned to take full advantage of the view out through the double doors into the garden and down Belle Vue's drive. Sitting there, Vicky breathed a happy sigh. As a writing retreat, the summer house would be just perfect. She promised herself the next time she walked up here she'd bring her laptop. It was such a beautiful place, she felt sure her writing would be inspired.

Carefully closing the door behind her, Vicky carried on along the path as it curved around the back of the summer house and meandered through some shrubs and a terraced rock garden before gently sloping down towards the pool.

'Hi,' Chelsea called, throwing her phone onto the recliner as she saw her. 'You can keep Matilda company for five minutes. I'm going for another swim. I need to cool off,' and Chelsea dived into the pool and started a fast and furious crawl down the length of it.

'Is she all right?' Vicky asked, watching her.

'I think someone sent her a text that has upset her,' Matilda explained. 'I do hope it was nothing to do with the relationship that went wrong. She was telling me earlier that she's come to terms with the fact that whatever happened was her own fault but can't forgive herself yet for being stupid. Chalking it up to experience and moving on is always hard to do, especially when you're young. Lemonade?' Matilda picked up a can and held it out to Vicky. 'Still cold and quite refreshing.'

'Thanks,' Vicky said, sitting on one of the teak loungers. 'Have you seen that wonderful summer house right at the top of the garden? I think I'm going to use it as my writing hut. If that's all right with everyone, of course.'

'I'm sure it will be,' Matilda said. 'It's so generous of Amy to share Belle Vue with us. I've never won anything in my life before and I have to keep pinching myself that I'm having a free holiday. It's so beautiful here.'

'It is,' Vicky agreed. 'And feels a million miles away from real life.'

Thoughtfully, she sipped her lemonade. Matilda was right. Moving on emotionally or physically was always a hard transition, whatever age you were. Making changes to her life when she returned home would take a lot of determination. Determination she hoped she possessed.

'I think I'll put my feet in the pool for ten minutes,' Vicky said. 'Then I'm going to grab my laptop and retreat to the summer house and do some plotting.'

DAY THREE OF THE HOLIDAY – JUNE 8

8

As agreed at dinner the previous evening, everyone congregated in the kitchen for breakfast the next morning, ready for Pierre to run them down to the station at nine to catch the train to Monaco. Matilda, although still unsure about her ankle, had decided to join them and had her stick firmly to hand as they boarded the train for the ride along the coast.

'So many tunnels,' Chelsea said as the train whooshed through another one.

'The long one as we leave Cap d'Ail will take us into the heart of Monaco,' Amy said. 'We'll grab a taxi and go straight up to the Palace. We should just about be in time for the changing of the guard at midday.'

'It's no Buckingham Palace, is it?' Vicky whispered to Matilda an hour or so later as they joined the crowd already in Palace Square in front of the main entrance to the Palace. 'It's so tiny in comparison. I know it's a silly allusion, but it makes me think of a decoration for the top of a wedding cake!' she laughed. 'I love it.'

Watching the guards in their full dress white summer

uniforms marching past, Vicky snapped a picture on her
phone and sent it to Anthony.

✉ Guess where I am today? Hoping for a glimpse of Princess
Charlene with the twins.

The short ceremony was over quickly, not much longer
than five minutes Vicky estimated, before the crowd started
to disperse. Amy led them over to where cannons were
placed overlooking the harbour at Fontvieille and the huge
arches of the entrance to the Stade Louis II football stadium
in the distance.

Turning her back on the view and looking at the Palace
and the other buildings, Vicky sensed there was definitely
something special about this place perched on The Rock
high above the Mediterranean. There was just something in
the air that was glamorous and exciting, not to mention the
sense of history underlying everything. Not even the large
number of tourists milling around managed to disperse that
feeling for her.

'Right, lunchtime,' Amy said. 'Follow me.'

She led them down one of the narrow ancient streets and
ushered them through a narrow doorway into a restaurant
already filling up with customers. A waiter showed them to a
table set in the corner of an unexpected, small courtyard
filled with tubs of lavender and lemon trees, handed them
menus and promised to return in 'cinq minutes' for their
orders.

Over lunch, Amy outlined the plans for the afternoon. A
stroll around the streets, a visit to the cathedral and then a
walk down to the harbour before making their way to the
Café de Paris for a spot of people watching around the Monte
Carlo Casino before catching a train home.

She glanced anxiously at Matilda. 'How's the ankle? You can take a taxi from here if you prefer and we'll meet up with you at the Café de Paris.'

'I'll walk down with you,' Matilda said. 'But I think taking a taxi to the top of town is a good idea.'

It was gone two o'clock before the four of them left the restaurant to start exploring the shops lining the narrow lanes on their way to the cathedral. Once in the cathedral, Matilda was the first of them to light a candle, Amy and Vicky followed, only Chelsea hung back.

'This is a catholic cathedral, isn't it? I'm not catholic,' she said sotto voce to Amy.

'Your religion is irrelevant. Think of it simply as a candle to remember someone you've lost and whom you miss,' Amy said quietly. 'Mine is in memory of my Aunt Tasha.'

'My mum. I miss her a lot,' Chelsea said. 'I'll light one for her.'

Leaving the cathedral twenty minutes later, they were all quiet, lost in their own memories. The dazzling sunlight that hit their eyes as they walked down the steps had them all searching their bags for sunglasses. Amy led them back towards Palace Square, past the dark bronze figure of Francis Grimaldi near the arch, and on to the pathway that led down to the port via a series of steps and slopes. The sunshine, along with the laughter and chatter of tourists, banished the sober feelings the atmosphere in the cathedral had imbued in each of them.

By the time they reached the port, Amy could see that Matilda was leaning heavily on her stick and rang for a taxi to take her to the top of the town. Once they'd waved Matilda off, promising they'd see her within the hour for a coffee in the Café de Paris, the other three started to walk along the front and then up the hill, past the Princess Grace Theatre, towards the casino.

Passing the theatre, Amy caught her breath as she saw a poster advertising the opening night of a ballet. She quickened her pace until she was almost running in her anxiety to put the theatre as far behind her as possible. The poster had brought back painful memories of the past and the thought that she'd be accosted at any moment by the one person she dreaded seeing. The sensible part of her brain tried to tell her it was unlikely they'd bump into each other once she got away from the theatre area, but she didn't want to take the risk.

'Whoa,' Vicky puffed. 'I can't keep up this pace. Why the rush?'

Amy slowed down. 'Sorry. I wasn't thinking. Let's have a wander along rue de Monte Carlo before we meet up again with Matilda? Some of the poshest shops in Monaco are there.'

Vicky glanced at her curiously before saying, 'Sounds fun, but please don't let me get my credit card out.'

'Don't worry,' Chelsea said. 'I'm definitely only window shopping. We'll hold each other back.'

By the time the three of them had oohed and aahed their way past the posh shops and were admiring the jewellers' window near the Casino, Amy's breathing had returned to normal.

Outside the Casino, there was the usual crush of tourists all vying with each other to have their photographs taken alongside the various luxury cars parked in front of the entrance steps.

Vicky held her phone out. 'Would one of you please take a photo of me posing against... against that one,' and she pointed to a white Aston Martin convertible. 'I know it's an incredibly naff thing to do, but,' she laughed, 'it's Anthony's dream car.'

Chelsea took the phone. 'You can take one of me afterwards. I fancy the red Ferrari.'

'I'm going to join Matilda,' Amy said. 'I've just spotted her over there,' and she waved to Matilda sitting at one of the tables on the pavement outside the Café de Paris.

Quarter of an hour later, the four of them were enjoying chatting and people watching when Amy saw her worst fear coming down the Casino steps, hand in hand with a woman. How could she have forgotten how high the chances were here in Monaco of bumping into the one man she'd been avoiding for the past five years? He always spent a lot of the summer there, in his small studio in one of the modern apartment blocks down by the heliport in Fontvieille. She hadn't forgotten really. Simply pushed the possibility to the back of her mind in her eagerness to give the others a day out.

The knot in her stomach tightened and, too late, she tried to shrink out of sight. His glance across the crowds caught hers, and she saw him start before saying something to the woman and leaving her as he ran down the rest of the steps, making his way over to Amy.

'Hello, Amy. This is an unexpected surprise.' The smile he gave her failed to reach his eyes.

'Hello.'

'What are you doing here?'

'I'm on holiday with my friends,' Amy gestured towards the others, praying that they wouldn't interrupt and tell him the truth.

'You could have rung the theatre. Left a message to say you were in town. We could have had lunch. We need to talk.' He stared at her before brusquely demanding.

'Where are you staying?'

'Not in Monaco,' Amy said quickly. 'Further along the coast. Your friend is waiting.' Pointedly, Amy looked at the woman now opening the door of the white Aston Martin. 'Goodbye.'

He sighed and shook his head as he looked at her. 'You can't run away forever, Amy. There are things that need sorting. You should have answered my calls. But right now is not a good time. I have to go. Just make sure you reply to the next letter.' He turned and strode purposefully to his car and slid into the driving seat.

They all watched as he edged the car out into the traffic and, with a wave of his hand in Amy's direction, drove off.

Vicky looked at Amy. 'Are you going to tell us who that was – or shall we all be terribly polite and British and talk about other things?'

Amy smothered a deep sigh and looked at the other three. 'That was my husband. Kevin Peake.'

'You mean your ex-husband?' Vicky said.

Amy shook her head. 'No. We're still married. And he's right. I did run away.'

DAY FOUR OF THE HOLIDAY – JUNE 9

9

Vicky carried a coffee and her laptop up to the little summer house and sighed happily as she sat in one of the comfortable wicker chairs admiring the view and drinking her coffee before she started work.

Today was the day she intended to start writing her novel. So far, she'd compiled a list of characters with a few descriptive details, a beginning, a middle and an ending for the actual story, a vague plot outline and a jumble of jotted notes. She was itching to get stuck into the actual writing now, knowing that, as she wrote, further scenes would come to her. Except this morning she couldn't stop thinking about the incident in Monaco yesterday. Amy's ashen face and the dead tone to her voice as she'd told them about Kevin had stuck in her brain.

When they'd got back to Belle Vue, after a subdued journey, Amy had excused herself and gone straight to her room. A terse Olivia had served the three of them dinner and passed on Amy's apologies. By mutual, unspoken agreement, they'd eaten and talked about everything else but Amy and

Kevin. Once dinner was finished, they'd all gone their separate ways for the rest of the evening.

Vicky couldn't help wondering about the story behind Amy and Kevin's failed relationship. They certainly looked ill-matched in appearance, apart from anything else. The woman holding hands with Kevin coming down the steps of the Casino had screamed the same high maintenance look as he did and was the exact opposite of Amy. Amy... well, Amy was lovely. Not that she wasn't smart and well-dressed, but it was in an understated, discreet and classy way, rather than an 'in your face', 'look at my designer labels' way. And she still moved so gracefully, like the dancer she'd once been.

As for Kevin, Vicky had recognised his type only too well. Arrogant. Self-entitled. Opinionated. A man who wouldn't care who he hurt to get to what he wanted. Poor Amy. Marriage had probably been a mistake on Kevin's part and Amy had been the one to suffer.

As Vicky sipped her coffee, her laptop pinged with an incoming email. Anthony. She smiled as she read it.

Really jealous of your visit to Monaco – maybe we can go together some day? How's the writing going? How are you getting on with everyone? I hope you are enjoying your break – missing you. Love A.

Quickly Vicky typed a reply.

It's wonderful. We'll definitely do Monaco together one day. You'll love it. Everyone here is lovely. I'll tell you about yesterday's small drama when I get home. I miss you too. Love V.

She pressed the send button and sat back. It was true – she was missing Anthony. They'd been apart for days at a time before when he was busy doing government things and she'd missed him then, but not like she did now. It probably had something to do with the fact that it was her away doing her own thing in a different country with Anthony being the one left at home. She felt strangely released from the guilt that had hung over her ever since she'd accepted the holiday, when she realised that.

The minute the email had whooshed off into cyberspace she remembered she hadn't answered Anthony's question about her writing. She needed to get on with what she was here for.

Vicky closed the email application and pressed the icon to open a blank page. Taking a deep breath, she typed *Trouble on the Riviera. Chapter One.*

Like Vicky, the morning after Monaco, Matilda was up and taking an early shower. Before breaking her ankle, at home she'd always gone for a long pre-breakfast walk on the Downs, enjoying the solitude and the glimpses of wildlife she occasionally saw; a tawny owl flitting across the sky, homeward bound as the sky brightened, a vixen and a cub purposefully crossing a path and disappearing into the undergrowth, and many different birds, of course. Her injury, just over four months ago, had put an end to those walks and she just hoped it would improve enough by the end of her holiday for her to get back into a walking routine. Although a bit stiff, her ankle had responded well to the walking yesterday and was definitely on the mend. So, from today, she intended to begin every day with a pre-breakfast stroll around the gardens and possibly one before dinner as well. The exercise would also help to get rid of some of the extra calories she was eating. If her ankle held up, she'd be as fit as a fiddle when she went home.

Closing her bedroom door behind her and walking down the shallow terrace steps to the path, Matilda turned left towards a part of the garden she hadn't explored. She'd barely walked five metres before Lola bounded towards her, tail wagging furiously.

'Morning, Lola, you coming with me? No biscuits, I'm afraid,' Matilda said, thinking she should try and find some if the little dog was going to accompany her every morning.

Together, they wandered along, Matilda stopping occasionally to admire the view down to the Mediterranean or when a particular shrub or plant caught her eye. As she walked, she thought about Amy and her marriage. She'd looked so vulnerable and helpless after Kevin had left and Matilda couldn't help wondering what had gone wrong between them. The next time she saw Amy on her own she'd ask if she'd like to talk about things, maybe she could offer some help in a small way from her own past experience.

Matilda remembered that feeling of helplessness and despair so well, but she could at least offer Amy hope, if nothing else. Tell her these things had a habit of working themselves out – sometimes in unexpected ways. She'd been far happier with the kindred spirit that was William. She still missed him so much it hurt. But the time was coming when she'd have to sort things out and make plans for living the rest of her life alone.

Matilda sighed. Decision time was hovering. She resolved to talk to Josh the next time she saw him. He knew her as well as anyone – their mother-son bond was strong. Josh had adored William too and felt his death keenly.

She was standing looking at a tree with lots of funny lychee like unripened fruit hanging from it and wondering what it was when Pierre appeared pushing a wheelbarrow. Lola greeted him like a long lost friend before sitting back on her haunches and regarding him hopefully. He laughed as he pulled a biscuit out of his pocket and gently gave it to the dog.

'Bonjour, Pierre,' Matilda said. 'Ça va?'

'Oui merci. Et vous?'

Matilda nodded. 'Merci. Please tell me, this tree? What is it? The fruit looks interesting.'

'C'est un Arbutus unedo. You Anglaise would call it a strawberry tree,' Pierre said with a smile. 'But you are too early to taste the fruit. It will be late summer before it is ready to eat.'

'That's what the fruit reminds me of,' Matilda said. 'Strawberries. One of my favourite fruits.'

'Moi, je preferé the raspberry, but I grow both. I will pick some for you,' Pierre said. 'For dinner this evening. Maybe Olivia will make a pavlova to accompany.'

'Thank you in advance,' Matilda smiled.

'You walk without a stick today,' Pierre said. 'Your ankle, it is healed?'

'I just need to exercise and strengthen it,' Matilda said. 'I walk a lot at home, so a walk around the garden before breakfast every day will help.' She glanced at Pierre. 'I want to go down into Cannes and that is a bit too far to walk. I'm hoping Amy will have a taxi number.'

'I am 'appy to take you, I 'ave some shopping to do,' Pierre said. 'I often chauffeur the guests.'

'Are you sure? You have time?'

Pierre nodded. 'Of course. 10.30, okay for you?'

Matilda nodded.

'Bon. Enjoy your walk and your breakfast.'

Matilda watched as Pierre trundled off with his wheelbarrow, with Lola following companionably at his heels, before making her way to the kitchen in search of coffee. She was delighted to find Chelsea there, already helping herself to a couple of pains au chocolat.

'Morning. Shall we keep each other company for breakfast or are you going back to your room?' Matilda asked.

'Definitely keep each other company. Here or out on the terrace – it's such a beautiful day,' Chelsea said.

'Let's sit on the terrace,' Matilda answered. 'Is Amy around this morning?'

'She was, but said she had to go down to the village quickly for something.'

* * *

At 10.30, Matilda found Pierre waiting for her by the bougainvillea at the front of the villa, ready to drive her into Cannes.

'That is such a beautiful colour,' she said, stopping to admire the huge spread of purple across the front of Belle Vue before turning to Pierre. 'If I had a proper garden at home, I'd be begging you for a cutting.'

'No need to beg. If you want a cutting, you can have one,' Pierre smiled, opening the car door for her. 'It would survive in a big pot.'

Matilda shook her head. 'Sadly, my balcony is small and already overcrowded.'

Pierre shrugged. 'Un petit problem. If you ever have the space, let Amy know and I'll send you a cutting.'

'Thank you.'

Matilda settled back in the front passenger seat as Pierre navigated around the slight horseshoe bend leading to the village, before turning onto the bord de mer. Both the sky and the Mediterranean were blue and the sun was glinting off the sea as the waves lapped the beach where children were already playing.

'I'd forgotten how beautiful it is down here,' Matilda sighed. 'Years ago, I came with my husband and our son. We stayed in Antibes and it was one of the best family holidays we ever had. We even talked about moving here one day.'

'Amy, she tells me she is taking you all for an outing to Antibes soon. It will bring back the good souvenir for you, n'est pas?'

'Souvenir?' Matilda said, puzzled for a moment. 'Ah, memories. Yes, it will.'

Good memories for certain, but tinged with sadness now that William was gone. If only Josh could be with her as she relived that precious holiday. Maybe she'd suggest a short holiday there together in the autumn if he was back in the country and not off helping on another crusade to save whales and dolphins with Sea Shepherd.

She hesitated for several seconds, unsure of Pierre's reaction, she didn't want him thinking she was gossiping, before saying. 'Amy has been quiet since we saw her husband in Monaco. Is there anything we can do to help her?'

Pierre's hands on the wheel stiffened and he gave a Gallic shrug of his shoulders. 'Peut-être you know a hitman?' A smile touched his lips as he glanced sideways at her.

'Sadly no. I wish I did.'

'Olivia, she tells her 'as to get on with the divorce now. It is hard, but there can be no going back.' Pierre's face as he pulled up at a red traffic light was stern and Matilda sensed how angry and hurt the whole business of Amy and her husband made him feel. As the car inched forward when the lights changed, Pierre glanced at her. 'Do you have something definite to do in town?'

Matilda shook her head. 'No. I just fancied a wander

around really. And maybe a coffee somewhere. I don't want to be a nuisance if you have things to do.'

'I have some errands from Amy and Olivia. Is an hour long enough for you?'

'I suspect my ankle will have had enough by then.'

'Bien. I park here,' and Pierre expertly manoeuvred the car into a small space on the bord de mer. 'I wait for you at that café,' he said, pointing over the road, 'In about an hour and we have a coffee together before we return for lunch. D'accord?'

'D'accord,' Matilda agreed. 'And the coffees are on me.'

They crossed the road together and then Pierre left to make his way to Marché Forville, while Matilda wandered along in what she hoped she remembered as being the direction of the famous rue d'Antibes for an indulgent spot of window shopping. Passing an estate agent's on the way, she stopped and looked at the upmarket luxury properties displayed in the window. 'Très cher' didn't begin to describe them – although some were so expensive, prices had been replaced by the letters POA. Which, in Matilda's book, translated as 'if you have to ask, you can't afford it'. There didn't appear to be any what she'd term as normal houses up for sale. Lots of apartments were in her price range though.

She turned away. No point in even thinking about changing from one apartment to another, even if the new one was in a different country with year-round sunshine and a communal pool, when what she really wanted was a proper house with a garden.

She meandered on. Through a marble tiled mall with a diverse range of shops, including a tabac, where she bought a couple of postcards. She needed to send Sheila one at least.

For several moments, she stood in front of one window display, wondering whether to answer the siren call of the soft leather jacket draped over the shoulders of a mannequin. She'd spent a lifetime longing for a leather jacket like it. The azure blue colour was beautiful. It would be a perfect addition to her wardrobe.

In the shop, the chic saleswoman helped her on with the jacket and then stood back, probably sensing that the garment had already sold itself to the elegant Englishwoman. Matilda looked at herself in the mirror and smiled. It fitted and she looked good in it. But a little voice was niggling in her ear: *Leather at your age?* Matilda batted that thought away. This jacket was classy and ageless. The next thought though, refused to be ignored. It was the kind of jacket that aided and abetted a glamorous lifestyle, which her life back in Bristol was anything but. She enjoyed the occasional dinner at a smart restaurant, a concert or a show at the Hippodrome with Josh, but the lack of a proper social life meant in reality that the jacket would spend more time in her wardrobe than on her back. It was a jacket that needed to be seen and admired. Reluctantly, she slipped it off and handed it to the sales assistant.

'Merci. Mais non.'

The sales assistant didn't answer, simply took the jacket back with a shrug.

Near the exit of the mall, a trio of men were busking. Matilda stopped to listen to them playing a medley of jazz for several moments before foraging in her purse for some euros and putting them in the saxophone case placed in front of them. She acknowledged the smiles of thanks from the men with a wave of her hand.

A quick look at her watch and she saw that she'd spent more time in the boutique than she realised. There was only about ten minutes left before she was due to meet Pierre back at the coffee shop. There was no way she could hurry, her ankle was twinging and without her stick it was impossible for her to walk fast. She just hoped she wouldn't keep Pierre waiting too long.

Pierre was sitting at a pavement table outside the café, thumbing a magazine, and stood up when she arrived and brushed her apology aside.

'Désolé. We do not have the time for coffee. I 'ave to get you back to Belle Vue and go to Olivia's. She's not well.'

Pierre took her arm as they hurried across the road to where the car was parked, explaining Amy had phoned him saying Olivia was ill.

Driving back up to the villa, Pierre concentrated on the road and Matilda sat at his side silently, hoping nothing was seriously wrong with his sister.

'Drop me off at the gate and I'll walk up the drive,' she said. 'Save you a moment or two. I can take the shopping up to the villa for you.'

'Merci.' And Pierre took off again for the village.

When Matilda walked into the kitchen with the basket of shopping, Amy and Chelsea were there setting out the lunch things and Chelsea was talking.

'Amy, I really don't mind doing it. In fact, I'd enjoy it. Please let me.'

'It is supposed to be a holiday for you,' Amy said, slicing through a baguette. 'We can go down to the village tonight. I can get an agency cook in for a couple of nights or we can eat out.'

'Giving the three of us a free holiday is generous enough – taking us out to dinner every night or employing a cook for the rest of the holiday is way too much. Please try and convince her to let me cook dinner until Olivia is better,' Chelsea said, turning to Matilda. 'I love cooking – it's never a chore to me. And I'd love to cook in this kitchen.'

'Olivia will probably be better again by the weekend. It just doesn't seem right for you to be cooking,' Amy said.

'Chelsea's right about the extra expense. I'm happy to help her in the kitchen if she needs a sous chef. And I'm sure Vicky will too,' Matilda said. 'It will be fun and add another element to our holiday.'

'Okay, I give in,' Amy said, holding both her hands up. 'Thank you, both. I'll fetch you a copy of the menus Olivia and I planned for the next few days, but, Chelsea, do feel free to do your own thing if you'd rather.'

Early evening and Vicky sighed contentedly as she treated herself to a pre-dinner bath. Bliss, she slipped further under the bubbles into the hot water. She loved this bathroom. She was definitely going to make the case for changing one of the showers back home to a full-size bath.

Not that their bathroom could ever be as luxurious as this one. It would never have gold taps or a claw-footed, free-standing bath but she'd happily settle for a simple IKEA bath with normal chrome-plated taps and perhaps a couple of rows of marble tiles as a splash-back surround creating enough space for candles. There was nothing quite like a long, rejuvenating soak to get the creative juices flowing. Not that she was currently thinking about her novel. She was thinking about Tom and Suzie.

Anthony hadn't mentioned the children in his email and she had forgotten to ask about them. What kind of mother did that make her? Definitely guilty of... what exactly? The truth was, the two of them were busy living their own lives and had virtually moved out of the family home, so she wasn't constantly worrying or wondering what they were up to. They'd both wished her a happy holiday when she'd told them about Belle Vue before dashing off in different directions. So she didn't have to give guilty feelings room in her conscience. Both Tom and Suzie would be in touch soon enough with either her or Anthony if they needed help.

Deep in thought, Vicky stretched out a foot and nudged the hot water tap open. Lying there, the thought occurred to her that once you were a so called grown-up, life became a series of milestones – first job, first car, first flat, first lover et cetera, et cetera, and then when you added children into the equation, it all gathered an unstoppable momentum. The first smile, tooth, step, birthday, first day at school, first— oh, the list was endless. The children grew and you got older with their passing birthdays without truly noticing your own. You were so busy watching and encouraging them and enjoying their achievements that you didn't realise, until it was too late, what had truly happened, or even what hadn't happened, in your own life.

All those milestones had flashed by as though on the busiest motorway in the world. Suddenly you were a mere step away from being middle aged. And there was no doubt about it, she and Anthony were at another milestone in their lives together with the children leaving home. Back to being that idealistic couple they were over twenty years ago. But that was the problem. All those family and life milestones had changed them as people. They both had a different mindset these days. Anthony's time seemed to be taken up 24/7 with being a backbencher and his constituency, leaving very little time for her.

Whereas, back home, she currently had nothing to occupy her days with other than her mundane normal housekeeping routine and a few hours every week helping out in the charity shop. She knew she and Anthony had grown apart in recent years as Tom and Suzie became more independent. The closeness of their early years together had been swallowed up and become a distant memory. Would they even survive as a couple as they approached their later years? So many middle aged couples divorced these days.

Vicky pushed the tap off with her toe. She was getting maudlin. She needed to snap out of it and think about something else.

Towelling herself dry with one of the super-sized white towels from the heated towel rail, Vicky tried to think about her story but found herself thinking of Amy again. Wondering what had gone wrong with her marriage. The evening they'd all arrived and introduced themselves over aperitifs and dinner, she and Matilda had spoken of their children, but Amy hadn't mentioned any. Maybe that had been the problem – she and Kevin didn't have – or couldn't have – a family together?

In a lightbulb moment, Vicky realised that Kevin the not-yet-ex-husband would make a good villain in her novel. Suitably camouflaged and unrecognisable of course. She'd kill him off, for Amy's sake.

Quickly reaching for her laptop, Vicky smiled as she made a few notes while the idea was fresh in her mind.

DAY FIVE OF THE HOLIDAY
– JUNE 10

10

After breakfast the next morning, Chelsea took the wicker basket she'd discovered earlier hanging in the kitchen cupboard, picked up her list, slung her slouchy tote over her shoulder and set off for the village. Amy had said there was a small market there a few mornings a week and today was one of those days. She planned on sticking to the menus Olivia had worked out already for the next couple of evenings but had realised she needed some more eggs, fresh cream and possibly some extra local cheese.

Walking down the plane tree lined small road leading to the village, Chelsea smiled happily to herself. Being in France, a world away from everything back home and having new people in her life, was helping to clear her head. Crossing the road to reach the market, Chelsea noticed a hairdressers next door to the Credit Agricole bank. Now she was swimming again, she knew the chlorine would play havoc with her long hair. Maybe it was time for a change. Impulsively, she pushed open the door and walked into the salon. A familiar smell of shampoo and hair lacquer hit her nostrils as she made her way to the desk.

'Bonjour, Mademoiselle. Puis je vous aider?'

Chelsea opened her mouth and realised the little bit of French she spoke had deserted her. She stared at the girl's name tag – Bibi – closed her mouth and prayed that inspiration would strike.

'I speak English,' Bibi said, smiling at her. 'If that helps?'

Relief flooded Chelsea. 'You do? Wonderful. I'd like a haircut please.'

Bibi ran a practised scarlet fingernail down the page of the appointment book in front of her. 'Gaspard could fit you in later. Twenty-five minutes? You want cut and blow-dry?'

'S'il vous plait,' Chelsea said, pleased that she could at least remember that most basic of phrases.

'You want to wait?' Bibi asked.

'I'll do my shopping and come back if that's okay?'

Bibi nodded. 'But don't be late.'

'I promise,' and Chelsea hurried out of the salon.

She practically flew round the market, carefully stowing things in the wicker basket, and began to make her way back to the hairdressers. Passing a newsagent with a stand of magazines and papers on the pavement, she was surprised to see an English edition of her favourite celebrity magazine. Quickly pulling it off the rack, paying for it and tossing it in her tote, she ran back to the salon.

Bibi took Chelsea's basket and her tote before sending her to sit at a washbasin, where a junior washed her hair. Once that was done and she was sitting there with her head wrapped in a towel, Bibi came over.

'Gaspard will be with you in a moment. He doesn't speak English, so I will translate. Please tell me how you would like your hair? A little shorter or more short?'

'Definitely more short,' Chelsea said. 'A pixie cut?' She looked at Bibi, hoping she knew the style she meant.

'Ah, peut-etre à la Audrey Tatou?'

Chelsea looked at her blankly. 'Who?'

Bibi reached out and took a style catalogue off a shelf. 'Here. Like this?'

Chelsea took one look and nodded. 'À la Audrey Tatou, definitely.'

When Gaspard appeared at her side, Bibi simply showed him the photo and left him to it, muttering 'Bon courage' as she went. Chelsea wasn't sure which of them she'd aimed the comment at.

As Gaspard flashed his scissors and the first long tresses of her hair fell to the floor, Chelsea closed her eyes, praying that Gaspard did know how to make her look like a French starlet.

Half an hour later, Bibi tapped her on the shoulder.

'You open your eyes now.'

Chelsea opened them and promptly covered her face with her hands. It took several seconds before she plucked up the courage to peer between her fingers and sneak another look at Gaspard's work. She'd never had a haircut like it.

'You no like?' Bibi asked anxiously. 'Gaspard is a good cutter. He is our star.'

Chelsea slowly took her hands away from her and looked at herself properly before letting out a huge breath.

'Gaspard is not a good cutter – he's absolutely brilliant. I love it. Thank you, thank you,' and she jumped up and flung her arms around Bibi.

Gaspard still had the scissors in his hands and was staring at her with an unreadable expression on his face. No way was she going to hug him. Instead she gave him a beaming smile and when he smiled and held out his hand, she shook it, vigorously.

'Merci beaucoup. Merci beaucoup.'

* * *

Vicky bit her lip as she concentrated and tried to think of a hobby for one of her female characters and how it could link into her main storyline. She needed it to be something easily accessible to a single mum and not too expensive to do. So that ruled out horse riding, tennis or joining a gym, to name but three expensive hobbies, leaving her with? Knitting? Jogging? Watercolours? Cooking? As a mum, cooking would be an everyday ritual, so why would she want to do it for a hobby unless it had a fun element. Vicky knew that personally it wasn't something she would do. Cake making? Could making batches of cupcakes be a relaxing thing to do for her character? Something she maybe did at home when stressed.

Vicky had been surprised by how relaxed Chelsea was last night preparing dinner, something she never managed to be in the kitchen. She'd have to pick Chelsea's brains and extract a few tricks for when she went home. But maybe baking cupcakes could be on the agenda for her heroine.

By the time Chelsea returned from the village, Vicky had given up writing for the day and was sitting by the pool, reading the Edith Piaf biography from her room. She looked at a Chelsea she barely recognised.

'Gosh. You look different. Your hair looks amazing. Really suits you. You look younger than ever.'

'Thank you. It feels great too,' Chelsea said. 'You not writing this afternoon?'

Vicky shook her head. 'No. Thought I'd have a break – I am on holiday after all – and mull over some scenes in my head. I was wondering too if I could ask you some questions? One of my characters needs a hobby. I'm thinking about having her bake cupcakes as a way of relaxing and I know nothing about cakes. Apart from those in Marks and Sparks food hall. If you're going swimming, we can do it later.'

'I'm staying out of the water today. Can't ruin the blow-dry,' Chelsea laughed. 'And I'm going to catch up on all the celebrity gossip with this,' and she waved the magazine at Vicky.

Vicky's heart skipped a beat as she recognised the cover photo. 'Out-of-date gossip. That magazine is last month's, so the gossip is at least six weeks old.'

'What? Oh damn. It didn't occur to me to check the date,' Chelsea said. 'I haven't read it anyway, so it'll be news to me.' She settled down on one of the loungers before glancing across at Vicky. 'You like reading the gossip mags then?'

'Not really. Usually just look at the pictures. I read that particular one in the dentist's waiting room and recognised the cover,' Vicky said, turning a page in her book in the hope that Chelsea would not keep talking about the magazine. No need to tell her she'd bought that very copy and stashed it away because there was a picture of her and Anthony in there arriving for a Parliamentary dinner. With luck, Chelsea wouldn't spot her as she was thumbing through the pages. If she did, Vicky would have to admit Anthony was more than a mere civil servant, but unless that happened, she was determined to keep her anonymity. She was enjoying being incognito as good old Vicky Lewis.

'Yeah, me too, especially the interiors of famous people's homes. But some of the pics of celebrities are so Photoshopped. I bet in real life they'd be unrecognisable. So shoot: what d'you want to know about baking?' Chelsea said, looking up from the magazine.

Vicky stood up. 'Actually, can we do it later? Maybe when we're in the kitchen tonight. I've just remembered I need to text my husband. I'll leave you to enjoy your celebs.'

'Oh, okay,' Chelsea agreed, absently, glancing back down at a page of photos.

As Vicky picked up her things and turned to go to her room, she was conscious of Chelsea watching her.

There was no way she could stay as Chelsea continued to look through the magazine. The photo of her and Anthony definitely hadn't been Photoshopped. There was every chance that Chelsea would see it and recognise her.

* * *

Amy had had only one idea in her head as she got in her car that morning – to get away from Belle Vue and spend some time alone. Coming face to face with Kevin in Monaco had unsettled her more than she'd expected. Leaving the village behind, she automatically joined the east-bound traffic on the main road and impulsively decided to make for Juan-les-Pins, one of her favourite places on the coast.

As she left Cannes behind and began the drive along the bord de mer, Amy found herself in a stream of slow moving traffic, which suited her mood fine. Driving slowly allowed her glimpses of some of the old belle-époque villas that littered this part of the coast. Built to impress at the end of the nineteenth century, several had been lovingly restored, but others were mere shells of their former opulence and open to the elements.

She and Tasha had often played a game of 'I wonder who lived in that house' as they drove along the coast road. Tasha had been interested enough to start to research the history of several of the villas and had told her some gossipy tales she'd discovered about the people who had lived and holidayed in the houses. Some of her favourite stories had involved L'Horizon, an opulent villa, out of sight on the cliffs in front of the railway line that ran along the coast that was visible only from the sea. Winston Churchill, Wallis Simpson and Aly Khan to name but three people had apparently partied there.

Amy's initial reaction to hearing about L'Horizon had been one of disbelief. 'Who would want trains thundering past so close to a luxury home? Rather takes the romance of it all away.'

Francois, Tasha's husband, had often spoken too of the tales his parents had told him from the early forties, when Cannes had been occupied by the Germans and daily life had been lived in fear. Rumour had it that several local resistance groups had operated in the area.

Today, driving past the locked and graffitied steel gate leading to the hidden villa, Amy glanced seawards, wondering if it was still intact or whether it had suffered a similar fate to some of the other villas and was now derelict. It was impossible to believe that a place with such a rich, opulent history had just been left to rot. Tasha had often teased her, saying she hoped her romantic rose coloured view of life would never be challenged.

Pulling up at the lights in Golfe Juan, Amy sighed. Not only had it been challenged, it had been so damaged and broken, she doubted she had a romantic vibe left in her body. Marrying Kevin Peake had seen to that.

Kevin. Amy had known Tasha had never taken to him. She'd never badmouthed him to Amy but had made it quite clear that she couldn't understand what Amy saw in 'that man', as she called him. The tension between the two of them on the few family occasions when they met had been palpable. It was the main reason she'd seen less and less of Tasha once she'd married Kevin. When she did come to France during the five years of her marriage, it had always been alone. If Tasha had guessed she wasn't as happy as she made out, she'd never probed, believing that Amy would talk to her when the time was right.

But Amy had hugged the hurt to herself. It was her mistake, up to her to deal with it. Besides, she couldn't bear to tell either her mum or Tasha how ashamed she was for not listening to them. As the rows had become more frequent, Kevin more volatile, she'd really struggled, trying to keep a brave face on things. Keeping her distance from family and friends had become second nature. Thankfully, when the break-up finally happened, everyone accepted her version of things: 'We discovered we wanted different things from life and decided we were better off apart.' Not even Fleur knew all of the details, the lies and the depth of her heartbreak behind the split. Amy took a deep breath. It was in the past. She'd moved on.

Juan-les-Pins was busy as usual, but Amy managed to squeeze into a parking space on the front. Sitting in the car, she took her mobile out of her bag and pressed the shortcut button for her mother, hoping it wouldn't go straight to voicemail.

'Darling! Everything all right?' Fleur said.

'Fine. You?' Amy answered automatically. 'I took everyone to Monaco recently. Guess who I saw?'

She sensed her mother's sharp intake of breath rather than heard it. 'How did you feel? I hope he didn't make a scene?'

'No, he was with someone – a woman – but he did say – like you've been saying for ages – I can't run forever.' Amy caught her breath.

Two small toddlers, looking like twins, were excitedly running towards the beach, as their young parents, clutching windbreaks, buckets and spades, as well as a large chill box, struggled to make their way along the esplanade. Amy felt the tears rising. Something she'd never have now – a family of her own.

She shook herself. Forced herself to concentrate.

'I think you'll probably receive another solicitor's letter for me soon.' Amy took a deep breath. 'I'm going to make an appointment with a notaire and get the divorce underway – and keep it going this time.'

'Good. It's definitely more than time. Does he know you're at Belle Vue? He won't turn up there to harass you, will he?'

'No, I said I was on holiday with friends,' Amy explained. 'And I think his lady friend will keep him occupied. Right, I'm off for a walk on the beach, followed by lunch and a glass of rosé in your favourite bar. Wish you could join me.'

'Me too, but it's not long to July now. Take care, darling.'

Walking along the wide promenade hoping the sea air would clear her head, Amy remembered her mother's question about how she'd felt meeting up with Kevin unexpectedly. In truth, the shock at seeing him face to face for the first time since she'd left him had left her feeling nauseous and shaken. But once those feelings had disappeared, she'd been relieved to discover that she felt nothing for him. Not a single loving emotion remained in her body as she'd looked at him. Just a dull ache for all she'd lost.

The lunchtime rush had begun when she reached the bar-cum-restaurant and Amy was lucky to be shown to a table with a view out over the beach. She ordered a small glass of rosé to sip while waiting for her croque monsieur and side salad and sat there happily watching the place fill up with holidaymakers all keen to sample some typical French cuisine, bowls of mussels and frites piled high and steaming in most cases.

Her head definitely felt clearer after the sea air and she was able to think dispassionately about the past and more positively about whatever the future might hold for her. A little niggling worry was whether Kevin would, in fact, put two and two together and turn up at Belle Vue. Amy dismissed the thought as unlikely if he was staying in Monaco with a female companion. He probably didn't remember the exact location anyway, it was so long ago, the one and only time she'd taken him there.

After lunch, Amy made her way back to the car, stopping en route to buy a large ice cream – a special treat for dessert. An hour later, she was driving home feeling much happier in herself and knowing she could handle whatever happened now with Kevin much better than would have been possible five years ago. The weight on her shoulders was beginning to lift.

Chelsea and Matilda were in the kitchen when Amy got back. Chelsea was thumping a piece of pizza dough into submission as Matilda looked on.

'Hi, you two. Everything all right?' Amy said.

Matilda nodded. 'Yes. But it is a good thing you went out this morning. Your husband turned up.'

'Kevin? He came here today?' Amy's stomach clenched as worry took hold of her again.

Chelsea slapped the dough down on the board again. 'We told him you weren't here and he wasn't welcome.'

'He kept asking questions,' Matilda said. 'How long you were staying here? Did you have a partner? Where was Tasha?'

'Did you answer his questions?'

Both Matilda and Chelsea shook their heads.

'No. We genuinely didn't know the answers to his questions – and if we had, we wouldn't have told him anyway. Pierre heard the car arrive and he... he encouraged him to leave quickly.' Matilda smiled as she remembered how Pierre had quietly and firmly told the younger man to leave if he didn't want to be hurt or for the gendarmes to be called. Despite the age difference, Matilda knew that Pierre was more than fit enough to deal with Kevin.

Amy sighed. 'I'm sorry you had to deal with this, but I'm equally glad I took off this morning.'

'If you want to talk to me while I'm here, sometimes it is easier to talk to a friend who does not know about the past,' Matilda said, before adding quietly, 'People always say you have to work at a relationship, but when things go wrong, there are some things that can never be righted or forgiven.'

Amy smiled at her gratefully. 'Thank you. That is so true, but I've had time to come to terms with everything and forget the unforgivable lies I was told. It's time to push it firmly into the past and move on.'

Matilda patted her gently on the arm. 'I was in an abusive relationship many years ago from which William rescued me. Like I said, I'm happy to listen if it helps at all.'

11

Matilda wrote the postcard to Sheila sitting on the terrace outside her room. Knowing how much Sheila loved flowers, she'd chosen a photo of the old part of Cannes, Le Suquet, where window boxes were in abundance decorating the pastel coloured houses.

Looking at the postcard after she'd written her message, Matilda imagined herself living in one of the houses, enjoying the good weather this part of the coast was famed for, wandering down to the market every day, meeting friends for coffee, exploring the town, taking a boat ride out to the Iles de Lérins that she could see lying low out in the bay. Matilda sighed. All the things she and William had planned to do together when he retired. She missed William so much. Moving to France had been their dream. Would she be strong enough to build a new life in a different country without him at her side? Or would she be better staying put and keeping safe the life she already had and knew?

Maybe she was foolish to even think about moving away from Bristol? After all, she had everything she needed on her doorstep there, plus Sheila had become a good friend and there were many happy memories buried deep in her subconscious. She knew those memories would accompany her wherever she lived, but she dreaded them fading away as her life moved on. And making new friends rather than mere acquaintances certainly got harder as you aged.

On the other hand, since William had died, her life had settled down into a predictable rut. A rut that would get deeper the older she got and the longer she stayed in it.

She smiled to herself, remembering them having one of those inevitable frank discussions about getting older and one of them dying, leaving the other alone. William had urged her not to shut herself away but to live her life in the way that was best for her if he should die first. Even meet someone new. She definitely wasn't to don widow's weeds and give up on life – he'd threatened to come back and haunt her if she did. She was to follow her own dreams.

Matilda sighed, recalling how determined William had been to make her promise that she would continue to live a fulfilling life even without him in it. Something she'd failed to do since he'd died.

'You need to be there for Josh as a fully functioning member of the human race, not a shadow in the corner. No retreating into yourself after I'm gone. Promise?'

Of course, she'd promised, but who would know if she didn't keep her promise. Only her and her dodgy ankle.

Matilda stood up and took the postcards and her pen back into her room. She'd forgotten to buy stamps, so posting the cards would have to wait until her next visit down to Cannes or the village. Right now, she was going to walk around the garden to exercise her ankle, which thankfully was gaining in strength every day.

Pierre, busy weeding the vegetable patch tucked out of

sight of the main garden, raised a hand and threw her a smile in greeting when Lola barked, alerting him to Matilda's presence, but he didn't stop working. Not wanting to be a nuisance, Matilda waved back and kept walking. She had some serious thinking to do.

* * *

Both Matilda and Vicky insisted on helping Chelsea prepare dinner, with Vicky freely admitting she was what her grandmother always called 'a plain cook'.

'I do like cooking, but I've never seemed able to get beyond the basics of family comfort food. You know, cottage pie, casseroles, roast chicken, that kind of meal. Cooking with you will be like having a masterclass in cordon-bleu cuisine.' Vicky glanced at Chelsea. 'You won't throw things at me, will you? Or shout? I've heard some chefs are very temperamental.'

'I promise not to throw anything – or shout,' Chelsea smiled. 'Right, aprons on and let's get to it.'

Working companionably around the central island, they were soon chatting away as they peeled and sliced vegetables, and watching Chelsea as she made a bowl of mackerel pâté.

Amy, popping into the kitchen to see how they were getting on, opened a bottle of wine and poured them each a glass. As they all toasted each other, Chelsea's phone beeped. Amy went to pick it up off the dresser and hand it to her, but Chelsea shook her head.

'It'll be my father. I'll call him back later. Right, the starter's done, main course is underway. Olivia had crêpes Suzette down for dessert, so I need to make some light pancakes.'

The phone clicked over to voice message and into the

silence that suddenly engulfed the kitchen, Simon Newman's voice rang out. 'Chelsea, if you don't ring me back before midnight tonight, I shall come to France tomorrow. I need to know exactly what's been going on. Understand? Before midnight tonight. I'll be waiting.' The phone clicked off. In the strained silence that followed, Chelsea gave a weak smile.

'My dad is a bit cross with me over... something that happened a few weeks ago,' she said, looking at everyone. 'Something I never told him about at the time, but someone else clearly has.'

'He didn't sound cross cross,' Matilda said. 'More concerned for you.'

'Would he really come here?' Vicky asked. 'Not always easy to get a flight when you want it.'

'Dad always travels by private plane,' Chelsea said. 'If I don't ring him, he'll be here.' She took a deep breath. As much as she wanted to, she knew she couldn't put off talking to him any longer. 'I'll ring him later. Right now we've got pancakes to make.'

Whisking the eggs and flour together, Chelsea tried to keep her mind focused on the job in hand and not think about the conversation she was avoiding with her father. She'd ignored all three of his text messages, so she wasn't really surprised he'd phoned. Knowing he would have no hesitation in following through on his ultimatum, she'd ring him this evening after dinner – and face his wrath. She knew she'd let him down big time.

It wasn't until later that evening when everyone had eaten and declared everything to be delicious, that she excused herself and went to her room. As she'd known he would, Simon picked up the phone almost before she'd heard the tone ringing.

'Hi, Dad.'

'You okay, Sunshine?'

Chelsea smiled. At least he was still calling her by his pet name for her. 'I'm having a lovely holiday,' she said.

'You know that's not what I meant,' Simon said. 'Why didn't you tell me about Kit, or whatever his damn name is? Learning the sordid details from friends was not good.'

'I'm sorry, Dad. I was ashamed and I knew I'd let you down.'

'I thought you understood you could tell me anything. I hate you being hurt.'

'I know, Dad. Who told you anyway?'

'Marcia's father. We play golf together occasionally. He doesn't have a good word to say for her husband. Was against the marriage in the first place and wants her to kick him out. You, apparently, were the latest in a long line of affairs.'

Chelsea was silent. And she'd thought she meant something to him.

'If he gets in touch, promise me you won't have anything more to do with him?" Simon said.

'I promise you that goes without saying, Dad. I'm concentrating on the business from now on. No room in my life for any man – except you, of course!'

'You'll meet someone worthy of you one day, Sunshine,' Simon said. 'Please don't become bitter and twisted. I want to see you happy.'

'I am happy,' Chelsea insisted. 'I'm having a lovely holiday – I've even taken over cooking dinner for everyone because the regular cook is ill.'

'You're working on holiday?'

'You know me, happiest when I'm cooking and this place is wonderful – you'd love it here. Belle Vue is a special place. Amy, the owner, is lovely too.' She hesitated before adding, 'I'm swimming again. The pool here is amazing. I've realised how much I've missed swimming, so that's something I'm going to get back into when I come home.'

'Sunshine, that's the best news I've heard in years. I was so sad you felt you had to give up after...' Simon's voice faded away.

'I know. But it's definitely back in my life from now on,' Chelsea said.

A few minutes later, Simon ended the call, saying he was a lot happier now he'd spoken to her. Chelsea stood looking out over the terrace for a few moments thinking about her dad. She'd been wrong in expecting him to be furious with her over Kit. She should have remembered how protective he was of her – and how much he cared.

DAY SIX OF THE HOLIDAY – JUNE 11

12

When Chelsea told Matilda that Pierre was driving her down to Cannes to do some shopping, and would she like to go with her, Matilda accepted immediately. 'Yes please. How d'you feel about lunch out? My treat – a belated thank you for your help with my suitcase at the airport.'

'Lunch sounds a great idea, but I really didn't do anything.'

'Shall we ask Vicky to join us?' Matilda said, ignoring her comment. 'D'you know where she is?'

'She's already typing away in the summer house – not sure she wants to be disturbed.'

As Pierre drove them down, they told him they planned on staying in town for lunch and would get a taxi back to the villa afterwards.

'Non, non. You call the villa and I come for you when you are ready.'

Pierre dropped them on the Boulevard de la Croisette, not far from the famous Palais des Festivals, and they made their way up to rue d'Antibes, via the mall Matilda had explored the other day.

'How's the ankle? You haven't brought your stick,' Chelsea said.

'It's so much better, I thought I'd be brave and chance leaving it behind today,' Matilda answered.

'You can always take my arm and lean on me if you need to,' Chelsea offered.

When Matilda stopped by the boutique and pointed out the jacket she was tempted to buy, Chelsea urged her to get it.

'It's a beautiful colour. Did you try it on? I bet you looked good in it.'

Matilda nodded. 'The leather is wonderfully soft and so comfortable. It's just that I'm not sure I live the kind of life where I'd wear it enough. Get my money's worth. It's so expensive.'

'I'd wear it every day.' Chelsea laughed. 'It would become my signature look.'

Leaving the mall behind, they crossed the road and Matilda stopped in front of an estate agents. An outside rack fixed to the wall held copies of the free monthly magazine showcasing hundreds of properties along the Cote d'Azur. Matilda took one and put it in her bag. Chelsea glanced at her curiously.

'Bedtime reading,' Matilda said. 'With a little bit of daydreaming. Right now I need to find the post office so I can buy stamps and post my cards. Pierre mentioned there was one in this direction somewhere.'

While Matilda queued for what seemed like forever at La Poste, Chelsea wandered off in the direction of an upmarket kitchen shop. When Matilda found her there, she was standing in front of a set of copper saucepans and sauté pans.

'Aren't these beautiful? Since I've been using Olivia's pans,

I've realised just how good they are to cook with. I'm going to have to get some, but not today,' Chelsea said regretfully before turning to Matilda. 'Shall we find somewhere for lunch?'

'I know just the place,' Matilda said. 'The Terrace Restaurant at the Carlton. Come on.'

'Wow. Really? It's expensive there, isn't it?'

Ten minutes later, they were sat at a table for two and being handed glasses of sparkling rosé to sip while they looked at menus.

'I know it's none of my business, but have you spoken to your father?' Matilda said, glancing at Chelsea. 'He sounded very concerned in that voice message.'

'He does worry about me.' Chelsea sighed before she added quietly, 'Especially since it's been just the two of us.' Her voice died away before she smiled brightly at Matilda. 'I did ring him and we're good. Planning a get-together when I get home.'

'That's good. The father-daughter relationship can be special. I know William would have loved a daughter after we had Josh, but it never happened. Now, what would you like to eat? I can see our waiter returning.'

Chelsea's cryptic 'just the two of us' remark left Matilda wondering about her mother. The mother that she had failed to mention so far, which could mean a number of things. But Matilda wasn't one to probe. Everyone was entitled to keep their secrets – especially if they were painful ones.

* * *

Chelsea sipped her wine and looked around. She'd never have ventured in here on her own. It was the kind of place her dad liked to eat at and was a real glimpse of how the other half lived in Cannes.

The terrace was full of people. Some were clearly holidaymakers enjoying a treat, a few businessmen and women, with phones switched to silence but placed on the table ready to be picked up instantly, were seated at various tables. Chelsea's attention was caught by three women sitting at a table in the corner of the terrace. 'Ladies who lunch' she decided, smiling as she saw a small dog poke its head out of a large tote its owner had placed on the floor beside her.

'You're spoiling me, treating me to lunch here,' she said to Matilda. 'It's the kind of place my dad would love. He used to come to the South of France a lot – I suspect he would have eaten here in the past. I'll have to ask him when I get back.' Instantly, she regretted bringing her father back into the conversation as she sensed that Matilda was waiting for her to say more. 'Have you been here before?' she asked quickly.

'Years ago – it's different to how I remember it,' Matilda replied. 'It's had a makeover and feels even more glitzy than it did back then. I thought, as you cook for a living, you'd like the cordon-bleu food they do here.'

'It's a real treat,' Chelsea said, smiling. 'Your blue jacket would ace it here. Oh. I'm not sure, but I think Eddie Redmayne is being shown to a table.' She shook her head. 'Nah. It's probably someone who looks like him.'

'I wouldn't be so sure,' Matilda said. 'There are already a couple of famous people in here. Probably more famous to my generation than yours though.'

'Do tell. Who?'

'Well,' Matilda leaned forward conspiratorially. 'See those three women over there?' She threw a quick glance at the table where Chelsea had seen the dog in the tote bag. 'The older blonde is an actress who made her name in a well-known children's film years ago. And the two men and woman over there – the man on the right is a well-known French TV news presenter, Jean-Pierre... sorry, I forget his surname.' Matilda stopped speaking, an expression of shock on her face as she stared across the restaurant for a couple of seconds.

'What's the matter?'

'The man with him is Amy's husband, Kevin.' Matilda said flatly. 'The woman is different to the one we saw him with in Monaco, so she's probably Jean-Pierre's companion.' Matilda sighed. 'I do hope he doesn't recognise us.'

'Doesn't matter if he does. I'm glad Amy isn't with us though,' Chelsea said, before taking a sip of her wine and looking at the group over the rim of the glass.

The waiter arrived with their food and for several moments they both concentrated on eating.

'This magret of duck is delicious,' Chelsea said once she'd taken the edge off her appetite. 'How's your monkfish?'

'Wonderful,' Matilda answered, reaching for the glass of Soave white wine she'd ordered to accompany it.

Matilda was clearly used to the finer things in life, Chelsea decided as she watched her.

'That property magazine you picked up? Just daydreaming or are you seriously thinking of moving down here?'

Matilda sighed. 'To be honest, I'm in a bit of a "bugger's muddle" and I'm not sure what to do for the best.' She smiled at Chelsea. 'One moment a cottage with a garden in the countryside, the Cotswolds or the Forest of Dean, appeals. The next, I can imagine enjoying life down here in the sunshine. William and I always planned to move to France when he retired. Sadly, he never got the chance to retire.'

Matilda fell silent for a few seconds and twirled her wine around in the glass before smiling at Chelsea.

'Regrets in life are inevitable, but regrets over not doing something and years later wishing you had are avoidable – you simply have to take a deep breath and get on with whatever opportunity presents itself.'

'Have you thought like that all your life?' Chelsea asked.

'No. It was William's influence. He was an impulsive man.' Matilda smiled. 'Given to see opportunity and fun everywhere. Unlike me.' She took a sip of her wine. 'Of course, those decisions sometimes bring their own regrets, especially the older you get, but at least they're regrets that prove you've lived rather than just existed.'

Chelsea looked at Matilda thoughtfully. 'Can we keep in touch when we go home, please?'

'Of course,' Matilda said, looking startled at Chelsea's words. 'I'd like that.'

* * *

Vicky closed her laptop down with a sigh. Two thousand words written this morning and her body was stiff with sitting. Still, it had been a productive few hours and she felt happy with the result. She stood up and stretched, trying to loosen the knot in her neck with a couple of head swivels.

She'd heard the other two going off earlier with Pierre and wondered how they were enjoying their foray into the shops. She rather wished she'd gone with them, but then she wouldn't have written a new chapter of her novel. Besides, Chelsea buying that particular gossip magazine had unnerved her somewhat. She'd hoped to get to know her new friends as Vicky Lewis, but here she was starting to do exactly what she'd done for the last ten years as an MP's wife – holding people at arm's length. Vicky sighed. She'd go to Antibes with everyone and get to know them a bit better.

Amy was at the kitchen table filling a small baguette with salad and some prosciutto when Vicky walked in. 'Hi, just the two of us today for lunch. Shall we keep each other company?'

'Good idea. I think I'll join you with a salad baguette,' Vicky said, looking at Amy and registering how tired she looked. 'You okay?'

'Bit tired. D'you want to eat in or out?'

'Oh, out,' Vicky said. 'It's such a treat eating outside every day.'

While Vicky made her lunch, Amy opened a bottle of wine and took it and two glasses out to the terrace.

'How's the writing going?' she asked as Vicky sat down.

'Fits and starts really. One day everything flows – like today. The next, I look at the utter drivel I've written and know I haven't got what it takes to be a writer and I should just forget it. But today I feel I can do it. Cheers,' Vicky said, raising her glass in Amy's direction. 'Oh, and by the way, I killed off Kevin this morning in chapter three, so no more worries from that direction.'

'If only,' Amy said, laughing. 'But thank you for the thought.'

Vicky had almost finished her baguette before she glanced at Amy. 'Has Chelsea said anything to you about me?'

'No. Any reason why she would?'

'She bought an out-of-date copy of an English celebrity magazine and there is a picture of me with my husband attending a parliamentary dinner in it.' Vicky managed to laugh. 'I'm hoping the woman in the photograph looks so different to me, the Vicky Lewis you all know, as to be unrecognisable.'

'Does it matter if she does recognise you?' Amy asked.

Vicky shook her head. 'Not really. It's just that I wanted to stay incognito for a little while longer. Get everyone to know me as me.' Vicky glanced at Amy. 'I'd never planned on being married to a politician. It's a bit like living on a merry-go-round in a goldfish bowl at times.'

Amy laughed. 'I can imagine.'

'The worse of it is that being a politician's wife, I seem to have lost myself along the way – buried under all the trappings that Anthony's chosen profession have piled on me.' She finished the glass of wine Amy had poured her before saying quietly, 'Anthony has upset a few of his fellow MPs, not to mention his constituents, with his directness and what some people regard as radical ideas. Because I'm married to him, it's taken for granted that I agree with him – which isn't necessarily true. Sometimes I feel we're no longer on the same wavelength and as the family dynamics change, I can see...' she sighed. 'Well, all I can see of the future at the moment is a life I don't particularly want to live.'

'Have you talked to him? Told him how you feel?'

'No. Once upon a time, we talked about everything. These days, talking is one of the things there's never time for. Big part of the problem, I think. Although we did have words about me coming here,' Vicky said, remembering how sorry Anthony had been about their argument afterwards. Could he be feeling as worried about their lifestyle as she was? 'I know you're right. I must talk to him when I return.'

'Not talking about things sounds the death knoll for so many relationships,' Amy said. 'It encourages the keeping of secrets too. Once that happens...' she shrugged.

'Is that what happened between you and Kevin? Secrets between you?' Vicky asked quietly.

'It only took one rather big secret,' Amy replied.

When she realised Amy wasn't going to say any more, Vicky pushed her chair back before picking up her plate and glass.

'Thanks for the lunch and the chat – it's helped to clear my mind.'

This afternoon, she decided, writing was going to be all about getting her thoughts about her and Anthony down on paper and setting out her feelings, ready to talk to him when she got home.

13

Amy couldn't help thinking about her conversation with Vicky as she pottered around in the kitchen after lunch. Being married to someone who, while not exactly famous, certainly lived in the public eye was difficult, she knew only too well, especially if you personally didn't like the attention. Maybe she'd ask Chelsea if she could borrow the magazine and see if she could spot Vicky and her husband. No, that would be a seriously underhand thing to do. She had to respect Vicky's privacy. Maybe by the end of the holiday, they'd all be friendly enough for Vicky to open up and tell everyone who her husband was.

Amy was still in the kitchen when Pierre came in with a basket of vegetables and fruit from the garden.

'Chelsea mentioned wanting some salad for dinner tonight,' he said, placing the basket on the sink draining board.

'Thanks. How's Olivia?' Amy asked, turning the tap on and preparing to wash the lettuce, tomatoes and rocket.

'Ça va. No change,' Pierre said. 'The doctor says it will take time. It's a nasty virus she has.'

'Is she up to having a visitor, do you think?'

Pierre shook his head. 'Best not – for your sake and the others. Peut-être in a day or two. Hervé is taking good care of her.'

At the mention of Hervé, Amy smiled. Olivia's bear of a husband would protect her to the end. The way she'd always thought Kevin would be her protector.

'Chelsea – she is a good cook?' Pierre asked.

Amy nodded. 'Very. But perhaps it's best not to mention that to Olivia at the moment?'

Pierre smiled and pulled his phone out of his pocket as it pinged with an incoming text. 'Bien. I collect the women from Cannes in an hour. Just time for me to do a little weeding in the top garden.'

After he'd left, Amy carried on cleaning the salad, feeling sad for Pierre. He was such a good man, but life hadn't dealt him the best hand, leaving him a widower in his thirties when his wife died in a tragic accident. Tasha and Olivia had hoped for years he'd meet someone new, but Pierre had always insisted he wasn't interested and had got used to living alone. Just like she herself had settled into life alone here in France. Pierre did at least have his daughter and her husband whereas she would never now have the consolation of a child, however much she might wish it was possible.

Amy took a deep breath and scolded herself for being maudlin because of the one thing in her life plan that had gone wrong, making her aware of her ticking, soon to be silent, biological clock. She loved living in France and running the retreat. She might not have the family she dreamed of having and was living a different life to the one she'd hoped to live, but it was a good life and she was in a happy place.

Seeing Kevin in Monaco the other day had been a shock, but at least it had jolted her into making an appointment with the notaire. She was finally doing something about ending their marriage and getting closure on her life with Kevin.

Placing the washed vegetables in the salad drawer of the fridge, she felt a sudden shiver overtake her body and she closed the fridge door quickly and turned away – only to come face to face with the man currently occupying her thoughts, nonchalantly leaning against the kitchen doorway.

Amy blinked rapidly. Had she somehow made him materialise in front of her by thinking about him? She hadn't heard a car arriving. But then he spoke and she knew the nightmare was all too real.

'Hello, Amy.'

Stunned, Amy looked at him. 'What the hell are you doing here?'

'I was having lunch in Cannes and thought it would be nice to pop in and surprise you. Offer you my condolences for the loss of your aunt. Talk about old times. How good we were together.' Kevin looked at Amy, an expectant tone to his voice, a complacent smile on his face.

Amy stared at him in disbelief. 'Old times? Good together? For over five years, you pretended to love me, but all the time you were lying to me.'

Kevin shrugged and sighed. As he opened his mouth to speak, Amy held her hand up.

'I don't want to hear any more lies. I just want you to go. How did you get in anyway? I didn't hear a car.'

'I parked on the road. The front gate was open. You should really take more care of things, Amy. Burglaries are on the increase down here,' Kevin said. 'Anyone could have walked in.'

'Well, you can just walk straight back out before I call for Pierre to throw you out.'

'We have things to discuss.'

Amy shook her head. 'No, we don't. Since seeing you and your lady friend in Monaco, I've spoken to a solicitor. So go and talk to yours. They can do the discussing for us.'

'I'd forgotten how "nice" this place was,' Kevin said, ignoring her words and waving his fingers in the air to indicate quotation marks around the word 'nice'. 'Very nice indeed. Tasha left it to you, did she?"

'You hated the place the one time I brought you here,' Amy said, ignoring the mention of Tasha.

'True,' Kevin nodded thoughtfully. 'But then I didn't know you would inherit it. Must be worth a fair bit these days.'

'Whether it is or not, it's mine and you can forget any idea of having a claim on it.'

'Not so fast, Amy, we're not divorced yet,' Kevin said, wagging a finger at her. 'So I think I have a legitimate claim. What's yours is mine et cetera,' and he gave her a smug look that made her want to punch him.

'Not for much longer. Another few weeks and I'll be free of you. Please leave now.'

Kevin shook his head. 'In a moment. I'd like to take a look around first. See exactly what we've inherited.'

'Kevin, if you don't leave now, I'll...' Amy faltered, knowing she wasn't physically able to throw him out. 'I'll call the gendarmes,' and she snatched up her phone from the kitchen table.

Kevin laughed in her face. 'They won't come out for a little domestic spat. I'll go when I'm ready.' And he went to make his way into the villa – only to find his way barred by Pierre.

'You're leaving or I'll call the gendarmes and have them out here in a matter of minutes. Local man is a relative and he owes me a favour,' Pierre said, glaring at Kevin. 'Out.'

Kevin raised a clenched fist and took a threatening step towards Pierre as Amy held her breath and waited for the inevitable punch, but it didn't come. Kevin abruptly lowered his arm, gave Pierre a look of pure spite, then looked at Amy and muttered, 'You've not heard the last of this.'

Pierre followed him out of the kitchen and Amy sank down on a chair. She was still shaking when Pierre returned.

'He's gone and I've closed the electric gates. Be a good idea to keep them shut for a bit. Ça va? You okay?'

Amy nodded wearily. 'I'm fine. Just a bit shocked.' She looked at Pierre. 'Thank you for coming to my rescue.'

Pierre shrugged. 'I knew when I saw him parking outside that he intended to creep in and surprise you.'

'I'm glad he changed his mind about hitting you,' Amy said.

'I wish he had hit me – I'd have enjoyed hitting him back,' Pierre said with uncharacteristic force. 'Your aunt never liked him, you know. Didn't trust him.'

'I should have listened to her, shouldn't I? And Mum.' Amy was quiet for a few seconds, remembering how the two of them had repeatedly asked her if she was sure about marrying Kevin. She'd been so convinced he truly loved her that she'd brushed their concerns aside.

'Will you be okay now while I go to Cannes and collect Chelsea and Matilda? Vicky is up in the summer house if you want company.'

'I'll be fine. They'll be wondering where you are if you don't go now,' Amy said. 'Just make sure you close the gates again as you leave, please.' The thought of Kevin reappearing in the villa without Pierre here didn't bear thinking about.

Getting her thoughts down on paper was proving to be way more difficult than Vicky had hoped. It was all too easy to simply sit in the doorway of the summer house admiring the view, soaking up the peaceful atmosphere and letting her thoughts wander. Pierre had nodded and given her a smile as he'd pushed a wheelbarrow along a lower path, an alert Lola sitting in it, head up, sniffing the air, looking like she was the bowsprit of a boat, with her paws over the front edge of the barrow. Pierre was now busy working in one of the flower beds on the terrace in front of her. Vicky watched him for some time as he loosened the soil around a small rose bush before starting to weed the rest of the bed.

Vicky forced herself to concentrate and write down the things she needed to say to Anthony, starting with how she hated living in the public eye. She didn't like the way she was expected to be 'the little woman' standing behind her man, urging him on to 'great things'. She didn't like the way their lives were dominated these days by political correctness. She no longer felt like a free agent – more like a puppet having her strings pulled, which was ridiculous really.

Before she'd come to France, Anthony had been going on about a forthcoming crisis vote to do with the NHS. His constituents had been telling him about how hard they'd be hit if the vote went through and they lost their local hospital, which was already threatened with closure and being merged with another in the Greater London area. He didn't see how he could vote with the government on this one and he was worried the whips would be out to make him toe the line again. She knew toeing the party line was becoming increasingly difficult for Anthony, but when she'd asked if he could abstain, he'd shaken his head. Showing a 'united front' was the government's catchphrase of the moment, according to Anthony.

Well, she was more worried about their personal 'united front' at the moment than the one the government was insisting on portraying. She wasn't the MP in the family and she definitely didn't agree with most of the policies that were being pursued. If she'd realised six years ago when Anthony had first won his seat, how much she'd be expected to contribute behind the scenes – well, she wouldn't have been quite so enthusiastic in telling him to go for it.

Smothering a sigh, Vicky glanced up from her list and saw that Pierre had abandoned his gardening and was running down to the villa, Lola chasing after him. Vicky half rose from her chair. Was there some sort of emergency? Or had Pierre simply forgotten something? She sank back down, undecided as to what she should do. Surely if it was an emergency, he'd have called out to her for help before running down the garden. She'd give it a couple of minutes and see if anything untoward happened.

Sitting there watching for Pierre to reappear and letting her thoughts drift, she realised the list of things she'd written down and wanted to say to Anthony seemed selfish in the extreme. But... but as much as she loved Anthony, and she did still, she had to talk to him about making changes in her own life. It would help, of course, if she had more of an idea of the kind of life changes she wanted, rather than sounding off like a spoilt child.

Raised voices from the driveway caught her attention and she stiffened as she saw Pierre closely following a man down the drive. Kevin. No wonder Pierre had been running to the villa. Poor Amy. Vicky watched as Pierre closed the electric gates the moment Kevin was off the property before turning and walking back up to the villa. Would Amy appreciate her going down? Or would she prefer her to ignore the incident? She'd leave it until Pierre returned to his weeding before she wandered down to check on Amy. See if she wanted to talk to about Kevin, woman to woman.

Five minutes later, Pierre came out and got into the car parked in front of the villa. Vicky watched as the drive gates opened and then closed again as Pierre drove away. Right, time to go and see Amy. Vicky hesitated as her laptop pinged with an incoming message. Anthony. She was about to leave it to read later, but the subject line caught her eye as she went to close the laptop down and she caught her breath at the words it contained. Words that drove all thoughts of going to check on Amy out of her head.

I've cocked up.

14

On the way back to Belle Vue Villa from Cannes, an angry Pierre told Matilda and Chelsea about Kevin's visit. Both promised him they would keep an eye on Amy and make sure she was okay.

As they got out of the car, Chelsea thanked Matilda for lunch, before saying, 'I'll take the shopping into the kitchen and see if I can find Amy. See you down by the pool in about twenty minutes?'

Once in her room, Matilda opened the terrace doors in the hope the gentle onshore breeze coming off the Mediterranean would cool the room. She took the houses for sale magazine out of her bag and lay down on the bed under the whirring ceiling fan, thinking about the last few hours. Chelsea wanting her to stay in touch had moved her deeply. Pierre's news about Kevin, on the other hand, had upset her and spoilt what had otherwise been a lovely day. She couldn't help but worry about how Amy had reacted. Thank goodness Pierre had been here. Anything could have happened if Amy had been alone.

Absently, Matilda thumbed through the magazine in an effort to distract her thoughts. Some of the houses were beautiful and luxurious and most definitely beyond her means, so she flicked through page after page, concentrating on the agents who dealt with the less expensive properties. It clearly wouldn't be easy to find a suitable house. Matilda sighed. She and William had often talked about the kind of house or cottage they would buy when he retired and they moved to France. Detached with a reasonably sized garden, possibly a pool, train and bus links nearby so they wouldn't need a car – William hated driving and she avoided it as much as possible – and within walking distance of a boulangerie and a restaurant. A reasonable view was one requirement they both had. And one that had led to one of the few arguments they'd ever had.

William had favoured a countryside view with the mountains in the distance and she fancied the coast with its changing sea moods. They still hadn't decided when William had sadly died. So she was free to choose to live on the coast without feeling guilty, but she'd have happily gone to live in the countryside instantly if it meant she still had William at her side.

Matilda put the brochure down and closed her eyes. Outwardly, she knew she gave the impression she was coping, but she still missed William so much. It didn't get any easier, no matter how many times she repeated to herself the old cliché 'time is a great healer'. Was moving to France on her own even a good idea? Staying in Bristol, she'd at least be surrounded by the familiar and constant memories of the life she and William had shared. Moving away, she'd lose that everyday physical presence of the buildings and places they'd both loved – and her memories, would they fade?

Josh had urged her not to make any major decisions in

the early weeks after his father died and she hadn't. But she couldn't just drift along on memories for the rest of her days. She needed to find some sort of purpose in life. Organising a move to France had the potential to keep her busy for months. A phrase some unknown woman had used on Radio 4 the other day sprang into in her mind unexpectedly – 'You have to be on the beach to catch the wave.'

Matilda smiled to herself. William would definitely have agreed with that sentiment. He'd always been one to jump in to new projects. His enthusiasm for life had been one of the many things Matilda had adored about him. He'd longed to move to France for some time; had even talked a couple of years ago about taking redundancy, retiring early and just taking off. Matilda regretted talking him out of it now. It had seemed sensible at the time to wait the two years for his official retirement. If they'd taken the leap then, William would at least have realised part of his dream for the two of them. She couldn't help feeling that he'd expect her to carry on and make the dream come true for herself.

She picked up the magazine. Decision made. She'd keep looking until she found a suitable house. The next time she spoke to Josh, she'd tell him her plans. Right now though she was going to go and sit by the pool, study the brochure properly and make a couple of viewing appointments. After all, she had nothing to lose but time.

There was no sign of Amy when Chelsea went into the kitchen with her shopping. Once everything was away, she went to her room and changed into her swimming costume, grabbed a towel and her ever-present phone and made for the pool.

Amy was swimming a slow crawl down the length of the pool when she got there. Chelsea sat on the edge and dangled her feet in the water as she waited for Amy to finish her swim and join her.

'Hi. How was Cannes? Busy?' Amy asked.

'Matilda treated me to lunch at the Carlton, which was awesome.' Chelsea glanced at Amy. 'We saw Kevin there. Pierre says he's been here?'

Amy nodded, a rueful look on her face. 'I'm going to have to keep the gates closed and locked from now on. Tonight at dinner I'll give everybody the code to the small side entrance for when you go out. I rarely use it, so I need to look it up; make sure I remember it correctly. It's a bit inconvenient but...' and Amy shrugged before getting to her feet. 'Fancy a cold drink? I'll go and get some.'

'Cool,' Chelsea said and slid into the water and powered away with a fast crawl. She'd managed fifteen laps before Amy returned, accompanied by Matilda holding her brochure.

The three of them settled down companionably, dangling their feet in the shallow end of the pool, drinking iced tea.

'This place is just so perfect,' Chelsea said happily. Matilda murmured her agreement. Chelsea looked at her before turning to Amy. 'I still can't believe I'm here really. Did you know Matilda's thinking about moving to France?' She picked up the brochure Matilda had placed on the ground beside her. 'There's some lovely houses in here,' she said, flicking through.

'A lot of them out of my price range,' Matilda said. 'But I'm sure the right villa is out there. I'll certainly have fun looking. Not sure how my son, Josh, will react though.'

'Well, I think it's a brilliant idea,' Chelsea said. 'I'm so looking forward to visiting when you move here. Just so you know, I plan on being your very first visitor.'

Matilda laughed. 'Don't hold your breath – it could be a long time coming. Ah, here comes Vicky.' Matilda paused before adding quietly, 'She looks a bit upset. I do hope nothing is wrong.'

'I think Vicky's got a secret,' Chelsea whispered.

Amy looked at her. 'Everyone has their secrets – and their reasons for keeping them. Probably even you. Please don't say anything.'

'Don't worry,' Chelsea said. 'I like Vicky. I'm not going to say anything to upset her. I'm just curious.' Hmm, that was interesting. Was Amy already in on Vicky's secret?

Amy held out a drink to Vicky. 'I hoped you'd join us.'

'Thanks,' Vicky said, taking the drink and sitting down to join the three of them and dangle her own feet in the water. 'Oh, that's refreshing.' She looked at the house brochure Chelsea was still holding. 'You're not thinking of selling this place, are you?' she said to Amy.

'No. I'll never sell Belle Vue,' Amy said. 'Matilda is toying with the idea of moving here.'

'Toying is the right word,' Matilda said. 'It's always been a dream but...' she shrugged. 'We'll see. Are you all right?' she asked, looking at Vicky. 'You looked a bit hot and bothered when you arrived.'

'I'm fine. Just not used to such high temperatures. I think it's time I braved the pool and had a swim. It should at least cool me down a bit.' And Vicky slipped off her sundress and cautiously walked down the pool steps and slowly eased herself into the water. The other three women watched her silently for a few moments.

'She's definitely upset about something,' Chelsea whispered.

Amy and Matilda nodded in agreement. All three fell silent as they watched Vicky swimming a methodical breaststroke.

* * *

Vicky, swimming slowly up and down the length of the pool, tried not to worry about whatever it was Anthony had cocked up. The message under that heart stopping subject line had been simple in the extreme:

Need to talk to you asap. Will phone at 7 this evening. Got to go to a press conference now. x.

The fact that he was having to attend a press conference told her that whatever he'd done would soon be public knowledge.

Various scenarios began to run through Vicky's mind. Drink-driving? No. Anthony never drank away from home unless he knew he had an official driver waiting for him. Could he have lied about something? Possible, she supposed, but Anthony was more likely to have bluntly – and possibly rudely – told someone the truth. He'd got better at political correctness over the last few years, but sometimes he forgot that he should bite his tongue and stay silent.

The word 'affair' floated unbidden into her brain. Vicky's steady breaststroke rhythm faltered and she almost sank beneath the water as the thought registered. Spluttering as she struggled to regain a steady pace, she thought about it. Could that possibly be the reason? An affair with one of the many women who worked in the Houses of Parliament? A few years ago, she would have laughed and dismissed the idea as absurd, her trust in Anthony complete. But things had been difficult and distant between them the last few months and Anthony had always been popular with her own female friends. She'd lost count of the number of affairs – secret and not so secret – she and Anthony had heard about down the years. It wasn't out of the question that he could have been tempted and had now been caught.

Turning on her back and floating for a minute or two, Vicky tried to convince herself that Anthony cheating on her was the least likely explanation. He just wouldn't. It had to be something else. Something she wouldn't find out until he rang this evening. In the meantime she'd carry on as normal, which meant getting out of the pool in a few moments and facing the others.

A burst of laughter broke into her thoughts. Turning her head to look at the others, she saw them playing about, posing for photos. A perfect diversion, and turning back onto her front, Vicky swam to the steps. As she climbed out, Chelsea took a picture of her.

'If that shows my cellulite you can delete it,' Vicky said, smiling. 'Shall I take one of you?' and she held out her hand for the phone.

Chelsea struck a pose, standing on one leg, kicking the other out behind her, with one hand on the back of a lounger and the other placed on the back of her head as she pouted at the camera.

'Very starlet-like,' Vicky laughed as she took the picture. 'Straight out of the 1950s.'

'Thanks,' Chelsea said, looking at it. 'Ooh, it's got a nice background shot of the villa in it too. I'm going to send it to my dad – show him where I'm staying.'

'Feel better for your swim?' Matilda asked, turning to Vicky.

'Yes, thank you. Much cooler,' Vicky replied, remembering the reason she'd given for finally going for a swim. 'But time for a shower now, I think. I'll see you all later in the kitchen for dinner-prep duties.'

Walking back to her room, she wondered about telling everyone who she was back in the real world. Whatever this cock-up of Anthony's turned out to be, was it serious enough for her to tell them he was her husband before they saw it in the papers or heard his name on the news and put two and two together?

Would they even hear about it? They were all living in a little French cocoon here with the only TV in the villa tuned into the French language. She deliberately hadn't heard any English news since she'd arrived. Wanting a complete break, she'd resisted the urge to look at the news channels when she had her laptop on. But that was about to change. She couldn't wait until seven o'clock for Anthony to tell her. Forewarned was forearmed, as they say. If it was an affair, then she'd at least be prepared for his confession.

She found what she was looking for on the BBC website. She sighed with relief when she saw it wasn't an affair before gasping with shock as she read through the details. It was something far worse for his career. He'd actually dared to pick up the mace from the table in front of the Speaker and walked several paces with it.

Vicky knew that the mace, a five foot long silver gilt ornamental club that actually dated from Charles II's reign, was carried in to the House of Commons chamber every day by the sergeant at arms and placed on the table of the house. Representing the authority of the monarch, without it in place the house could not meet or pass laws. To say that it was a sacrosanct item of government was putting it mildly.

The media were having a ball with the news and speculation about the outcome was rife. All she could think of as she read was that it was so out of character for Anthony to act in that way. There was no possibility he could deny doing it because the whole incident had been seen by so many MPs and, of course, recorded by the in-house cameras. He'd been handed an immediate suspension for ten days, but it was going to take far longer than that for him to live this incident down.

Vicky prayed that his true friends would rally around him with support. By the time she returned home next week, surely something else would have become headline news. Maybe she should cut this holiday short and return early? She'd suggest it when Anthony rang this evening. It was the last thing she wanted to do, but if Anthony needed her there, she'd do go home willingly.

15

Amy, leaving Matilda and Chelsea down by the pool and taking advantage of a quiet hour where everyone was doing their own thing, made for her desk in the bedroom, determined to get to grips with her paperwork, including the dreaded tax. This year she resolved to be on top of the mountain of paperwork that running the retreat seemed to generate before the summer season was in full swing.

But first she needed to send an email. An email confirming an appointment with the notaire. They had everything to hand and were just waiting for her to sign a paper or two and instruct them to go ahead. Today she was finally ready. As the email pinged off into the air, Amy sighed. Now she could push all thoughts of Kevin stirring up trouble in the future into the furthest recess of her mind and concentrate on the accounts.

The small fifteen inch tv on the side of the desk, tuned into an English lifestyle programme via satellite, was switched on merely as background noise. This afternoon though, Amy had studiously avoided watching anything –

until a breaking news bulletin from the Houses of Parliament came on and caught her attention.

She watched in amazement as the presenter outlined the outrageous action that had taken place in the house earlier, involving a certain Anthony Pinehill who had now been suspended. Amy switched the TV off and sat back. Could this possibly be Vicky's husband? Thoughtfully, she opened her laptop and googled his name. Within seconds, she'd found a picture of him and Vicky that confirmed it. No wonder Vicky was so hot and bothered earlier.

Amy sat there for a few minutes, wondering what to do. Would Vicky be upset if she told her she knew who her husband was and the trouble he was in? Or would she appreciate a friendly offer of commiseration and the chance to talk about it? She knew she herself would appreciate a friendly word and she quickly came to the decision that she had to go in search of Vicky. She'd start with the summer house.

Walking up through the garden, Amy wondered how to broach the subject with Vicky. Come straight out with, 'I know who your husband is and also the trouble he's in,' or wait and see if Vicky broached the subject herself? The latter would probably be best, but she'd wait and see how receptive Vicky was to her company once she realised Amy knew the true situation.

As she turned onto the last meandering path in front of the summer house, Amy saw Vicky sat outside, her laptop unopened on the small table next to her. Amy could feel her watching and waiting for her. When Vicky jumped up and fetched another chair from inside before settling down again, Amy breathed a relieved sigh. Ah, that was a good sign of her presence being welcome, and Vicky would like to talk.

'Hi,' Vicky said, speaking quickly. 'I love Belle Vue Villa.

The view is wonderful from up here. You are so lucky. Pierre is a great gardener and... and—'

'Vicky, I've heard about your husband, Anthony Pinehill, on the news,' Amy interrupted gently.

Vicky sighed and her shoulders dropped. 'I guessed that's why you've sought me out.'

'I just wanted to offer an understanding ear if you'd like one,' Amy said. 'Are you all right?'

Vicky made a noise between a splutter and a groan. 'I guess.'

'Have you spoken to Anthony?'

'Not yet. He's ringing me at seven.' She glanced at Amy. 'I don't know what to do about the kids. They're both busy with work but are certain to hear the news,' Vicky shrugged helplessly. 'And I can't help but feel I ought to be there for Anthony. That somehow this mess is my fault for not being there.'

'That's nonsense and you know it,' Amy said.

'But it's so out of character for Anthony to do something like this. If I'd been home perhaps he'd have talked to me and I could have prevented it.'

'I don't think it was a premeditated action,' Amy said. 'I think it was one of those spur-of-the-moment regrettable things we are all capable of doing from time to time.'

Vicky nodded thoughtfully. 'You're probably right. Anthony has been very frustrated lately over things beyond his control really. I'll know more when I've spoken to him this evening.'

'Why don't you tell him he's welcome to join you for the rest of your holiday?' Amy said impulsively. 'Away from all the drama, the two of you would find it easier to talk.'

Vicky looked at her in surprise. 'Honestly? He'd insist on paying his way though. Thank you. Oh, but...'

Amy raised her eyebrows and waited.

'What about the others? D'you think they'd mind?'

Amy shook her head. 'Of course they wouldn't – they would need to know who he is and why he's here though.'

'Would you tell them about his suspension please?' Vicky said. 'I'm not sure I can without bursting into tears.'

'Of course I'll tell them. Now, can I get you a coffee – or a stiff gin?' Amy smiled as Vicky shook her head.

'No thanks. I'd better keep a clear head.'

'If you're sure you're okay, I'll get back to my paperwork. Try not to worry too much. The media do tend to blow things out of proportion. I'm sure everything will sort itself out.'

Amy left Vicky saying she'd try and do some work and opening her laptop. She made her way back down the garden, via the pool this time. She'd seen Matilda and Chelsea were still sunbathing and reading there as she'd walked to the summer house. No time like the present for breaking the news to them about Vicky's husband and explaining that he might well be joining them.

Once Amy had quietly explained about Vicky's husband and the trouble he was in, Matilda voiced the opinion that to talk about them would be to gossip. 'And gossip can turn malicious very quickly,' she'd added. 'So it's best avoided whenever possible,' and she'd turned resolutely back to reading her book.

* * *

It was early evening when the three of them met up in the kitchen to help prepare dinner. The menu for the evening was a simple one: Parma ham and endive salad for starters, fish in white wine sauce with asparagus and sauté potatoes, the usual cheese board and chocolate mousse. Chelsea had made the mousses yesterday to give them time to set, so there was very little really to do in the way of preparation.

'Have you heard how Olivia is?' Matilda asked as she peeled potatoes.

'Pierre says she's on the mend, but it's going to take weeks rather than days for her to recover completely,' Amy said, glancing across at Chelsea. 'I know you've got a business to get back to, but it's a pity you can't stay on for a couple of weeks. You can't, can you?' she asked. 'I'll pay you.'

Chelsea shook her head regretfully. 'Oh, I wish. I'm really sorry, but I can't leave Elsie to cope on her own any longer. I know we've got lots of bookings lined up for the next month.'

'No worries, it was just a thought,' Amy said. 'I'll organise an agency cook.'

A subdued Vicky walked into the kitchen just then. Everyone choroused out, 'Hi,' followed by a slightly tense silence in the air for a couple of seconds with no one knowing quite what to say, before Matilda smiled at her and broke the silence.

'Sorry to hear about your husband's troubles. Try not to worry – these things generally sort themselves out.'

'Try not to let it spoil your holiday here,' Chelsea said, picking up a large bundle of asparagus and holding it out to Vicky. 'Need to break off about two inches of stem from each one and put them in the steamer ready for later,' she explained. 'Some chefs would have you peel the remaining stalks, but I like to leave them as they are. Okay?'

Vicky nodded.

'Drop the stems in here,' Chelsea said, handing her a saucepan. 'I can make soup for later in the week with those blended together with a couple of potatoes and some cream.'

'I'll do these,' Vicky said. 'And then I need to go back to my room to take Anthony's call.'

It was five to seven when Vicky threw the last stem into the saucepan. 'Sorry, I have to go now.'

As she turned to leave Amy sent a quiet, 'Good luck,' in her direction. Vicky didn't answer but acknowledged the comment with a smile and a wave of her hand as she left the kitchen.

'Must be very difficult for her being so far away,' Matilda said, sighing.

'I forgot to mention it earlier, but I've suggested she ask her husband to join her for the last few days of the holiday. I assured her neither of you would object,' Amy said, looking at both of them.

'D'you think he'll accept?' Chelsea asked.

Amy gave a short shrug. 'We'll have to wait and see. Maybe Vicky will be able to tell us at dinner this evening.'

* * *

Vicky sat on the terrace outside her room with her laptop and Skype open, ready and waiting for Anthony's call. She stopped herself from surfing the news sites looking for any further developments that might have happened in the last few hours. Anthony would no doubt give her the latest updates.

When the laptop buzzed with the incoming call, she pressed the button and waited for Anthony's face to appear as the connection was made. Tired and dishevelled, he looked unlike his normal self. Vicky was about to pre-empt him with, what on earth did you think you were doing with the mace, but said instead, 'Are you okay?'

Anthony nodded. 'Tired, but okay.'

'I've seen the news,' Vicky said quietly.

'I was hoping to tell you before you saw it, but...' Anthony's voice trailed away.

'Why did you do it? Were you drunk or something? You know the rules of parliament as far as the mace is concerned.'

'To be honest, I had a bit of a red mist come down when it was clear the way that the government wanted to go was in direct opposition to what is needed in my constituency. At least I didn't drop the mace like Ron Brown did thirty years ago. I did manage to put it back down safely.'

'Was it over the hospital merger?' Vicky said, knowing how passionate Anthony felt about that particular subject.

'Yes. My job is to tell the truth and represent my constituents. Today I felt no one was listening. Until I swore at them,' he added with a rueful smile. 'That earned me another day of suspension for unparliamentary language.'

'Is that on top of the ten days I saw in the news?'

'No, it's included in that. Tom and Suzie have both texted me – they don't seem to blame me. Seem to think it's a bit of a hoot their dad being in trouble. Mum, of course, is torn between being totally supportive and proud of me and embarrassed by the publicity.'

'Do you want me to come home?'

'No. I miss having you around, but there's nothing you can do. Stay and enjoy your holiday. How's it going anyway?'

'It's fine,' Vicky paused. 'Amy has suggested you might like to come and spend some time here with me. Would you like to? It would take the pressure of you and give you a brief rest.'

'How d'you feel about it?' Anthony asked. 'I know you wanted time away from everything, me included, to think and—'

'I think it's a good idea,' Vicky interrupted. 'We could at least talk about things in a neutral environment. Might even be able to fit in a trip to Monaco for you – once we've talked. Because we do need to talk about the future.'

'Well, if you're sure, I think it's a brilliant idea. Please tell Amy I accept, but I insist on paying my way. I'll check out flights this evening and let you know when I'll arrive. I think I'm allowed to leave the country!'

Vicky smiled at the thought of Anthony coming to Belle Vue Villa. They could be plain old Mr and Mrs Pinehill for a couple of days, enjoying a brief respite in the South of France.

'I'll ring you again as soon as I have more news,' Anthony said.

'Okay. Love you,' and Vicky closed down her laptop.

The others were all sipping a before dinner rosé aperitif and enjoying some slices of baguette spread with tapenade when Vicky joined them on the terrace.

'How is your husband?' Amy asked anxiously.

'Unrepentant about today's events,' Vicky said, accepting a glass of wine. 'And he'd like to accept your offer of coming to stay for a few days. If that's all right with everybody?' She turned to look at Chelsea and Matilda, who both nodded their agreement. 'I suspect he's checking out flights even as we speak.'

'As long as he doesn't plan to arrive tomorrow. I was thinking tomorrow might be a good day for our outing to Antibes,' Amy said.

Vicky smiled at her. 'Depending on flights, I suspect it will be nearer the end of the holiday so we can travel back together. Antibes tomorrow will be good. Just what I personally need to take my mind of things. Santé,' and she raised her glass in the general direction of everyone before taking a large gulp of her drink.

DAY SEVEN OF THE HOLIDAY – JUNE 12

16

After a night where she'd tossed and turned for a couple of hours before sleep finally claimed her, Vicky was bleary-eyed but cheerful when she joined the others in the kitchen for breakfast the next morning. Last night after dinner, she'd managed to get hold of both Tom and Suzie on their phones. Thankfully, they didn't seem upset by the furore around Anthony – if anything, they seemed to find the whole episode amusing. Tom, with typical youthful honesty, had admitted he thought the antiquated rules governing a relic from the past laughable and completely outdated. Vicky wished she could find it in herself to agree with him, but until the whole episode was over, she couldn't.

After a quick breakfast, the four of them piled into the car ready for the trip to Antibes. Amy drove through Cannes before joining the bord de mer going east and once again pointed out various things of interest to the other three as she drove. Although still quite early, people were already claiming their places on the beach for a day of sunbathing. Out in the Mediterranean, the last of the early-morning mist was hanging over the Iles de Lérins. Already, a few luxury yachts were anchored in the reach between the two islands, their passengers ready to go ashore to explore one or other of the islands, or to simply spend a relaxing day out on the water.

Matilda, gazing out of the car window, said, 'I love the abbey on Saint Honorat. Harmonious is the word I think that best describes the island. William and I had a wonderful day there years ago. And Sainte-Marguerite too, has such a serene feel to it, despite the fortress that housed the infamous Man in the Iron Mask in its cells.'

'It's a different world over there, isn't it?' Amy agreed. 'Hard to imagine it's part of the Cote d'Azur really. Aunt Tasha actually used to go on retreat at the Abbey. Said it was a life affirming experience every time she went.'

'I can imagine,' Matilda said.

The traffic increased as they drove along the coast road and they all fell silent as Amy concentrated on her driving. As they reached Juan-les-Pins, Amy swung inland away from the crowds.

'We'll come back via Cap d'Antibes, but this way will hopefully be quicker for us to get to town.'

A quarter of an hour later, Amy had parked in the underground car park in the centre of Antibes and the four of them were making for one of the nearby cafés.

Over coffee and delicious flaky almond croissants, they decided to stay together in a group, like they had in Monaco, rather than each go off individually.

Amy looked at Matilda anxiously. 'If your ankle starts to hurt, you must say.'

Matilda nodded. 'I hope it won't – it is much better. I'm really looking forward to just wandering around and remembering my holiday with William. Although it is a lot busier these days,' she said, looking around at the milling crowds. 'And so much building work going on, but I suppose that is to be expected.'

'Does anyone want to visit the Picasso Musée?' Amy asked.

'I'd like to if there is time,' Vicky said. 'But I'm happy to slope off there on my own if nobody else is keen.'

'Okay. How about we finish coffee, then wander down to Place National, I'll show you where we're having lunch and then whoever wants to can make for the museum and the rest of us can mooch around the old town before lunch – there's lots to see and some great shops hidden away down the narrow streets. Our table is booked for one o'clock. Then, this afternoon, we can walk out to where the larger yachts moor and dream of living a life of luxury before wandering back into town. There's usually a craft market on at this time of year.'

'Sounds like a plan,' Chelsea said.

'As we missed Cap d'Antibes on the way here, we'll go back that way and stop off for a glass of wine on the beach at Juan-les-Pins. Is that okay with everyone?' Amy asked. When the other three smiled and nodded their agreement, she stood up. 'Come on then. Let's introduce you to Antibes.' At least acting as guide for the day was guaranteed to take her mind off her own problems with Kevin.

Passing a tabac-cum-marchand de journaux as they strolled down the narrow road, dodging both cars and people, Vicky stopped in front of the pavement rack displaying papers and magazines. She glanced at the headlines on several papers before pulling out an English newspaper and going inside the shop to pay for it.

When she came out, Amy was waiting for her. 'The others are over there,' she said, pointing in the direction of a small boutique on the other side of the street.

'You okay?' Amy asked.

Vicky nodded. 'I don't know why I bought this really – I've read it all on the internet anyway.' She sighed. 'Seeing it in black and white in a physical form though does bring it home to me just how serious it is.' She pointed to the picture of Anthony halfway down the front page. 'At least it's not the main headline.' She stuffed the paper into her bag on top of her phone that she'd switched off for the day. There had been a few text messages, including one from her mum last night offering support, and she guessed there would be a few more today. She'd answered her mum, but the rest she'd deal with when she got back to Belle Vue. Today she was going to enjoy her day out in Antibes.

'Has Anthony booked his flight?' Amy asked.

Vicky shook her head. 'I haven't heard yet. I'll feel better when he's here and we can talk face to face.'

Together, they crossed the road, and as Chelsea and Matilda left the boutique and joined them, Amy pointed to the restaurant she'd booked for lunch.

'Looks good. Can you point me in the direction of the musée please?' Vicky asked.

'Keep going down here and make for the market. You'll see the signs then.'

'Thanks. Anybody want to join me? No? Okay, I'll see you at lunch,' Vicky said.

Once through the market, Vicky quickly found herself outside the imposing old Grimaldi Chateau, the fortress-like building that housed the musée. She paid the entrance fee and began to wander slowly around, soaking up the atmosphere – especially on the upper floors which Picasso had used as a studio in 1946. It was the work he'd done during that time that made up the bulk of the current exhibition.

Stepping out on to the terrace to look at some sculptures, Vicky caught her breath at the panoramic views of the coastline both to the east and the west. She stood there for some time studying the sculptures, as well as drinking in the air and the beautiful vista before her. When she finally turned and re-entered the chateau, she realised the staff were gently encouraging everyone to make their way to the exit as the musée would close soon for the two hour lunch break. Vicky just had time to buy a couple of postcards in memory of her visit before she was ushered outside.

She glanced at her watch. Three quarters of an hour to kill before lunch. To join the crowds who were milling around and try to find the others? Or explore the little alleyways leading away from the market and the tourist crowds? No contest really. And Vicky set off to discover the parts of Antibes that were hidden from view.

Chelsea sighed happily and waved her hand in the air as she looked around the restaurant garden. 'This place is, is... so French. It's got a fountain, a canopy of wisteria, ancient risqué garden statues and the sky above is *so* blue. Outside in the street, everything is rush, rush, rush, you'd never guess there was this oasis of peace hidden away. It's just a perfect setting. Thank you for bringing us here,' she said, turning to Amy.

'The food's usually good too,' Amy replied, smiling at her. 'I have to confess it's one of my favourite places for lunch in

Antibes. Now, what do you both want to drink while we wait for Vicky? Shall I order Kir aperitifs all round? As I'm driving I'll need to be careful, so I'll be on the sparkling water with my meal.'

Both Chelsea and Matilda said a Kir sounded good. 'We'll decide about wine when we order our food, shall we?' Chelsea asked.

'I hope Vicky hasn't got lost,' Matilda commented.

Amy shook her head. 'Anyone would point her in the direction of the market and this place is easy to find from there. But if she's not here in five minutes, I'll text her. She's got a lot on her mind at the moment, I expect she's forgotten the time.'

The waiter was placing three drinks in front of them when a breathless Vicky arrived. Amy quickly asked for the fourth Kir and the menus.

'Sorry, sorry. I thought I had loads of time before lunch and I went further than I realised,' Vicky said.

'How was the exhibition?' Chelsea asked.

Vicky pulled a face. 'Very small and a bit of an anticlimax actually, but I'm glad I went. There's a spectacular view from the museum terrace. Thank you,' she said as the waiter placed her drink on the table. 'I went for a wander afterwards – took lots of photos of old doors. I even got an idea for my book. Santé,' she said, raising her glass. 'This is lovely,' she said, looking around. 'A hidden gem.'

'Isn't it? Our waiter is quite a hunk too, isn't he?' Chelsea whispered, watching said waiter as he approached a nearby table. 'Fits right in with the beautiful garden,' and she flashed him a dazzling smile.

'I thought you were off men,' Matilda said, smiling.

'Mmm, so did I,' Chelsea replied. 'But he could make me

change my mind. Pity we're only here for the day. He could have given me some French lessons.'

'Let's decide on food,' Amy said, laughing.

Once the food and the wine to accompany it were ordered, the four of them sat happily chatting under the shade of the canopy of white wisteria covering the wooden pergola beams above their heads.

'Our holiday is going so quickly,' Chelsea sighed. 'Less than a week and the three of us will all be back to our old lives. Days like this make me want to stay in France permanently.' She jumped up and took her phone out of her bag. 'Need a pic or two of us all here. Matilda, you stay sitting, Vicky and Amy, can you stand either side of her please.' Chelsea snapped a couple of photos. 'I really want one of us all together – hang on,' and she caught the eye of the waiter. When he came over, she smiled at him and held out her phone, hoping he would understand.

'You want me to take a photo of you beautiful ladies?' he said, before leaning into Chelsea and saying quietly, 'It is indeed a shame you only visit for the day. If you want French lessons, you only have to say.'

'You speak English,' Chelsea gasped, embarrassed. He'd overheard her earlier. She could feel the heat in her cheeks rising.

'Of course. I also speak Italian, Spanish and a little Danish. We have many international visitors here in Antibes.' He gestured for Chelsea to join her friends. 'Smile.' And he pressed the shutter.

'Merci beaucoup,' Chelsea stuttered as he handed her phone back.

'You speak a little French already. It was my pleasure. I fetch your lunch now.' He winked at her before turning and walking towards the kitchen.

Chelsea sank back down onto her chair. 'I want to curl up and die,' she said. 'He must think I'm a complete idiot – or whatever the French equivalent is.'

'I doubt it,' Vicky said. 'You probably made his day.'

'Let's see the photos,' Amy said.

Chelsea handed her the phone. 'Here you go.'

'The one of us all is rather good,' Amy said, scrolling through. 'May I print four copies out when we get back to Belle Vue?' She handed the phone back.

Chelsea looked at the photo. It was definitely one to keep. 'Of course. I'm going to send a copy to my dad right now. Show him my new friends.'

She quickly typed a message, added a couple of kisses and sent it. She knew her dad would love seeing her happy and laughing. But she didn't think she'd mention her faux pas with the waiter.

* * *

Matilda took a sip of the rosé wine the three of them had chosen to accompany their lunch before placing the glass down on the table. Sitting back thoughtfully, she shut out the buzz of conversation around her and let her memories bubble to the surface.

She hadn't mentioned it to the others, but she'd had lunch here before. William had heard about the wonderful food to be had in a garden restaurant in the heart of Antibes from a friend and had been determined they would sample its delights. Their secluded table for two that day had been opposite to where she sat now and the wisteria hadn't yet embraced the entire pergola. A large parasol had been necessary that day to give them shade. The fountain was the same, there were more sculptures than she remembered and the various plants and shrubs dotted around had matured well.

Matilda picked up her glass again as she remembered the conversations she and William had had time and time again during that holiday. Conversations that centred around their shared dream of moving to France. She'd laughed at him one evening, saying, 'No matter the subject of the conversation in the beginning – books, politics, films – it always ends up the same. It seems all roads lead to France for us.' William had laughed with her before holding her hand and saying soberly, 'We must do our best to make it happen, Matty.'

She smothered a sighed. They'd failed though. Life had caught them up in other plans – work plans that took William further and further away from his dream. But then she smiled to herself. William was the only person who'd ever shortened her name to Matty. She so missed being Matty.

'Earth to Matilda,' Chelsea's voice broke into her daydream. 'Are you all right? You've got a funny look on your face.'

Matilda nodded. 'I'm fine. Just inwardly reminiscing about a happy holiday long ago. Now, is anyone else going to indulge in a dessert with me? I see my favourite tiramisu is on the menu.'

'Oooh, I'll have one of those too,' Chelsea said, but both Amy and Vicky shook their heads, opting to have just coffee.

After lunch was finished, the four of them sat there, relaxed, chatting away and happy to let the world slip by. It was almost four o'clock when Amy said, 'Come on, let's go and ogle the luxury yachts.'

Once they'd sorted out the bill between them, they started to make their way from the garden out through the restaurant. Matilda smiled as she saw the young waiter standing politely by the door, saying 'Au revoir', slip a piece of paper into Chelsea's hand. A Chelsea who blushed and smiled as she responded with her own muttered 'Au revoir'.

Amy led the way along a narrow street and, after passing underneath an arch, they were down by the harbour. Following the road round to the right, they walked alongside the waterfront. The boats moored here, stern end in towards the quay, were a mixed variety. Some were clearly houseboats, with the occasional cat peering out from behind curtained windows. There were wooden hulls moored alongside modern sleek fibreglass ones and neglected boats with 'À Vendre' signs attached to their rails waiting for a new owner to buy them and make them beautiful again.

People were milling everywhere, dodging around each other and the chauffeur driven upmarket cars – Bentleys, Aston Martins, Mercedes – that swept past them, ferrying their owners to and from their luxury yachts. When, a quarter of an hour later, the four of them finally reached the long length of quay where a dozen or so mega yachts were moored, Amy said, 'And this, girls, is affectionately known as Billionaire's Quay.'

They walked the length of the quay slowly, before turning and beginning to make their way back.

'They're like mini cruise ships,' Matilda said, gazing in amazement at the boats. 'But nicer somehow. I can't even begin to imagine having the kind of money needed to own one.'

'Look – there's a helicopter taking off from the helipad,' Chelsea said, pointing. 'Wonder who's on board that.'

They all stood watching as the helicopter gained height before bearing away to fly along the coast in the direction of Nice Airport.

'Come on,' Amy said. 'Let's get back to the real world and

have a wander round the Marché de Chineurs, that should be set up and open now. See if there are any bargains.'

Half an hour later, the four of them were mooching around the brocante stalls that varied from pottery and wooden crafts, to books, vintage and second-hand clothes, collectible kitchen utensils, jewellery and postcards. Some things were clearly old, even antique, whilst others were brand spanking new. Matilda and Vicky stood by one of the clothing stands and Matilda heard Vicky's sharp intake of breath.

'Seen something you like?' Matilda asked.

Vicky nodded. 'That coat,' she said, pointing to a mannequin at the side of the stall with a lightweight velvet coat draped over it. 'Isn't it wonderful? A real Amazing Technicolour Dreamcoat, isn't it? I love it.' And she reached out to gently stroke a velvet sleeve with its myriad of colours. 'I had a similar coat years ago when I was a student. I wore it until it dropped to pieces. I felt so cool and bohemian whenever I wore it.' Vicky looked at Matilda. 'It gave me confidence to do things.'

The stallholder, her short blonde hair highlighted on the left side with a single wide stripe of scarlet, approached. 'You try,' she said, taking the coat and holding it out to Vicky.

Vicky hesitated for a second before slipping her arms into the sleeves.

'It fits you,' Matilda said. 'And not only that, it suits you.'

Vicky smiled. 'I wonder how much it is. Combien ça coûte?' she said, turning to the stallholder. When the woman told her the price, Vicky turned to Matilda. 'I'm going to buy it. I feel it was meant for me.'

* * *

As she'd promised, going home, Amy took the coastal road out of town. Along Cap d'Antibes, down past the Eden Roc Hotel hidden out of sight, past the Belles Rives Hotel and the shell of the much loved Hôtel le Provençal before parking alongside the beach in Juan-les-Pins.

'I thought we'd stop and maybe have a salad baguette with our glass of wine here and then tonight we'll have a midnight feast around the pool. Okay with everyone?'

'Brilliant idea,' Chelsea said. 'We can have a paddle too. Can't come to the beach and not paddle.'

'Come on then, let's get some food,' Amy said. 'There's a mini supermarche just over the road.'

Twenty minutes later, they were all sitting on the beach with salad baps, four plastic glasses, a bottle of rosé and a bottle of water.

Unscrewing the wine, Amy poured three glasses. 'I'd better stick to water again for now,' she said.

Chelsea was the first to finish her snack and she slipped her sandals off before rolling her jeans up her legs as far as she could. 'It's paddling time,' she said and ran down to the water's edge. 'It's freezing,' she yelled back at them as the first of the waves lapped her feet. 'But refreshing. Matilda, are you coming to join me? It would do your ankle good.'

'She's right on both counts,' Amy said, watching as Matilda undid the strap of her sandals. 'It probably will do your ankle good, but the water never really warms up until July or August, so it will be cold.'

Matilda nodded. 'It's a long time since I paddled, but I can't miss this opportunity,' and she followed Chelsea down to the water's edge.

Amy glanced at Vicky. 'I'll watch our things if you want to join them.'

Vicky shook her head. 'No. I'm happy sitting here looking

at the sea and thinking, thanks.' She glanced across at Amy. 'I meant to ask before – how are you after the Kevin episode?'

'Wishing I'd done something sooner about officially kicking him out of my life,' Amy admitted. 'But at least it's underway now. I've got an appointment with the notaire soon.'

'Will he turn up at the villa again, d'you think?'

'If he does, I'll call the gendarmes – and make sure certain people know about his actions. Kevin hates any kind of personal stuff leaking to the media.'

Before Vicky could say anything, Chelsea and Matilda were back from paddling and the conversation was over. By the time two pairs of feet had dried enough to slip back into sandals, the setting sun behind the distant Esterel mountains had turned the sky the colour of molten lava, swallowing everything in its path.

'Wow,' Chelsea said, holding her phone up to take a picture. 'That is some serious sunset.'

As Amy drove them homewards, she smiled to herself. The three women were laughing and chatting away to each other like old friends.

Once in the villa, Amy said, 'I'll see you all down by the pool in about half an hour for a late supper. It's a little early to call it a midnight feast but...' she smiled and shrugged.

'Can we do anything to help?' Chelsea asked.

'A hand carrying stuff out maybe? I took a few things out of the freezer this morning and the rest is just baguettes and charcuterie.'

'Okay. We'll dump our stuff and join you in the kitchen,' Vicky said, speaking for them all.

As the food and wine were ferried down to the pool, Amy picked up her iPod before closing the kitchen door and going down to switch on the pool's underwater lights. The solar lights dotted around the pool were already alight and she put a match to the citronella candles on the table before pressing the play button on her iPod deck.

Matilda, opening a bottle of rosé and one of white wine, stopped to listen as a female voice began to sing a well known French ballad à la Edith Piaf.

'I hope everyone likes Zaz. I can play something else if not,' Amy said.

'Personally, I think the choice is perfect,' Matilda said. 'She's very good and very French.'

* * *

Chelsea, sitting on the edge of the pool, dangling her feet in the water felt happier than she had for ages. Life here at Belle Vue was good. Uncomplicated. Unlike real life. The events of the past few months, years, were slowly fading into the obscurity that was her past life. She'd changed, but the important thing was she'd survived. Unlike her mum. Suddenly all her happy feelings vanished.

'What's the date today?' she asked, turning urgently to look at the others.

'The twelfth,' Vicky answered. 'A few more days and the three of us will be waving all this goodbye. Back to reality with a bump, I suspect.'

Chelsea bit her bottom lip and nodded absently. To think she'd almost missed the date that was etched on her heart. The anniversary of her mum's death. Something she blamed herself for despite being told it was an unavoidable tragic accident.

'My mum died five years ago tomorrow. And I still can't help feeling it was my fault,' she added in a whisper, desperately trying to stem the tears that were threatening to fall. 'I miss her so much.'

Vicky was at her side instantly, sitting down and dangling her own feet in the pool as she put her arm around Chelsea and squeezed her tightly, but Matilda was the first to break the silence that Chelsea's words fell into.

'Oh, my darling girl. D'you want to talk about it?'

Chelsea shook her head. 'Not really – nothing changes the fact it was my fault we were on the motorway when the lorry had a puncture and careered into us. I'd been ten minutes late meeting up with Mum. If I hadn't been late, we wouldn't have been there at that moment.'

'Chelsea, it wasn't your fault. It was a tragic accident. I'm sure your dad has told you that time and time again,' Vicky said gently.

'He doesn't know. I've never told him, I felt so guilty. I couldn't bear the thought of him knowing I'd killed Mum.' Chelsea took her feet out of the pool and swivelled herself around to look at them. 'This is the first year Dad and I haven't spent the day together. We usually take flowers to the cemetery and then have lunch somewhere and talk about Mum. I'm not sure how he's going to cope on his own tomorrow.'

'Did you see a trauma counsellor after it happened?' Amy asked.

Chelsea shook her head.

'I think maybe you should. I know when Tasha died – and it was expected because she was ill – I was absolutely shattered, and she was my aunt, not my mother. Seeing a counsellor helped me. I can't imagine what it feels like when your mother is suddenly not there. I'm so sorry.'

'If nothing else, you should talk to your dad when you get

home,' Matilda added. 'I'm sure he'll be horrified to hear you've been blaming yourself all this time.'

'I'm not sure I can,' Chelsea said. 'I think it's five years too late.'

'Nonsense,' Matilda said. 'It's never too late to talk.'

'Maybe I'll try when I get back.' Chelsea sighed. 'It's been such a lovely day – I'm so sorry if I've spoilt the evening.'

'Don't be silly – you haven't spoilt anything,' Amy said, leaping to her feet and starting to hand around various dishes. 'We're your friends, willing to help in any way we can. Come on, we're supposed to be having a midnight feast – so let's eat.'

* * *

Vicky, nibbling some goat's cheese with a slice of baguette and listening to Zaz singing in the background, smiled to herself as she wondered how her mother would have reacted to the young singer's cover version of a favourite Edith Piaf song. Before she left France next week, she'd have to track down a Zaz CD and buy a couple – one for herself and one for her mum.

She glanced across to Chelsea, sitting with Matilda at one of the small white wrought-iron tables further along the pool terrace. She felt so sorry for her having to cope with losing her mother in such a tragic way. Words were always inadequate in such a situation. Tomorrow was sure to be a difficult day for Chelsea, maybe she'd suggest doing something together, something that would take her mind off the anniversary. Coffee in Cannes maybe?

'More wine?' Amy asked, standing in front of her with the rosé bottle and a glass.

'Thanks. And thank you for today. It's been lovely. And

this feast in the garden is the perfect end to the day. I've never seen a pool with underwater lights before. Together with the solar lights, there's a magical *Midsummer Night's Dream* atmosphere down here this evening.' Vicky laughed. 'I half expect Titania to appear in a diaphanous gown and join us for a while before fading away again and leaving us to our present-day worries.'

'Any word from Anthony?' Amy asked.

'A couple of text messages. He's having a problem getting a flight. Hopefully I'll hear something soon.' She took a sip of her drink before saying quietly so the others couldn't hear, 'I was thinking that maybe the three of us could suggest coffee in Cannes to Chelsea tomorrow morning. Try and take her mind off the date. Good idea? Or best left?'

'It would have to be you and Matilda – I'm busy in the morning, I'm afraid. Leave it until tomorrow before suggesting – make it seem more spontaneous,' Amy said. 'Anybody else like a top-up?' she asked, holding out the bottle to the other two.

'Please, and I'm going to indulge in some more of that gorgeous pâté,' Chelsea said.

As Amy moved away, Vicky felt her phone vibrate in her jeans pocket. Anthony. Glancing at the brief text, she heaved a sigh of relief. He'd managed to get a flight and would arrive for the last two days of her holiday. Quickly she sent a reply.

✉ Great. The change will do you good. You'll love the villa. xxx.

She put the phone back in her pocket thoughtfully and went to tell the others the news.

At least they'd be on neutral ground while they talked about his suspension and how he saw the future. Both their futures. If anything, the short time she'd been at the villa had made her more determined than ever to live her own life the way she wanted. She didn't intend to seek Anthony's permission. Just his co-operation. And his promise not to mind.

* * *

Matilda finished her wine, placed the empty glass on the poolside table and looked at the other three women.

'I have a confession to make,' she said quietly.

Startled, they all looked at her in surprise, wondering what was coming.

'I've registered with an estate agent and tomorrow I'm looking at four houses and one apartment.'

'Exciting,' Amy said.

'I think I'm too old to be having a mid-life crisis,' Matilda said. 'But I'm still dreaming of a life in France, so I thought I'd better check things out while I'm here. Of course, nothing may come of it but...' she shrugged. 'I have to at least try and see if the dream William and I had is viable. I'd love the company if any of you would like to come with me?'

'I'll come,' Chelsea said. 'I love looking at property and daydreaming about the kind of house I might buy one day. Besides, I can make sure anything you buy has a spare room for when I visit.'

'I'd normally jump at the chance,' Vicky said. 'But with Anthony coming, I know my time to write will disappear, so as much as I'd like to, I don't think I'd better.'

'Any other day I'd have loved to have joined you,' Amy said. 'I have an appointment in the morning but could join you in the afternoon? I can certainly ask Pierre to drive you down to the estate agents.'

'Thank you. I have to be at the agents in Cannes at 10.30,' Matilda said.

'Are any of the houses near here?' Vicky asked.

'One is in Cagnes-sur-mer. Two are in Antibes, I think. The one I really like the sound of is in the village,' Matilda said. 'And there is an apartment in a new block in a nearby marina – I'm not sure of the exact location.' She was silent for a few seconds before turning to Amy. 'I know the film that inspired your generosity to offer us all a free holiday was set in an Italian castle and not a villa in France, but Belle Vue is just perfect. If I can find somewhere even half as wonderful, I'll be very lucky.'

'I bet the castle was just a film set somewhere,' Chelsea said. 'Probably wasn't even in Italy. I haven't seen the film, so I can't compare it with here.' She took a swig of her wine before realising the other three women were all staring at her. 'What?'

'You've not seen *Enchanted April*?' Amy said. 'How did you answer the questions?'

'Umm, I googled them,' Chelsea said, before biting her bottom lip and looking at them anxiously.

'Googled it!' The other three spoke as one, looking at her in shock.

'I was just killing time one afternoon. I couldn't believe it when I won. Please don't hate me.'

'Of course we don't hate you, but there is a forfeit to pay,' Amy said mock seriously, trying not to laugh at the expression on Chelsea's face at her words. 'You will be made to watch the film and possibly answer questions on it before you are allowed to leave Belle Vue.'

DAY EIGHT OF THE HOLIDAY – JUNE 13

17

The next morning, Chelsea was up so early to swim the daily thirty lengths she'd promised herself she'd do that she witnessed the sun rising. Wrapping herself in a towel afterwards, she sat on one of the poolside loungers for a few moments, watching the rosy pink hues fade away, leaving a cloudless pale blue sky that would slowly darken into the azure blue heralding a beautiful South of France summer day.

Today, she knew from experience, was going to be a long day, filled with remorse and guilt that overshadowed happy memories of her mum. It seemed impossible that it was five years ago that her world had imploded. Thankfully, the sheer horror of the accident had faded in her mind and she'd learnt to cope and live with its awful consequence, but the guilt of knowing it was her fault they were in the wrong place at the wrong time had never faded. She alone was responsible for the permanent mum shaped hole that now featured in her life.

Thinking about what the others had said about talking to

her dad, Chelsea brushed a hand against her cheeks, wet from the tears that had started to fall without her realising. Were they right, saying it was never too late to talk? What good would it do? It wouldn't alter the facts, but learning the truth could turn him against her, and she couldn't risk that. She needed him in her life. He was all that was left of her family. He was her rock.

She sighed. No. She couldn't share her guilty secret with him.

Chelsea clutched the towel around her tighter and stood up. She'd shower, have some breakfast and then phone her dad before joining Matilda for their day of house hunting. And then, this evening, she'd cook one of her mum's favourite meals for dinner. Keeping herself busy would help pass the day.

Her mobile rang while she was eating a pain au chocolat. 'Dad. I was going to ring you in a minute. How you doing?'

'Okay. You?'

'Feels weird not being there to go with you to the cemetery, if I'm honest,' Chelsea admitted. 'Have you got our usual flower arrangement?'

'Sunflowers, daisies and poppies,' her father said. 'All the favourites.'

Chelsea remembered the argument they'd had on the first anniversary. They couldn't decide which flower her mum had favoured most out of the three, so they'd ordered a large arrangement containing all three. It had become a tradition.

'Will you take a photo for me, please,' Chelsea said.

'Sure thing, Sunshine. Talking of photographs, thank you for the two you sent. Love the new haircut.'

'Thanks. You doing anything after you've been to the cemetery?'

'Heading into work, nothing special. What are you up to?'

'I'm going house hunting with Matilda. She's the older woman in the photo and is thinking of moving over here permanently. She and her husband had this dream, but he died.' Chelsea's voice faded away before she took a deep breath. 'Do you have a leftover dream, Dad? A dream that you and Mum planned to do together?'

There was a short silence at the other end of the phone before her father answered. 'No. We pretty much did everything that we'd planned to do – except, of course, growing old together.'

Chelsea hesitated. 'Do you ever think about meeting someone new? Being happy again? Growing old with someone else?'

'Occasionally. It would have to be a special woman to take your mum's place. But I'm not unhappy.' There was another brief silence before he added, 'Anyway, enough about me. We need you to meet someone decent first.'

Chelsea laughed. 'I'll let you know when that happens – although a waiter did give me his telephone number when we were in an Antibes restaurant.'

'I'd rather it was the maître d'hôtel than a mere waiter,' Simon said, a teasing note in his voice.

'Dad, that's very snobbish of you. He spoke four or five languages. I got the feeling he intends to be more than a mere waiter in a few years.'

'In that case, I'm sure he's a good prospect. Have you heard from Elsie? She coping all right with the business while you're away?'

'Haven't heard for a couple of days, too busy probably. I'll drop her a text later today. Right, I'd better get going. Tell Mum I love her and miss her. Phone me later? Love you,' and Chelsea ended the call just as Matilda came looking for her.

Pierre dropped the two of them outside the estate agent's

office, where an enthusiastic and smartly dressed man in his thirties greeted them.

'Bonjour. I'm Troy and I'm yours for the day.' As they walked to his car parked in a nearby back street, he explained the itinerary he'd planned. 'We'll start with the house at Cagnes-sur-mer. The owners are expecting us in half an hour, so we have plenty of time. Afterwards, we'll make our way back to Antibes for the two properties there you want to view. And then back to Cannes for lunch. This afternoon, we'll meet up again and I'll take you to see the garden apartment in Mandelieu-la-Napoule – in a very nice complex, that one – and finally the one in Cannes la Bocca, before I drop you at Belle Vue.'

Traffic on the A8 was busy and Matilda and Chelsea sat quietly, letting Troy concentrate on his driving. Twenty minutes later, he turned off the autoroute onto a one way system before heading into a quiet street with several villas on one side and a high bank on the other. He pulled up in front of one with a large 'Vendre' attached to its front gate.

'Here we are, ladies. Very conveniently located, this one, for transport and the shops. Here comes Madame Smythe.'

'Love the rambling rose hedge,' Chelsea whispered to Matilda as they got out of the car.

'Mmm,' Matilda murmured, before turning to shake Madame Smythe's hand and follow Troy into the house.

The tour of the house didn't take long and they were soon standing outside in the garden. Matilda smothered a sigh of relief. Finally, something she could be positive about. 'Lovely garden. You must work hard on it.'

'I'm going to miss it. Lovely sitting out here in the evening. Would you like a coffee?'

'I'm afraid we don't have time,' Troy said. 'On a tight schedule this morning.'

'Thank you, anyway,' Matilda said, her attention drawn to a loud rumbling noise. She and Chelsea both turned to look in the direction it was coming from. Thirty metres away on the bank across the road, a train whooshed in and began disgorging its passengers onto the platform. Passengers who had a clear view of everything and everyone in the garden as they walked to an exit. Chelsea raised her hand in response to a cheeky little boy, who smiled before waving at them vigorously. Thirty seconds later, the train rumbled on its way.

'Well, Troy did say transport was convenient,' Chelsea said sotto voce in Matilda's ear, trying not to laugh at the absurdity of having TGVs virtually in your garden.

'Well, that's one off the list then,' Matilda said as Troy drove them back to Antibes. 'I hope none of the other places you're showing me have such obvious drawbacks?'

'You don't harbour a secret love of trains then,' Troy said, a suspicion of a smile on his lips.

The drive back to Antibes was trouble free and Troy was soon parking in front of a villa in a quiet street at the top end of town.

Matilda and Chelsea followed him as he opened a gate and led them down a long path that curved around flower beds before ending in a short flight of steps stopping in front of a scarlet front door framed by a white wisteria.

Troy unlocked the door, explaining as he did so, 'The owners are at work all day, so feel free to tell me what you think as we go round.'

'I love this conservatory,' Chelsea said as Matilda wandered over to the double French doors to look out over the garden, where several trees provided shade over the pool.

Upstairs, the three bedrooms and two bathrooms were spacious and immaculate. Matilda sighed as they went back downstairs and out into the garden. 'It doesn't feel very

French, does it? It could be a suburban house in England,'
she said to Chelsea. 'No interesting little quirks. And it's overlooked from all sides.'

'True,' Chelsea said. 'But you could add some French
touches, grow the hedges taller.'

Matilda shook her head. 'No. It's a nice enough house, but
it doesn't feel right for me. Sorry,' she said, turning to face
Troy. 'Next one please.'

The next one was only five minutes away down the hill.
The third house in a cul-de-sac, it was clear from the moment
Troy opened the large electric gate that the villa needed decorating and the garden shrubs and trees were in desperate
need of pruning.

A trough of lavender by the side of the steps at the front
door smelt heavenly and Matilda couldn't resist running her
fingers over the deep blue flower heads as she walked into a
narrow hallway. Two huge dressers against one wall made
approaching the sitting room difficult and that area too, was
stuffed with leather sofas, tables and a third dresser. Two
small sunrooms overlooking the garden and a pool were
behind patio doors and filled with boxes.

Matilda sighed when she saw the size of the kitchen. It
was minuscule and badly in need of modernising. As was the
downstairs bathroom.

Troy opened a set of French doors and the three of them
walked out onto the terrace. Above them, a coloured glass
canopy fixed along the back of the villa provided shelter from
the sun. Standing there looking around, Matilda imagined
herself living in the house, making it her own. Being happy
there. Suppers out here on the terrace with friends. Swimming in the pool. Josh staying. But there was so much to do to
the place, did she really want the hassle? She and William

would have had fun doing the place up together, but on her own in a foreign country?

She turned to find Troy looking at her expectantly.

Matilda shook her head. 'I'm not sure. I do like the villa, but it does need work. Probably more work than I want to take on. I'll have to think about it.'

Troy drove them back to Cannes, promising to see them again after lunch. Matilda and Chelsea made their way to one of the many restaurants by the market, taking the last available pavement table at the one where they liked the look of the menu. Once they'd both settled on the plat de jour, and a carafe of wine had been placed in front of them, Chelsea said, 'That last villa certainly has potential. I could see you living there.'

'Could you?' Matilda asked. 'I could see William and me living there together, but I'm not sure about me on my own. Although getting it modernised and decorated would certainly give me plenty to do. A purpose in life again.'

Chelsea glanced at her. 'How long were you married?'

Matilda looked down at her drink, biting her lip. 'It would have been our thirtieth wedding anniversary last year.'

'Oh, Tilly, I'm sorry you didn't get to celebrate together,' Chelsea said, placing her hand over Matilda's that was resting on the table.

'You called me Tilly,' Matilda said, fighting back the tears. 'My mother was the only person who's ever called me that. William always called me Matty. Nobody else these days shortens my name.'

'I promise I won't again,' Chelsea said. 'It just slipped out. I didn't mean to upset you.'

'No, you didn't. I'd love you to call me Tilly from now on. Makes me feel young and happy.' And Matilda squeezed Chelsea's hand.

* * *

Vicky spent the morning, whilst the others were out house hunting, up in the summer house trying to do the writing she'd promised herself she'd do, but instead she found herself spending far too much time gazing at the view and letting her mind wander. She'd been surprised to realise just how fond she was becoming of the other women. Strangers a few days ago, they had become people she cared about.

Yesterday's outing to Antibes and the late-night feast afterwards had made her realise how much she was enjoying the holiday and the company of the other women. There had been a feeling of real camaraderie around the pool last night.

Her few close girlfriends all came from the past – Lisa and Bella from school and university – Kylie and Jena from flat sharing when she was single and newly arrived in London. Not that she saw much of any of them these days. They kept in touch via Facebook, but not in real life, where they were all too busy to actually schedule a meet up. She still saw Emily and Sally, women she'd met at the school gate when the children were younger, but it was a long time since she'd made any new real female friends.

Her friends nowadays tended to be the wives of Anthony's colleagues and weren't really the type of women Vicky felt comfortable with. High maintenance was the phrase that sprang to mind and summed most of them up. But she liked all three women she'd met here. They were all so different and yet she could sense a bond of true friendship was drawing them all together. She would definitely make an effort to keep in touch after they left at the end of the holiday.

Chelsea's story last night had been so sad and Vicky knew that she wasn't the only one whose heart had gone out to her. She'd seen sadness reflected too, in Amy and Matilda's eyes as they'd listened to Chelsea. Trotting out old clichés along the lines of 'Your mum wouldn't want you to feel guilty over what was a tragic accident. She'd want you to live a happy life' had seemed trite and useless. All Vicky had wanted to do was give Chelsea a big hug. Matilda had been so right to encourage Chelsea to talk to her dad.

Vicky forced herself to stop looking at the view and tried to concentrate on chapter nine. Strange how this writing lark made one start analysing things and speculating about people and characters. Matilda for instance. She was a bit of an enigma. Quiet and self-contained, but at times there was a vulnerable air about her – something that Vicky suspected she struggled to hide. Whilst determined to make a new life for herself, she clearly missed her husband desperately.

Sitting there, Vicky's thoughts drifted to her own life and Anthony. How would she cope if he suddenly died? Or they separated? Badly, was the honest answer to both questions. As cross as she was with him over this current diabolic shambles in his political life, she knew they'd survive beyond that particular problem, even if the worst happened and he lost his parliamentary seat. It was their personal lives that needed sorting. When he got here, she was more determined than ever to talk to him and make him understand that whatever happened in his career, things at home had to change.

18

Amy was in her room, about to take a quick shower and get ready for her meeting in Cannes when her mother rang.

'I posted you the latest missive from Kevin a few days ago. Have you received it yet?' Fleur asked.

Amy glanced across to the desk where she'd left the newly received envelope and its contents on top of the folder with all the others. 'Yes, thanks. All well with you and Dad?'

'We're off to Cornwall for the weekend soon. I've been thinking about you and your problem.'

Amy sighed inwardly. The last thing she wanted this morning was a lecture, however well-meaning, from her mother. 'Mum, I can't talk right now. I've got a meeting in town in half an hour. I'll call you back later, okay?' With a flash of guilt, she ended the call. She should have told her mum that her meeting was with the notaire, but she knew that although Fleur's reaction would be a heartfelt 'thank goodness', there would also be several questions. Questions that Amy didn't know the answers to yet. She'd phone home later to say sorry and tell her she'd finally been to the notaire.

Standing under the hot water jets of the shower, using her favourite Jo Malone shower gel, Amy thought about the upcoming meeting. The meeting she'd delayed and delayed. Inheriting Belle Vue Villa had been the incentive she'd needed to leave Kevin and she'd put all her energies into making the retreat work, promising herself that once her business was established, she'd start divorce proceedings. At her first meeting with the notaire, two and a half years ago, she'd come away feeling daunted with the amount of paperwork the French authorities required her to produce. Life in France was good, Kevin was out of her life and her urgent need to get away from him had disappeared. Despite Fleur's nagging to do something, it had become a case of out of sight, out of mind – until this week.

After her shower, Amy pulled on a pair of white capri pants and a blue sleeveless top that she knew would be cool as the day got hotter, grabbed the file of papers and the envelope from the desk and left the villa. Driving down to town, she tried to concentrate on what was likely to happen at the meeting, but thoughts of Aunt Tasha and her mother kept crowding into her mind. Thoughts that made it vital for her to do the right thing.

Amy found a space to park near the train station and walked up to and crossed over the busy junction of Boulevard Sadi Carnot before making her way down a side street.

She stopped in front of a tall building with a brass plate fixed to the wall, alongside an old-fashioned wooden door, announcing the offices of *Lefevre, Mathias. Notaire*. Amy took a deep breath and pressed the intercom buzzer.

'Oui?'

'Madame Martin pour un rendezvous avec Monsieur Lefevre.'

The door lock buzzed. Amy composed herself before

pushing it open and walking into a carpeted hallway. Finally, after years of indecision, she was doing something about her sham of a marriage. As she was ushered into the notaire's office, she sent up a silent prayer that she would be able to keep Kevin's hands off Belle Vue. That was the most important thing. He'd seemed extremely confident when he'd threatened her with the fact that he had a legitimate claim to her inheritance and he intended to get it. If he did have a claim, she was resolved to fight him all the way, knowing how much Tasha would hate her beloved villa falling into Kevin's ownership.

Half an hour later, Amy, deep in thought, left the notaire's and walked slowly back to where she'd parked the car. Mathias Lefevre had been charming, taken her folder of papers and given them a quick glance, before gently reproving her for not coming back to see him sooner. To her question 'Will Belle Vue have to form part of any divorce settlement?' he'd pursed his lips.

'Inheritance here in France is not the same as in Angleterre. We handle it differently. I will study the papers and the dates to find your answer in this case. Next visit, I will have an answer for you.' And with that she had to be content.

The house phone was ringing when she got home and she picked it up before the answerphone could switch in.

'Is that Amy Martin?' a man's voice asked.

'Yes.'

'Are you alone? Matilda Richardson is not with you?'

'Who are you and why are you calling? And why are you asking about Matilda?' Amy said sharply. 'Is there a problem?' She heard an intake of breath over the phone.

'I'm sorry, I didn't mean to worry you. I'm Josh, her son. And there is no problem, although I'm hoping you can help me with something. But, first, you didn't say if you were alone? I don't want Mum overhearing this conversation.'

'I'm alone,' Amy said, relaxing now she knew who was on the end of the phone. 'Matilda has gone out for the day.'

'Good. Has she told you it's her birthday on the fifteenth?'

'No, she hasn't.'

'I was wondering...' Josh hesitated. 'Would it be possible for you to organise a secret birthday meal for her. With a cake and things? I'll pay for the extras, of course.'

Amy laughed. 'That won't be necessary. I'm more than happy to throw Matilda a surprise party and have a cake made.'

'Really? Thank you. There is another complication though – I'm planning on turning up and surprising her.'

'I know she'll be thrilled to see you,' Amy said. 'Do you need somewhere to stay? If you do, you're more than welcome to a room here.'

'That's really kind of you. That would be great. Thank you. I'll see you on the morning of the fifteenth then. And remember, not a word to Mum.'

'My lips are sealed.' Amy laughed as she hung up.

Vicky coming into the kitchen at that moment looked at Amy, her gaze curious.

'That was Josh, Matilda's son,' Amy said, crossing over to the wine rack and selecting the last bottle of pink champagne to place in the fridge and making a mental note to buy some more. 'We have a secret birthday party to organise for your last evening,' she said, smiling at Vicky. No need to tell her or Chelsea the other part of the secret. Less chance of the news unintentionally slipping out when they were all chatting together.

'It's Matilda's birthday? It will be fun surprising her.'

'Yes, I'm hoping Chelsea can quietly make a cake without her noticing. I can always go to the patisserie if not. I think a barbecue would be fun and easy to organise without drawing attention to it being a party.'

'I'm sure Chelsea will insist on making a cake for Matilda. The two of them seem to be growing close,' Vicky said.

Amy glanced at her watch. 'It's a little early, but shall we have lunch together down by the pool?'

'Good idea,' Vicky replied, looking at the basket of salad things Pierre had left on the work surface by the sink. 'I never eat salad at home – here, it's my go-to for lunch. That and the wonderful baguettes,' she added.

Ten minutes later, sitting down by the pool under the shade of a large parasol, Vicky sighed with contentment. 'Listen to those cicadas. Back home next week, if I sit in the garden, all I'll hear will be traffic.'

'Would you like to move and live in the countryside?' Amy said.

'Now the children are living more or less independent lives we could downsize and cut costs, maybe even go mortgage-free – although that wouldn't happen in London. I fancy somewhere in the West Country, Bath or Bristol appeal, but London is where Anthony needs to be at the moment.'

'Any more news on what's happening? Or when you can expect him?'

Vicky shook her head. 'No. I'm on a self-imposed news blackout, to be honest. I'd rather wait and hear everything from Anthony. At least I know then it won't be fake news. I must admit I was hoping to have heard details about his flight by now. All I know is he's got one for the fourteenth.'

'Maybe he'll give you his eta this evening,' Amy said.

Vicky nodded absently. 'Hope so. I wonder if Matilda's

seen a villa she likes today. It's a big step, moving to another country on your own. You were very brave to do it.'

Amy was silent for a moment, swirling her wine around her glass. 'To be honest, it didn't feel brave. In some respects, at the time it seemed preordained – my marriage falling apart at the same time as my favourite aunt dying and leaving me this amazing villa. Suddenly I had an escape route. The perfect place to run to and hide away from the world.' She smiled ruefully. 'I came here to lick my wounds and keep my promise to Tasha.' She glanced at Vicky. 'Both my aunt and my mother disliked – hated even – my husband. Tasha's dying wish was for me to divorce him and she intended to give me the means to do so.' Amy brushed a tear away. 'It wasn't until the reading of her will that I realised what she meant. I just wish I'd had the sense to kick-start divorce proceedings when I moved here. Now it seems I might have to fight Kevin to keep the villa.' She took a deep breath. 'But fight I will.'

'How did you and Kevin meet?' Vicky asked curiously. 'I know the old cliché, opposites attract and all that, but you strike me as being an unusual couple.'

'I was a dancer in another life, as you know, and Kevin produced a show I was in. We fell in love – well, I thought we did – and he persuaded me to give up dancing, marry him and become his personal assistant. So I did. More fool me,' Amy said. 'In my defence, I was nearly thirty, had never achieved the coveted role of principal dancer within the company and in my heart I knew that it was unlikely to happen. Always the understudy, that was me.' Amy smiled ruefully. 'And my feet were showing signs of a ballet dancer's nightmare – bunions. Besides, I thought once we were married we'd have a family. Giving up dancing professionally seemed the sensible thing to do at the time.'

'I'm so sorry it didn't work out for you,' Vicky said. 'You seem to have found your niche though, living here and running the retreat.'

Amy smiled, glad that Vicky hadn't said she was young and there was still time to meet another man. Maybe there was. But she'd accepted years ago now that her dream of having her own family would remain that forever – a dream of what might have been.

'I am happy living in Belle Vue and running retreats, even if it's not the life I expected or envisaged having for so long,' she said slowly, looking at Vicky. 'As a way of life, it works for me – and it's definitely one that I'll fight to keep, if necessary.'

* * *

It was late afternoon when Troy dropped Matilda and Chelsea back at the villa.

'Thank you,' Matilda said. 'I haven't seen anything today that really inspires me to buy, but please do keep me on your mailing list.'

'Of course. But do seriously think about that apartment in the marina complex. It's got so much going for it.'

Matilda nodded. 'I'll definitely give it some more thought,' she said, knowing full well that she wouldn't. The apartment itself, with its view out over the Mediterranean, had a certain appeal, but the thought of living in the complex made her shudder inwardly.

As they walked into the villa together, Chelsea said, 'Troy's right about the facilities at the marina complex. You'd never be bored. In fact, you'd probably never have to leave the place, there was so much to do on-site – swimming, tennis, boules, a restaurant, a bar and a social club. All that before you go down to the harbour and set foot on an actual boat.'

'You forgot the monthly book club,' Matilda said, laughing. 'I found the thought of all that activity exhausting. Not my scene at all. Although the book club might have been interesting.'

Chelsea laughed. 'It did all sound rather full on. Right, I'm going to dump my stuff and then get on with prepping dinner.'

'I'm going to have a quiet ten minutes in my room and then go for an amble around the garden,' Matilda said. 'Clear my head from all Troy's jargon and hard sell.'

'Catch you later then,' Chelsea said and made for her own room.

Opening her laptop to quickly check her emails, she saw her dad had sent her one with a picture of the flowers he'd placed on her mum's grave. She quickly typed a thank you note before scrolling down and stiffening in shock. Today of all days, there was one from Kit. She hadn't heard a peep from him after her humiliation at the hands of his wife and stupidly she'd forgotten to block him. She caught her breath, reading the single word in the subject line, 'Sorry.'

Chelsea stared at the screen for half a minute, her mind reeling, her heart racing. Was he serious? She could feel the anger that had consumed her all those months ago rising up again inside. She could take the opportunity to tell him exactly what she thought of him. Spew out the words of contempt, the nasty names she'd shouted aloud into the empty air of her bedroom. Did 'Kit' even realise his life could have been in danger if they'd ever come face to face at that time?

Her fingers hovered over the keypad as she hesitated. Should she answer him? Chelsea waited for several seconds, trying to rationalise her thoughts, before she decisively pulled the lid of the laptop down and closed it. She'd read the email itself later. She needed time to calm down. To think things through.

Amy was in the kitchen having a drink of water when Chelsea walked in.

'Hi. Did Matilda find her dream home today?'

'No,' Chelsea shook her head. 'But we had fun.'

'I had a phone call from her son earlier,' Amy said. 'It's her birthday the day before you all leave. He wondered if we could surprise her with a cake?'

'I'll make one,' Chelsea said instantly, looking at Amy. 'We could arrange a secret party too?'

Amy nodded. 'I'd already decided to do that. As it will be the last evening, I thought we'd have a barbecue.'

'It'll make our last evening here extra special,' Chelsea said, methodically starting to lay out the ingredients she needed for dinner. 'I thought I'd cook my mum's favourite meal tonight,' she said quietly. 'Coquilles St Jacques for starters, roast chicken with all the trimmings for main and pavlova for dessert.'

'Sounds delicious,' Amy said before turning to Chelsea, a gentle look on her face. 'Has today been difficult?'

Chelsea nodded. 'In more ways than one. I did speak to Dad before I went out with Matilda and he's sent me a photo of the flowers he took to the cemetery. Looking at houses with Matilda did help to take my mind off things though.' She tipped some potatoes into the sink and started to peel one.

'I lost Tasha about the same time as your mum died,' Amy said quietly. 'She was my godmother as well as my aunt and I still miss her dreadfully, so I can understand a little of how you must feel about your mum. Certain anniversaries like today will always be difficult to get through.'

'You weren't responsible though, were you?' Chelsea said, trying and failing to hold back the tears. 'You can't possibly understand the guilt I feel over living while she died. It never goes away. It's always there in the back of my mind.'

Amy was at her side immediately and put her arms around Chelsea and hugged the younger woman tightly before she sighed. 'I'm sorry. You're right. I can't comprehend the guilt you are carrying. It was presumptuous of me to think I could understood what you continue to go through.'

Chelsea sniffed and wiped her cheeks with the back of her hand. 'I'm sorry. I didn't mean to blub all over you. I think having an email from Kit, today of all days, has pushed me over the edge.'

'The guy you dated who turned out to be married?' Amy asked gently.

Chelsea nodded.

'In the words of the song, Let it go.' Amy gave Chelsea a final squeeze before smiling at her. 'Now, is there anything I can do?'

'Grate the cheese for the scallop sauce?' Chelsea suggested, relieved that her cross words hadn't upset or hurt Amy. She knew Amy had only been trying to console her, but she also knew there was no getting away from it. The guilt over her mother's death would stay with her forever. Even if she lived to be a hundred, she'd never get over, or forget, the part she'd played in it.

Matilda sat on the terrace outside her room drinking a cup of tea and enjoying the quiet of the garden, cicadas notwithstanding. She could see Pierre hard at work digging over a patch in the vegetable garden. She'd wander down that way in a few moments and have a chat with him. She'd discovered, talking to him over the course of the holiday, that he had a dry wit and his genuine down-to-earth opinion on any subject was always worth hearing. She suspected he'd been regarded as quite a catch in his younger days, with that twinkle in his eye. He always seemed pleased to see her too, didn't make her feel a nuisance for interrupting him.

Matilda's mind was darting all over the place as she drank her tea, throwing up more negative thoughts than positive ones regarding the big change of lifestyle she was contemplating. Was this sudden urge to move to France a fad? A reaction maybe to being a widow? Would she and William have actually sold up when he finally retired and leapt into a new life over here? As William had done nothing but drawn up plans and talked about it for months before he'd had the final fatal heart attack, she had to believe that, yes, they would have moved over here. And she would have come more than willingly with him.

Matilda stood up and took the cup and saucer into her room and rinsed them under the hot water tap in the bathroom sink. She'd have that walk in the garden, see if she could clear her head and talk to Pierre.

Pierre was starting to put his tools in the wheelbarrow that accompanied him everywhere in the garden. Lola, his faithful companion, barked a welcome at Matilda and she bent down to pet the little dog.

'Find a villa you like today?' Pierre asked, smiling at her.

'No. Nothing gave me that "this is the one, I could live here happily" feeling.'

'Like taking a wife, you definitely need a coup de Coeur when buying a house,' Pierre said, his face inscrutable.

'There was one that almost had that heart stopping moment but...' Matilda shrugged and lifted the cane basket with its small hand tools into the wheelbarrow as Pierre balanced the spade and hoe and began to push the barrow down the path. 'The last one Troy took us to was down in the village and I was really hoping it would be "the one" as I like it around here, but it was so small and ugly, I couldn't bear it,' Matilda sighed. The path being narrow, she walked to one side of the barrow, talking to herself more than directly to Pierre. 'I think I'm going to have to come back later in the year for a serious look – that is, if I decide moving here is what I truly want to do. Maybe it's a silly idea and I'd be better off just forgetting the whole thing.'

She was so wrapped up in her own mutterings that it was a minute or two before she realised that Pierre had stopped a few yards behind her and was talking on his phone.

'D'accord. À bientôt.' Switching off his phone, he joined Matilda. 'You come with me to the village. We 'ave time before dinner. I show you something.'

'Right now?' Matilda said.

Pierre nodded. 'Oui. It is important for you to see.'

* * *

Vicky sighed happily to herself as she pressed 'save' on her laptop and closed it down. For the past hour, the muse had definitely been with her. She'd barely been able to keep up with the flow of words as she typed. Finally she was getting to grips with this story.

She stood up and stretched in an effort to loosen her neck and shoulders, stiff with hunching over the laptop. Glancing at her watch, she decided she had time for a quick soak in the bath before going down to the kitchen to help Chelsea with dinner.

As usual, the huge bath filled with perfumed water and bubbles was wonderful and Vicky lay there, her eyes closed and her shoulders under the water, completely relaxed, losing all track of time. Lying there, blissfully peaceful, the bathroom scene in *Enchanted April* popped into her mind. Lottie had invited her husband, Mellersh, to join them and the day he arrived, he decided to take a bath in the old-fashioned bathroom. When the Italian staff tried to explain the workings of the temperamental boiler to him, he'd humoured them by smiling and agreeing before ushering them away. The resulting explosion of the boiler he didn't understand the workings of had been impressive and Vicky laughed to herself as she remembered it.

The ping of her mobile signifying an incoming text brought her back to reality with a jolt. Reluctantly, she clambered out of the bath and slipped into the towelling robe before picking up and checking her phone. Anthony.

✉ Be with you about midday tomorrow xxx

Tonight was her last night of freedom then. Immediately, she felt guilty for thinking like that about Anthony's arrival. But she couldn't help it, even though she was also looking forward to seeing him. This holiday on her own had given her space to be herself for days at a time rather than snatching the occasional hour out of a life dominated by family and politics. To say she'd enjoyed being Vicky again was an understatement. She knew she was looking better too. Her skin had acquired a gentle tan and she'd lost her usual city girl pallor.

Selecting a pair of white jeans and a scarlet floaty chiffon top from the wardrobe, she stroked her new velvet coat she'd hung up alongside. She couldn't help but wonder what Anthony would make of it when she wore it. It was a lifetime ago since she'd worn anything as bohemian. By tomorrow evening she'd be back in the role of Anthony's supportive wife – standing at his side, facing the world together. A role she didn't want to relinquish, but she wasn't ready to resume it quite so wholeheartedly as she had in the past. Getting Anthony to understand her needs and to change the basics of how things were in their marriage would be difficult if he wasn't ready to compromise.

'Sorry, it looks like I'm too late tonight to help,' Vicky said when she walked into the kitchen minutes later.

Chelsea had everything under control and was just putting a few aperitifs on a plate.

'Can you take these out to the terrace please,' Chelsea said. 'Amy's out there already. I'll bring the rest.'

Amy was talking on her phone as Vicky put the plate on the table. 'No worries. We'll see you when you get back.' She clicked her mobile closed. 'That was Matilda saying she might be late for dinner tonight and not to wait for her. Pierre is apparently whisking her off to the village for some reason.'

'Dinner will be another hour anyway,' Chelsea said. 'She might be back by then.'

'I hope she'll be here in time. This will be the last evening it will be just the four of us,' Vicky said. 'Anthony will be here tomorrow.'

'I've never met an MP before,' Chelsea said. 'Is he frightfully grand?'

Vicky laughed. 'No, he's not. He can be a bit serious and earnest about things he believes in but he's... he's just normal really.'

'I don't want to worry anyone, but I think we'd better get

indoors,' Amy said. 'The sky was blue just moments ago – now look at it.'

'Looks like the end of the world is nigh – it's so black,' Vicky said, standing up and picking up the plates.

'It might just be we're in for some heavy rain,' Amy said, collecting cushions from the chairs. 'Although I can hear thunder rumbling around in the hills. Fingers crossed we're not about to get one of our infamous flash floods.'

19

Pierre held the passenger car door open for Matilda. As she settled herself in and thanked him, Lola jumped on her lap. 'Oh. Are you coming too?' She looked at Pierre. 'Is she allowed? Amy won't worry if she can't find her?'

Pierre shook his head. 'It's okay. Amy knows Lola often comes with me.'

'Is there any point in me asking where you're taking me?' Matilda said as she stroked Lola.

Pierre shook his head. 'Non. I'm hoping we arrive before the rain,' he said, looking up at the darkening sky. He turned the car left onto the road leading to the village and a few minutes later turned left again into a small cul-de-sac that was more a lane than a proper road. A turfed island in the middle of the lane at the halfway point with a tall willow tree, its fronds bending and flying sideways as the wind increased, reminded Matilda of an English village green. Eight or ten typical Provençal villas with their painted yellow walls and blue shutters were set along the lane at various angles, gardens and hedges dividing them from each other.

Pierre drove slowly down the lane, giving Matilda time to look around. 'All the gardens are so beautiful. Especially that one,' she said, pointing to one. 'What a lovely place,' she said as Pierre turned onto the drive of the villa opposite the garden she'd admired. 'Is this where you live?'

'Non. It is the holiday home of an Italian cousin. He and his wife spent all their holidays for years renovating the place. These days, he rarely gets to visit, he's so busy, and I keep an eye on it for him. Let's get inside,' and Pierre took a bunch of keys out of his pocket

Large drops of rain were falling as they got out of the car. Slowly at first and then quicker and harder as they ran up the drive towards the front door, Lola scampering ahead of them. Pierre pushed a key into the lock, opened the door and ushered Matilda inside.

The light and space inside the villa took Matilda's breath away. It was so different to what she'd been expecting. White walls, curved arches, minimal furniture. The sitting room with its limed and distressed beams and three sets of French doors overlooked the garden and pool. Even with the rain now thundering down outside and the wind reaching gale force, the house felt cosy and secure. She walked through into the kitchen with its marble worktops, state-of-the-art Italian fixtures, some wonderful wall tiles and a scarlet fridge which should have jarred amongst all the pale colours but was somehow perfect.

Matilda turned to Pierre. 'I know Italy is lovely, but if this were mine I 'd want to live here forever. It's a wonderful house. Your cousin has great taste too, in the way he's decorated it.'

Pierre looked at her seriously for several seconds. 'My cousin, he 'as the plan to sell the maison this summer. If you like, you can buy.' A loud clap of thunder followed his remarks and they both turned to look out of the kitchen window as the rain hammered down even harder than before.

Stunned not only by his words but also at the ferocity of the storm now raging, Matilda gazed out at the garden, unable to speak. This beautiful house was up for sale. Could it be hers?

Pierre's mobile rang. Answering it, he listened intently before swearing and closing it down. 'Merde.' He moved closer to a window and stared out before turning to Matilda. 'That was Amy. There is already a flood on the road between here and Belle Vue. The drains are blocked and can't cope with this deluge. The road is closed for the next hour at least until the pompiers pump it clear.'

'So we are marooned here?' Matilda said. 'It doesn't matter to me, but I hope you don't have any plans for the evening?'

'I promised to call in and see Olivia, but she'll not be expecting me in this weather.' He shrugged. 'Fancy a coffee?'

'Please. Your cousin won't mind us helping ourselves? But may I take a look upstairs first?'

'Feel free,' Pierre said.

The wooden stairs had a gentle curve in them at the bottom and halfway up there was a landing almost the size of a room, with a small glass topped table on which a pottery vase containing silk flowers had been placed – three sunflowers and three poppies. Above the table, a leaded glass window with different shaped pieces of coloured glass – yellow, red, and green – complemented the colours of the flowers.

The hallway of the top floor was light and airy, thanks to

four large skylights. Three double bedrooms, all en suite, and a family bathroom opened off the wide hallway. A smaller room with a single bed and wardrobe overlooking the side garden was a child's bedroom with Disney characters painted over one wall.

Standing in what was clearly the master bedroom at the front of the villa watching the rain lashing down, Matilda jumped as a sudden flash of lightning lit up the room and was instantly followed by a thunderclap that shook the whole house. The storm was now right overhead. The lane outside had become a tumbling stream under the latest onslaught, but the drains on either side of the road appeared to be coping. A tantalising smell of coffee drifted into the room from the kitchen below. Matilda turned and went downstairs, eager for a coffee but also to take the opportunity to quiz Pierre about the villa.

A cafetière stood on the small bistro-type table tucked away in an alcove at the end of the kitchen, two cane chairs alongside it. Pierre placed a couple of traditional French coffee bowls and two plates on the table.

'A few mini croissants are defrosting in the microwave,' he said, pushing the plunger down on the coffee. 'My cousin, he always keeps pastries in the freezer.' He poured the coffee and pushed one of the bowls over to her as the microwave pinged. 'Voila,' Pierre said, placing the plate with its selection of tempting mini pastries on the table. 'We pretend it's breakfast time, non?' His eyes twinkled mischievously at her.

'Non, no, I mean oui, I think.' Matilda laughed nervously. An unexpected frisson in her body as Pierre smiled at her raised an equally unexpected improper question in her mind. What would it be like to live in this house and have breakfast with someone new? Someone like Pierre? Now where had that insane thought come from? She wasn't some gauche woman desperate to fill the empty space in her life with a man. She quickly picked up a delicious looking apricot tart and took a bite.

The weather outside showed no signs of improving. The wind was howling around the house in strong gusts and the rain splattering against windowpanes was heavy, but right at that moment, Matilda couldn't think of anywhere she'd rather be. This house made her feel safe.

'So you think you buy the house?' Pierre asked, his eyes watching her carefully. 'It's a happy house and you suit it.'

Matilda looked at him, surprised. She suited the house? What did he mean by that remark?

'It's the kind of villa I've dreamed of living in. It all depends on the price. I won't be surprised if it's out of my reach.'

'I tell you the price – you can always make an offer.'

When he told her the amount his cousin wanted, she gasped.

'Oh.'

'Trop chèr for you? Je suis desolé. I really thought I was doing the right thing bringing you here. But now I make you unhappy,' Pierre said, genuine regret in his voice.

'No, no. It's near the top of my budget, but I think, maybe with a bit of juggling, it's within reach.'

Pierre jumped to his feet, pulling his phone out of his pocket. 'Bien. I tell him to take a few thousand euros off the price and voila – the house is sold. Two happy people.'

'Wait, wait. I need to think about it. Talk to Josh. Put my house in England on the market. So much to think about and do,' Matilda said. She took a deep breath. 'I love this house. Buying it would be a dream come true. But… but the inescapable fact is that I'm terrified.'

'Why?'

'As much as I dream of moving to France, I'm afraid I'd be making a huge mistake. That I'm too old for such a change. That I'm not strong enough, physically or mentally, to cope with everything on my own.'

'Mais ton âge n'est qu'un chiffre,' Pierre protested. 'Merde. I can't remember how to say that in English.'

'I think it's probably the same saying we have in English,' Matilda said. 'Age is just a number.'

'It must be true then,' Pierre said. 'If both the French and the English agree.'

'I know but...' Matilda shrugged her shoulders. 'It can't help but have an effect on things.'

Pierre took the empty plates and bowls over to the sink before turning to face Matilda. 'Have you read any of the essays of James Baldwin, the American novelist and activist?'

Matilda shook her head, surprised at the change of subject. 'I've heard of him, but no, I've never read any of his work.'

'He lived for several years in a villa down here near Saint Paul de Vence. He was a great one for quotes. Quotes like this one.' Pierre's voice softened. 'The moment we break faith with one another, the sea engulfs us and the light goes out.'

Matilda closed her eyes and sighed. 'As I understand that, you're trying to tell me that even though William is dead, if I don't follow our dream through, I'll be letting him down and breaking the faith that we always had in each other.'

Pierre nodded. 'Oui.' He hesitated before continuing, 'But you also have to find the courage to live your own life and move on without him. You've got so much still to live for. Don't waste the coming years in regret. Keep looking forward.'

There was a long silence before Matilda took a deep

breath and said, 'Go on then. Phone your cousin. Tell him if he'll take five thousand euros less than the price you told me, I'd like to buy his house. While you talk to him, I'm going to have another wander around.'

Upstairs in the master bedroom, Matilda sank into a comfy chair that had been placed near the window. Was she doing the right thing? Shouldn't she at least have told Pierre she'd think about it for twenty-four hours before deciding? Matilda fiddled with the wedding ring that she still wore. If only William could tell her what to do. She knew she loved this house, knew too that William would have jumped at the chance of the two of them living here and was already imagining the kind of life she'd have living here. Gardening, lunches with new friends on the terrace, wandering down into the village, finding favourite shops. Oh, the life she could imagine would be so good.

She stood up, hearing Pierre bounding up the stairs, and held her breath as he joined her, a big smile on his face.

'Well?' she said.

Pierre nodded. 'Congratulations. You'll soon be the proud owner of this villa and living in France. It is subject to one condition though,' he added.

As Matilda waited to hear the condition, she felt her heart sink at his words.

'My cousin, he would like one last holiday here this summer. It is June now, he suggests he comes in August as usual, signs the papers, et cetera, has a holiday and then the first of September it is yours.'

Matilda breathed a huge sigh of relief. 'That's fine. It will take me time to organise things when I get home.'

'Bien. I already told him oui,' Pierre said, smiling. 'Storm's dying away. We should be able to leave soon.'

'These flash floods are amazing. The clouds are disappearing and the sun is trying to break through,' Matilda said,
looking out of the window. 'Normal Cote d'Azur weather is
already returning. And look, there's a rainbow forming. How
lovely is that?'

Pierre nodded. 'The bottom of it appears to be growing
out of your new garden.'

Matilda couldn't help grinning at him. 'I wonder if there's
a pot of gold under it.'

Pot of gold or not, she knew the rainbow with its foot in
her new garden was a sign from William, telling her that she
was doing the right thing in buying this villa.

* * *

For the first time, dinner that evening at Belle Vue had been
eaten at the pine table in the kitchen while the storm raged
outside.

'That pavlova was amazing,' Amy said, putting her spoon
down with a sigh. 'The whole meal was delicious. Thank you.
A fine tribute to your mum.' She picked up her glass and
raised it in Chelsea's direction. 'She'd be very proud of you.'

'Thank you,' Chelsea said. 'Today has been hard, but I
think being in France made it bearable in so many ways
because it was easier to put things to the back of my mind.'
She looked at Amy and Vicky. 'I don't mean that in an
uncaring kind of way. It's just that there is nothing here to jolt
me into a guilty memory – no photos or memories of Mum
here. I didn't see Dad either, or go to the cemetery, which is
always difficult. Going house hunting with Tilly too, was a
fun thing to do.'

'You call Matilda, Tilly?' Vicky said in surprise.

Chelsea nodded. 'It slipped out unintentionally and she

said she liked it. Anyway, before she gets back, this birthday surprise party for her, are we all going to give her a birthday present? We could club together for something from all of us or we could get individual pressies. What d'you think?'

'Be nice to give her three presents,' Vicky said. 'Make it more of a celebration, having three gifts to unwrap.'

'Good, that's settled then,' Chelsea said. 'I'll make her a cake tomorrow.'

They all heard a car door slam and, seconds later, a smiling Matilda walked into the kitchen.

'My mother would say you look like the cat who's got the cream,' Amy said.

'Pierre took me to look at a wonderful villa – and I'm buying it,' Matilda replied. 'It's just the other side of the village.'

'If it's the one that belongs to his Italian cousin, I know it. It's really lovely,' Amy said.

Matilda nodded. 'That's the one.'

Amy went to the fridge. 'I think this calls for a celebration,' and she took out the bottle of champagne. 'I was saving this for... another occasion, but I can replace it tomorrow. We can celebrate your villa and also have a glass while we're watching the film.'

'What film?' Chelsea asked.

'*Enchanted April,* of course,' Amy said. 'It's time you saw it and we're running out of evenings. Come on, we'll watch it in the sitting room.'

'Tilly, I saved you some dinner if you want it?' Chelsea said.

'Please. You all go ahead. I'll eat and join you afterwards,' Matilda replied. 'I've watched the film so many times, I'm almost word perfect.'

'I remember the first time I saw it was in the old open air

cinema in Monaco under a starlit sky,' Amy said as she inserted the DVD. 'Tasha and Francois, her husband, were meeting friends there and insisted I joined them. Such a magical experience.' Amy smiled as she remembered the occasion. 'Right, everyone comfortable?' and she pressed the start button.

When the credits rolled up the screen an hour and a half later, Chelsea was the first to speak. 'I wasn't sure I was going to enjoy that, but I did. I shall buy a copy when I get home as a reminder of this holiday.'

'Two more days and we'll all be on our way home,' Vicky sighed. 'It's been wonderful.' She glanced around at everyone. 'Anthony arriving tomorrow will obviously alter things for me, but I just want to say – I feel we're all friends now and hope we can keep in touch when we leave here.'

'Definitely,' said Chelsea. 'Like Lottie, Rose, Lady Caroline and Mrs Fisher, we're no longer strangers but friends who look out for each other.'

* * *

When Chelsea got back to her room that evening, she threw herself down on the bed and lay there staring up at the ceiling. The fifth anniversary of her mum's death was nearly over and she'd managed not to spend the whole day in tears and feeling guilty. There had been a couple of times she'd nearly lost it, but thankfully no one had noticed. Or, if they had, they'd kindly given her time to compose herself. Amy had been kindness itself when she'd snapped at her earlier. So understanding.

The film this evening had been a good diversion too. Expecting it to be old-fashioned, even boring, she'd been surprised at how much she'd enjoyed the story of four very different women looking to briefly escape the monotony of their early twentieth century humdrum lives. The world they'd inhabited was so different to the one she lived in almost a hundred years later. She was lucky to have been born towards the end of their century. To have the freedom of the twenty-first century rather than the restrictions of the early twentieth.

Chelsea glanced at her watch. Strange, Dad hadn't phoned. She'd had her phone with her all evening, expecting him to ring after what was always a difficult day for them both. Usually, after the cemetery visit, they spent the day together, mooching around favourite places and reminiscing. Since he'd moved to his new penthouse apartment down in the harbourside development in the centre of Bristol, the evening had been spent there, looking at photos and talking about her mum, keeping her memory alive. Afterwards, they'd order in a takeaway and eat it watching the dockside activity: the quay lights coming on, bars opening for pre-theatre drinks, friends greeting each other before claiming a waterside table for dinner. A taxi would be ordered and arrive at ten o'clock to take her home to her own flat. Chelsea not being there today would have broken her father's routine. If he didn't ring before she went to bed, she'd ring him. Check he was all right.

Chelsea stood up and fetched her laptop from the table. The piece of paper the waiter in Antibes had slipped into her hand lay alongside. He'd written his name next to the number, Yannick. Chelsea smiled, remembering how embarrassed she'd felt at the time. If she'd been staying in France longer, she might well have rung him for one of those French lessons he'd offered to give her. He was very handsome. Probably for the best that she was going home soon. The last thing she needed in her life right now was a man. One, who in all probability, flirted with all his English customers and already had a French girlfriend, or even a wife, tucked away somewhere. There was no way she was going down the married man route ever again. Which reminded her. Kit.

Chelsea clicked on his 'sorry' email and read the short message with increasing incredulity:

Can we meet and talk about us putting the past behind us and getting back together? Despite everything that has happened, I still love you.

A string of xxx's followed.

A wave of nausea swept through her body as she read, bile at the back of her throat making her feel physically sick. No apology for the lies he'd told. No mention of his marriage; the way he'd cheated on his wife; No shame over his behaviour. Was his ego so big that he really thought she'd forgive him, fly back into his arms and they'd live happily ever after? That definitely wasn't going to happen, but should she reply to him? Call him all the ugly names she could think of before she kicked him out of her life forever?

Chelsea sighed. She knew she was over him, responding to his pathetic message with insults was pointless. She marked the message 'junk' and blocked the sender's address before deleting it and closing the laptop. Kit-gate was in the past, where she intended it staying.

Time to ring her dad and then go to bed. She listened to the ringing tone for what seemed like forever before it clicked into answer mode.

'Hi Dad, just ringing to check how your day went. I'll catch you tomorrow.'

She waited a couple of seconds. Simon usually picked up as soon as he heard her voice, even if it wasn't a convenient time. Not tonight. Thoughtfully, Chelsea pressed the end call button. Today of all days she'd expected him to be there in his apartment. If he wasn't there – then where the hell was he?

DAY NINE OF THE HOLIDAY – JUNE 14

20

The next morning, Vicky was up early as usual and made her way to the summer house carrying her laptop and a cup of coffee. Instead of opening the laptop immediately, she sat in her favourite chair, looking out over the garden and sipping her drink. The holiday had gone so quickly. She was going to miss starting her day here, in what had become her own personal space, when she was back in London. The absolute quiet at this hour of the day, before the intrusion of the noises from life waking up down on the coast arrived on the breeze, had been wonderful. Inspiring. The garden at home was never free from the hum of London traffic, even in the middle of the night.

Vicky finished her drink and opened the laptop. She'd promised herself she'd have written at least fifteen thousand words of her story before the holiday was over and she currently needed another three thousand. With Anthony arriving later today, this would probably be the last morning she'd be up here on her own so early. She really needed to make the most of it.

Thinking of Anthony, Vicky sighed. So much to sort out in both their lives. He was sure to be stressed and uptight when he arrived. And cross with himself for causing the situation he found himself in. She knew she too was full of conflicting emotions. Wanting to stand by him, but at the same time needing to distance herself from the political world and find her own. Selfishly, she found herself wishing his acceptance of Amy's generous offer hadn't curtailed her own time alone for the last two days of the holiday. It would be good though, to spend some time together on neutral ground and hopefully Belle Vue would cast it's magic and they would be able to talk, not argue, about where and what they would do in the future.

One of the things Vicky was determined about was not to be sidetracked away from trying to live her life the way she wanted to. It had to change. Anthony needed to understand how important this was for her at this stage of her life. Maybe she'd get a part-time job to give her a tiny bit of financial independence. One thing she'd definitely do when she got home would be to set out a schedule of time on her own when she could write without interruption. And there was no time like the present for getting stuck in.

Two hours later, she'd added fifteen hundred words to the novel and was feeling stiff. Switching off the laptop, Vicky stood up and stretched. Time to go back to her room for a shower and breakfast, but before she could put the chair back in the summer house, Chelsea and Matilda arrived with coffee and a basket of croissants.

'Hi,' Chelsea said. 'Sorry if we're interrupting, but we thought we'd have breakfast up here with you. We need to talk to you about something.'

'I've just finished, so no problem,' Vicky said, accepting the coffee and taking a croissant. 'Talk away.'

'We were wondering about buying Amy a thank you present,' Matilda said. 'Giving the three of us this holiday was so kind.'

'Brilliant idea,' Vicky agreed. 'Any thoughts as to what we can get her?'

'Something that lasts longer than simple flowers or chocolate,' Chelsea said.

'A plant for the garden? Pierre may be able to suggest something?' Vicky suggested thoughtfully.

Matilda nodded. 'I'll ask him.'

'A coffee-table book with glossy pictures about the Riviera?' Chelsea said. 'We could all sign it then.'

'Problem is, we don't have a lot of time to find something, do we?' Vicky said. 'There's only today and tomorrow. When Anthony arrives later, I plan on giving him a quick tour of the village and then taking him to Cannes. I do need to buy a couple of presents for Tom and Suzie, so I could have a look and see if anything inspires for Amy. I'll get your agreement before I buy anything.' She glanced at Chelsea and Matilda. 'Do we need to set a budget?'

'No, I don't think so. The cost will be split three ways,' Matilda said. 'So we just need to find something decent from the three of us. Chelsea, is that all right with you?'

Chelsea nodded absently, her attention down on the drive. 'Somebody is arriving. The electronic gates have been opened. Oooh, nice car. Amy's come out onto the terrace.'

'That's a luxury car,' Vicky said. 'It's earlier than the eta Anthony gave me, so I doubt – and sincerely hope – that he didn't get an earlier flight and splurge out on a top-of-the-range hire car.'

The three of them fell silent and watched as a man got out and Amy went forward to meet him.

'Definitely not Anthony,' Vicky said with a sigh of relief. 'I wonder who he is?'

Chelsea let out a strangulated shriek as she jumped up. 'I know exactly who he is. What I don't know is what the hell he's doing here?' And she sprinted off down the path towards the house, leaving Vicky and Matilda looking at each other.

* * *

Amy was doing some stretching exercises at the barre in her bedroom when she'd heard the gate buzzer go. She froze and prayed. 'Please not Kevin again.' Quickly running through to the hall where the main intercom was placed, she pressed the button. 'Bonjour?'

'Hi. Parlez-vous Anglais s'il-vous plait?'

'Yes.'

'I do apologise for turning up unannounced, but I'm here to see one of your guests. Could you let me in please?'

Amy, relieved it wasn't Kevin, pressed the entry button before belatedly realising she hadn't asked his name, or who he had come to see, and she'd just let a complete stranger into the grounds. A well-spoken stranger whom she could only hope was not going to be an unwelcome visitor.

Standing on the driveway watching the man climb out from behind the wheel of the expensive 4 x 4, she felt her heart lurch unexpectedly. He was in his late forties and definitely on his way to being a very attractive silver fox. Amy sighed. She was wearing her normal exercise gear of leggings and a sweatshirt. She could forget any idea of making a good first impression as the owner of Belle Vue.

'You must be Amy Martin,' the man said, holding out his hand and taking hers in a firm grip when she responded.

'Yes, I'm Amy – who are you?'

'I'm Simon Newman, Chelsea's father.'

Before he could say any more, Chelsea herself ran onto the terrace and cannoned into the man, flinging her arms around him. 'Dad. What are you doing here?'

'Long story, Sunshine. I need to talk to you.'

'I'll be home in two days. Couldn't it wait until then?'

Simon shook his head. 'Sorry, no.'

Chelsea frowned. 'Has something horrid happened?'

Simon looked from Chelsea to Amy. 'I really need to talk to my daughter in private, but I could murder a decent coffee?' He looked at Amy hopefully.

'Dad! You're are freaking me out. Just tell me.'

'Chelsea, why don't you take your father to your room and I'll bring you a cafètiere along, okay?' Amy said quietly.

'Thank you, Amy. Lead on, Chelsea,' and Simon put his arm around his daughter's shoulders. He threw Amy a grateful smile, but she caught a glimpse of a worried expression on his face as he turned back to Chelsea.

'It's this way,' Chelsea said and the two of them left the terrace.

Amy made her way to the kitchen. She hoped whatever it was that had prompted Simon Newman to turn up here unannounced, wasn't going to be too upsetting for Chelsea. She'd already had enough tragedy in her young life without the universe throwing more problems at her. Spooning coffee into the cafètiere, Amy thought about Simon. Her first impression of him was definitely a positive one. There was also something familiar about him niggling at her brain. Could she have met him before somewhere? Chelsea saying he always travelled by private plane and the expensive hire car he'd arrived in indicated that he was a seriously wealthy man. In which case he'd move in circles way beyond her reach, so it was unlikely they would have met socially. Amy resolved to ask him if they'd ever met before if she got the chance later before he left.

*   *   *

Chelsea's first thought when she'd realised it was her father getting out of the car was one of delight. Then, as she ran down the path towards him, fear gripped her. Something must be wrong for him to turn up unannounced. Something so bad he needed to tell her face to face, which would explain why he hadn't answered his phone last night.

'Why are you here, Dad?' she demanded as soon as they reached her room. 'Why didn't you warn me you were coming? Are you ill?'

'No, I'm not ill. I just need to talk to you urgently.'

'Is it about Kit?' Chelsea demanded.

'No. Why? Have you heard from him?'

'Yes. He wants to meet and talk about getting back together,' Chelsea said.

'I sincerely hope you haven't agreed. Did he tell you his wife is divorcing him?'

'No, he didn't. Anyway, I've blocked and deleted his mail without answering it.'

'Good.'

They both turned at a quiet tap on the French doors and saw Amy pointing to the tray she'd placed on the terrace table.

Chelsea opened the doors and Simon followed her out onto the terrace, calling out 'Thank you' to Amy's retreating back.

Chelsea poured two cups of coffee and pushed the plate of biscuits Amy had provided towards her dad.

'This is a lovely villa,' Simon said. 'Beautiful position. Amy is nice too.'

'Yes, she is. Come on, Dad – answer the question. Why have you come here to talk to me?'

Simon took a mouthful of his coffee before answering. 'Heard from Elsie recently?'

'No. Elsie's ill, isn't she?' Chelsea said sighing heavily. 'That's why you've rushed down. To fly me back. I did wonder why she hadn't answered my last couple of texts.'

'There's no point in you rushing back. Two more days won't make any difference,' Simon said slowly. 'Elsie is ill, but it's not as simple as that,'

'What d'you mean? She's either ill or she's not.'

Simon looked at her. 'Did you know Elsie has a drink problem?'

'I know she likes a drink at the end of the day to relax, but a problem? No.' Chelsea shook her head in disbelief.

'There is no easy way to tell you this so...' Simon took a deep breath. 'Elsie is apparently an alcoholic who couldn't cope with the debts her drinking has got her into.'

'What?' Chelsea stared at him, horrified. 'How could I not have noticed she was drinking too much?'

'People become very adept at hiding their guilty secret. And they have to want to help themselves before anyone can help them. Sadly, I don't think Elsie is at that point yet.' Simon rubbed his face agitatedly. 'I'm afraid it gets worse – for you and the business. A day ago, she cancelled all the bookings for the next two months, emptied your business bank account and did a runner. Nobody had been paid and neither had any of the outstanding bills.'

'I feel sick,' Chelsea said, failing to fight back the tears. 'And so, so sorry for Elsie. If only she'd told me I'd have tried to help her.' She looked at her dad. 'How did you find out about all this anyway?'

'Tina, your kitchen help, rang me to say everything was locked up when she arrived at work yesterday morning and she couldn't get hold of Elsie. She contacted me, as you were away, to see if I knew what was going on. So I met Tina at the kitchen. I'm afraid I had to break a glass door pane to get in – don't worry, it was fixed within the hour.' Simon hesitated.

'And?' Chelsea looked at her father, disbelief etched across her face.

'The thing is, Tina wasn't surprised that Elsie had done a runner. Said she knew she'd got in over her head with a bad crowd.' Simon reached into his jacket pocket. 'I found a letter addressed to you on the table.' He pulled out an envelope and handed it to Chelsea. Absently, she took it. 'It wasn't sealed so I read it, which is how I know about the bank.' Simon smiled sadly at his daughter. 'Tina discovered the cancellations when she looked in the day book.'

Chelsea's fingers were shaking as she took the letter out of the envelope and read the words through a blur of tears. 'Can't cope any more... so sorry... I'm in BIG trouble... I need the money... I have to get away... please forgive me...'

Chelsea looked at her dad. 'If only I'd been there this week. Maybe she'd have confided in me before doing this?'

Simon shook his head. 'I don't think anything or anyone could have stopped Elsie running away. You aren't to blame.'

'I wonder where she's gone?' Chelsea said. 'I thought Kitgate was bad enough, but this is... is so much worse. What the hell do I do now?'

* * *

After leaving Vicky in the summer house, Matilda wandered

down through the garden. Yesterday's euphoria over buying the villa had dulled somewhat and Matilda was back to worrying about the consequences of her impulsive decision.

There was no doubt that she loved everything about the villa and could see herself living there, but the thought of organising everything and moving on her own was daunting. And Josh – what was he going to say about her moving? Would he be around to help her with things when the time came? She needed to tell him what she was planning. If she'd thought about it yesterday, she could have taken some pictures on her phone, but she'd been so excited at the thought of actually buying the villa that taking photographs had completely slipped her mind. Perhaps she'd take a walk over there this afternoon. The villa had seemed quite close when Pierre drove her there, just the other side of the village. No more than a ten minute walk. Her ankle was so much stronger; she hadn't felt any painful twinges when she stood and walked on it for days now. She could at least take a few pictures of the outside and the garden and then she'd text Josh, telling him her big news and attach a picture or two.

Walking past a rose tree covered with beautiful white blooms, Matilda stopped to smell the perfume. Standing there, eyes closed, holding one of the large creamy white flowers close to her nose, she inhaled the sweet smell. William had always adored white roses and this one was a particularly beautiful specimen. She'd definitely take Pierre up on his earlier offer and ask him for a cutting of this rose for her new garden. It would take time to establish, but a tree by the terrace at the back of the villa would allow the perfume to drift into the house when the doors and windows were open.

'Bonjour, Matilda. That is my favourite English rose,' Pierre said. 'It does well down here.'

Matilda opened her eyes, startled. She hadn't heard him approaching.

'It's beautiful,' Matilda said. 'I was going to ask you about a cutting for my new garden?'

Pierre shook his head. 'No need. There is one already in your garden. I planted it for my cousin.'

Matilda smiled at him. 'Another sign I'm doing the right thing.'

Pierre looked at her, puzzled.

'The rainbow yesterday and now white roses in the garden. They were William's favourite flower,' she said. 'He called them the flower of light.' Matilda hesitated. 'My bouquet when we married had a dozen white roses to symbolise everlasting love.'

'How long have you been a widow?' Pierre asked gently.

'Two years this November,' Matilda said. 'As impossible as that is for me to believe.'

'I remember time stood still for me for months when my wife died. I turned around one day and nine months had disappeared. I have no true recollection of that time,' Pierre said quietly.

'I understand completely. You were existing on autopilot.'

'Exactement. Ma fille – she was twelve at the time. It was when I forgot her next birthday that I realised I had to pull myself together for her sake. Looking back, it was harder for her than me, I think,' Pierre acknowledged. 'No mother and a father who was only half alive for a long time.'

'It must have been hard for both of you, your wife dying so young,' Matilda said. 'How long were you married?'

'Thirteen years. Vous?'

'Last year would have been our thirtieth wedding anniversary.' Matilda hesitated. 'I knew William though, for a few years before we married. He rescued me from... from the biggest mistake of my life.' Matilda was quiet for several seconds. 'I owe him so much.'

'I think you and your husband 'ave a good and 'appy marriage?'

Matilda nodded. 'Yes. We did. That's what makes it so hard to live without him.'

'But you have your son and I have my daughter who give us both the reasons to live. And my daughter, she make me a grandpapa soon.'

'How wonderful,' Matilda said. 'I'm hoping Josh will meet someone too, and have a family in the future.'

'Have you told him about the villa?'

Matilda shook her head. 'Not yet. I was thinking about walking down there and taking some photos so he can at least see the outside and the garden.'

'I take you when I finish work this afternoon. Afterwards, maybe you join me for aperitifs before I bring you back in time for dinner?'

'Thank you. I'd really like that.'

'A tout la heure,' and Pierre strolled away down the path towards his gardening shed. Watching him go, Matilda found herself smiling for no particular reason other than she felt happier than she had in a long time.

21

Vicky put the chairs back in the summer house after Chelsea and Matilda left, before picking up her laptop and taking a last lingering look around and closing the door. After Anthony arrived, she doubted that she'd get the opportunity to escape up here again to write. Maybe she'd get up early and sneak away for an hour or so tomorrow morning before Anthony woke.

Back in her room, she ran a deep bath – oh, the luxury – and sank into it with a sigh. She didn't think she'd ever forget the delight of discovering such a luxurious bathroom that first day. This had been such a great holiday, sad to think it was almost over. That she'd be back in the same old routine this time next week unless she managed to convince Anthony otherwise.

Anthony. Another hour, two at the most, he'd be here. What kind of mood was he going to be in? Had anything else happened regarding his suspension? His constituency? Were they standing behind him? Would he fit in here for the last forty-eight hours or would the atmosphere between the four of them be spoilt? And what exactly was she going to say to him?

He'd known she was unhappy when she left for the holiday, but had the escalation of his parliamentary problems pushed any thoughts of her away? Had he even missed her? Had she missed him? Well, while she had mixed feelings regarding his coming here for the last few days of her holiday, she was looking forward to his arrival and showing him some of the local landmarks, but had she truly missed him?

Vicky pushed the tap lever to let more hot water flow into the bath and thought about it. Yes, there had definitely been times when she'd missed Anthony terribly, but she'd also enjoyed being alone and able to concentrate on her writing as well as trying to work out what she wanted from the future. Although she still had no definite plans on that score, apart from a vague idea that she needed to run past Anthony. This holiday had definitely helped her sort things out in her own mind. She felt stronger and more determined to, not fight her corner exactly, but to at least stick to her guns about her desires for the future – both personally and career-wise.

Towelling herself dry, Vicky thought about the day ahead. Her plan, once Anthony arrived, was a quick coffee and introduce him to anyone who happened to be around before going down to Cannes for a spot of present shopping and lunch.

She reached for her phone and opened the memo file to start a list of what she needed to do in Cannes. Seconds later, she irritably snapped the phone case closed. She was buying holiday presents for two people, a birthday present for Matilda, possibly a small memento for Chelsea, and looking for a joint thank you present for Amy from them all. Five things. She didn't need to make a list, for goodness' sake.

Routine and responsibility were already edging their way back into her life and she was still on holiday.

Vicky had just finished dressing when she heard a car arrive. This time it was Anthony and she went out to greet him as he parked alongside the luxury 4 x 4 that had arrived earlier. As he stepped out of the car, Vicky registered how hollow cheeked and tired looking he was. Her heart went out to him and as she stepped into his embrace she hugged him tightly.

'I've missed you. It's so good to be here. You look different,' Anthony said, holding her away from himself slightly. 'The French air clearly agrees with you.'

'I can't explain it, but this place has a special, soothing, aura about it.'

'It is beautiful,' Anthony agreed, looking around.

'Come on,' Vicky said. 'Let's put your case in my room and then we'll have a coffee. Not sure who's around for you to meet right now, but you'll see them all at dinner this evening anyway.'

When they walked into the kitchen Amy was on her own and greeted them with a smile and an offer of coffee.

'I can't thank you enough for suggesting I join Vicky here,' Anthony said. 'The media have been hounding me somewhat. It's good to escape their clutches for a few private days.'

'I'm sure it is,' Amy agreed. 'And I know Vicky is going to enjoy being your tour guide.'

'I thought I'd take Anthony down to Cannes today and then tomorrow we could take the train to Monaco rather than drive,' Vicky said.

'Don't forget the party tomorrow night,' Amy said.

'One of the reasons for Cannes today. I need to find a present for Matilda, as well as a few take-home presents.'

Vicky smiled. 'Chelsea all right?' she asked, eyebrows raised as she looked at Amy. The posh car was still parked outside, so presumably Chelsea's surprise visitor was still around too. 'She seemed a bit agitated when she saw she had a visitor.'

As if on cue, the kitchen door opened and the man Vicky had seen arrive earlier walked in, carrying a tray with an empty cafètiere and cups.

'Oh, I'm sorry. Not interrupting anything, am I?' he apologised. 'I wanted to return these and thank you again.'

'Vicky, Anthony, meet Simon – Chelsea's father, here on an unexpected visit,' Amy said, introducing everyone but deliberately not mentioning surnames.

Vicky, sensing that Anthony was uncomfortable in case he was recognised, said. 'Right, better make a move. Nice to meet you, Simon. See you later, Amy,' and grabbing hold of Anthony's hand, she propelled him towards the door. 'Cannes, here we come.'

Simon looked at Amy in surprise as he placed the tray on the table. 'Do I smell? They couldn't have hotfooted it out of here any faster if the place had been on fire.'

Amy bit her lip, wondering what to say – and decided the truth was the best and only option.

'That was Anthony Penhill and his wife, Vicky,' she said, waiting for Simon's reaction. When he didn't say anything, she added, 'He's an MP.' Perhaps Simon hadn't heard about the trouble Anthony had got himself into. Not everyone followed the shenanigans of Parliament. 'His wife was one of the competition winners along with Chelsea.'

'I know who he is. Bit notorious at the moment.'

'I invited him so he could get away from being hounded by the press.' Amy looked at Simon. Was he judging her? Amy could feel her hackles rising. It was none of Simon

Newman's business who she invited to stay. His next remark though, surprised her.

'That was a nice thing to do,' Simon smiled at her. 'From what I hear, he's a genuine bloke and a good MP. The country needs more like him.'

Amy busied herself emptying the cafètiere and rinsing it before turning to face Simon. 'I hope your urgent need to see Chelsea wasn't bad news for her?'

Simon ran his fingers through his hair. 'I'm afraid it was. Her business partner has done a runner. I wanted to be the one to tell her rather than have her find out when she got back.'

Shock registered on Amy's face. 'Oh, poor Chelsea. How's she taken the news?'

'On the chin, but she blames herself. Says she'd noticed Elsie wasn't her usual self recently and she should have done something to help her. She had no idea, though, that Elsie had a drink problem.'

Amy sighed and shook her head. 'Your daughter would take on the problems of the world if she could. Does she still have a business to go back to?'

'Doubtful. I need to talk to her about what she does now. I'm taking her out for lunch today – I don't suppose you'd like to join us?' Simon looked at her hopefully.

'I'd love to but...'

'Good,' Simon said, interrupting her. 'No buts allowed.'

'Just as long as I won't be in the way for you and Chelsea to talk,' Amy said. 'How long are you here for anyway?'

'I thought I'd stay a couple of days. Which reminds me, I need to book a hotel,' and Simon pulled out his mobile and began to scroll through a contact list.

'Why not stay here?' Amy said impulsively. 'I have one room left. It would give you both more time together.'

Simon stilled and his fingers stopped swiping the phone screen. When he looked up at her, it was impossible for Amy to know what he was thinking before he put the phone away and answered her.

'I'd like that very much,' he said quietly. 'It's years since... since I've stayed in a place with such a welcoming atmosphere.'

* * *

Vicky found it strangely difficult sitting next to Anthony as he negotiated the traffic-filled road along the coast and into the harbourside area of Cannes. She could sense tension coming from his body as he drove, but whether it was from worry about his suspension or his unfamiliarity with the road and a left-hand drive car, she wasn't sure. Whatever the cause, she decided it would be best to stay quiet and let him concentrate on his driving rather than break the silence by trying to chat. She was relieved when he took the right-hand fork into the car park situated on land which jutted out into the Mediterranean and from where the boats sailed to the Iles de Lérins. They would enjoy the longish walk past the boats moored alongside the harbour wall leading to the town.

Lots of holidaymakers walking slowly along the narrow pavement forced them both to adapt the same pace. When they finally reached the end of the quayside at the bottom of the town, Anthony stopped to look at a couple of elderly men sitting on an old wooden fishing boat mending their nets and exhaled a deep breath. Vicky smiled, being around boats always helped him relax. Growing up with a father who was a keen sailor, it was probably inevitable that Anthony would gravitate towards water and boats. Family holidays when

Tom and Suzie were young had always tended to be based in West Country seaside resorts.

'Come on,' she said. 'If we cross over here, past the Hotel de Ville, I can show you the Marché Forville as we make for Rue Meynadier. Amy says there are all sorts of shops along there, so I should find presents easily. If not, after lunch we'll make for Rue d'Antibes.'

Vicky was pleased that after walking the length of Rue Meynadier she had found all but one of the presents she needed. A Porsche baseball cap for Tom, a colourful floaty top for Suzie, a silk scarf for Chelsea and for Matilda's birthday she decided a beautiful glass candle lantern for her new home would fit the bill perfectly. She'd failed, so far, to find anything inspirational for Amy as a joint thank you present, but right now the midday heat was getting to her and she wanted to sit down and have a cold drink.

Anthony carried the shopping bags for her as they made their way down a narrow street towards the front where there would be more choice of somewhere to eat lunch. Anthony vetoed the first restaurant they came to on the grounds that it wasn't busy and on that basis it couldn't be very good. Thankfully, the next one they came to gained his approval and Vicky sank down gratefully onto a chair at the last vacant table.

When the waiter brought their menus, Anthony ordered a beer for himself and a half carafe of ice-cold rosé for Vicky as well as a jug of water. They barely glanced at the menu once they realised that 'mussels et frites' was the dish of the day. A meal they both adored.

Sitting there waiting for their food, sipping wine and people watching, Vicky waited for Anthony to broach the subject of his suspension. When he simply sat there in happy silence, she knew it was up to her to start the conversation but it wasn't until they were both eating that she asked her first question.

'So, are you going to tell me what caused your moment of madness with the mace?' she asked.

'Basically it was frustration with the system and the feeling that I'd let my constituents down,' Anthony said and his face turned serious. 'There's something I need to talk to you about.'

Vicky looked at him, dreading what was coming. 'You're in more trouble?'

'No. It's just...' Anthony hesitated. 'I'm thinking about giving up politics. It's not what I signed up for. I feel like a lone voice amongst all the bureaucracy. I want to give the PM my resignation before the next election, if you agree.' He stopped speaking and looked at her. 'Resigning will make a huge difference to both our lives.'

Vicky gazed at him, speechless. She'd never have guessed that was Anthony's intention. The possibility of him losing his large majority or even his seat at the next election had, of course, flitted through her mind, but Anthony voluntarily resigning from parliament was unexpected. Ever since he'd been elected, he'd seemed to be in his element and determined to do his best by his constituents. 'But I thought you loved being an MP,' she said. 'Are you having some sort of midlife crisis?'

'It's not a midlife crisis where I'm buying a Harley or running off to find myself, but it is a crisis in that I feel a failure and that I've let everyone down.' Anthony took a drink of his beer. 'The pressure has been building for months. I'm sorry I didn't discuss it with you before – forgive me?'

'Of course,' Vicky said. 'I have to ask, though, was the incident with the mace a wake-up call or the final breaking point?'

'Both, really,' Anthony said. 'I need to be able to look my constituents in the eye and I couldn't do that knowing I've failed to keep their much-needed hospital open. The government are determined on a policy with the NHS that I don't agree with and can't support. I've also realised I'm tired of fighting government decisions and losing.'

Vicky reached across the table and took his hand and squeezed it hard with her own. 'It's just one fight you didn't win. You've won others. You've been a good MP. Your constituency will miss you if you resign.' She might have wanted her own life to change but it appeared that Anthony's life too, was about to undertake some unexpected changes.

'I'll still be their MP for at least a few more months. There's a year before a general election is due – unless something happens and the PM calls an earlier one.'

'Any idea what you want to do next? Return to IT?'

'Definitely not IT but...' Anthony shrugged. 'A couple of vague ideas. It will be a case of putting some feelers out, seeing what options are available and discussing things with you.'

'We haven't done a lot of talking to each other recently, have we?' Vicky said. 'I was planning on speaking to you about the future – our future – when I got back.'

Anthony finished his beer. 'What you said when you won your holiday, about it being a chance to rediscover the old you that had disappeared under the responsibility of family life, resonated with me. I'd like to find the real me again.' He looked at her. 'Has the holiday worked? Have you found the old Vicky?'

'Let's say it's a work in progress,' Vicky answered. 'It's something else we need to talk about. Let's enjoy the next day or two down here, talk a bit about the future, perhaps throw a few ideas around, but maybe save the serious discussions for when we get home.'

'Sounds like a plan to me,' Anthony said. 'I have to say, I feel like a weight has been lifted now that I've talked to you.'

Vicky finished her rosé while Anthony settled the bill and then, by mutual consent, they began to make their way down towards to the open space of Allées de la Liberté. As they walked past the statue of the Englishman, Lord Brougham, credited with discovering Cannes when it was just a small fishing village, Vicky smiled.

'Look there's a brocante fair. Come on, let's have a wander round – we might find a souvenir or two to take home with us.'

Stalls of every description had been set up: paintings, bric-a-brac, artisan handmade wooden toys, silk scarves, jewellery, cards, cartoon portraits, summer hats, a stand with restored shabby-chic furniture. The crowds milling around and spending their money testified to the fair's popularity. Vicky stopped to browse a book stall selling new and old books in both French and English. A book displayed in the English second-hand section marked 'Collectable first edition 1922' caught her attention.

'Look', she said to Anthony. 'I think I might have found the perfect present for Amy.' The hardback book, with the publisher's original board slipcase placed alongside, had a coloured frontispiece as well as six coloured plates and was in a remarkably good condition. 'I wonder how much it is?' and she glanced across at the stallholder. 'Le prix, s'il vous plait?'

'Seventy-five euros. You want?'

Vicky nodded. 'Please. Merci beaucoup.' She turned to Anthony. 'Fancy finding a hardback copy of *The Enchanted April*.'

'D'you want me to haggle the price down for you?'

'No, thank you. I think it's a fair price and split three ways, it's not a lot. I'm supposed to check with the others before buying anything, but I know they'll agree with this. It's just the perfect present for Amy.'

'A lucky find indeed,' Anthony said. 'Shall we make our way to the car and go back to the villa? I quite fancy a swim and a lazy couple of hours in the sun.'

As they walked past the boats on their return journey to the car, Anthony stopped by a wooden ketch sporting a For Sale notice before turning to Vicky.

'Here's an idea. How about buying a boat and sailing away for a year and a day like the owl and the pussycat?'

Vicky laughed. 'You're not serious?'

'Sort of. You know I've always loved the idea of having a boat. Obviously, I couldn't take a whole year out, but I do like the thought of a long holiday away from everything when I'm finally free. What d'you think?'

'I think it's one of those ideas we talk about when we get home,' Vicky said.

Anthony was still acting as though he was the only one needing to make plans. The fact that she still hadn't told him about her needs and ideas for the future was her own fault. She'd brushed away his one question about finding her old self. But at least they'd agreed to have a serious discussion about what would happen next when they'd returned home and before he handed his resignation in. What his reaction would be to her vision of the future, though, was anyone's guess. And could she really wait until they were back home before she told him about her own dreams for the future?

22

After Simon had brought his overnight bag in from the car, Amy showed him to the Ernest Hemingway room, leaving the smaller Henri Matisse room for Josh when he arrived tomorrow.

'I hope you'll be comfortable in here,' she said, feeling strangely apprehensive in case he didn't like the room, which was silly. Aunt Tasha had set up Belle Vue with the best of everything, and while it wasn't ultra luxurious like a five star grand hotel, everything was of a high standard. All her guests so far had adored the rooms, there was no reason to think Simon would be the exception.

'It looks extremely comfortable,' Simon said. 'I love the fact you've given the rooms names rather than numbers.'

'When I inherited it from my Aunt Tasha, the villa was already a well-established auberge and I knew I was taking a slight risk changing from that business plan to start a retreat. As I was hoping to attract writers, artists and other creative people, I thought naming the rooms after well-known south of France characters and putting a book either written by them or about them in each room would be fun.'

Simon glanced towards the book on the bedside table. 'Please tell me the one for this room isn't *For Whom the Bell Tolls*?'

'No, it's *A Moveable Feast*,' Amy said, laughing. 'I'll leave you to settle in. I need to find Matilda and see if she has any plans for today as everyone seems to be doing their own thing. I'd hate for her to feel left out.'

'Invite her to lunch with us, if she's at a loose end,' Simon said.

'Thanks. I'll see what she says.'

Amy found Matilda sitting on the terrace outside her room, tapping away on her iPad. 'You look busy. I was wondering whether you had any plans for today?' Amy said, sitting on the spare chair alongside her. 'Vicky and Anthony have gone into Cannes, Simon has invited me to join him and Chelsea for lunch and you're more than welcome to join us too.'

Matilda looked at her puzzled. 'Who's Simon?'

'Sorry, I forgot you don't know about him – he's Chelsea's dad. Came in that big car this morning. I've offered him a room here, which he's accepted, so he'll be here for your last two evenings. He's a nice man – easy to get along with.'

'First Anthony and now Simon,' Matilda said thoughtfully. 'It's getting more and more like Lottie and Rose's story every day.'

Amy looked at her for several seconds before the penny dropped. 'Of course! They both invited the men in their life to stay at the castle, didn't they? Big difference though – Simon is not the man in my life.'

'But you've invited him to stay,' Matilda pointed out.

'Yes, but that's for Chelsea's sake, he's had to tell her some bad news about her business partner.'

'Oh, the poor girl. Is she all right?'

'Seems to be,' Amy said. 'So, lunch?'

'Thank you, but no. I'm emailing Josh at the moment, telling him my news about the villa,' Matilda said. 'I've tried ringing him, but it goes straight to voicemail. I just want him to know what I'm up to, but if I leave a message asking him to ring me, he'll think something is wrong.' She sighed. 'I know I'll see him sometime this summer, but I do so want to tell him my exciting news.' Matilda smiled at Amy. 'So frustrating when you can't get hold of people.'

Knowing that Josh would be with his mother tomorrow but not allowed to tell her that, Amy could only nod in agreement.

'Are you sure about lunch?' she asked.

'Quite sure. When I've finished my email, I'll have a light snack here and then go down to Cannes,' Matilda said. 'I need to ask the estate agent to take me off his mailing list and I fancy a spot of window shopping.'

'Have you asked Pierre to run you down?'

'No. He's driving me to see the villa again this evening to take some photos and has invited me to have aperitifs with him afterwards, so I thought I'd get a taxi this morning. I don't like to keep bothering him,' Matilda said. 'I can't keep taking him away from his work.'

'I'm sure he doesn't find it a bother,' Amy said, making a mental note to invite Pierre to the surprise party tomorrow evening. 'But if you want it, the number for a taxi is by the telephone in the kitchen.'

'Thank you.'

'I'll leave you to it then,' Amy said, standing up. 'Enjoy the day.'

'You too,' Matilda replied, turning back to her iPad.

Back in her room, Amy changed into a white short sleeved cotton shirt, which she tucked into a pair of smart blue jeans, and slipped her feet into her wedged espadrilles. Not knowing where Simon planned on taking them, she figured she was smart enough for any lunchtime restaurant, and casual enough for a pizza café if that was what he had in mind. She gave herself a spritz of her favourite Chanel Allure perfume and was ready.

Chelsea and Simon were already in the 4 x 4 when she went to find them, Simon in the driving seat and Chelsea in the back.

'You can sit up front with your dad if you want to,' Amy said. 'I don't mind sitting in the back.'

'No, it's fine. You can have the panic seat,' Chelsea said and laughed at the look on Amy's face. 'Don't worry, Dad's a fast driver, but he's actually quite good.'

The restaurant Simon drove them to along the coast was right on the beach in a small cove and one that Amy hadn't been to for years. The last time had been with her parents and Aunt Tasha before she became ill.

'I haven't been here for ages,' she said, looking at Simon. 'I thought only locals knew about this place. You must know the area well.'

He nodded. 'Used to spend a lot of time down here. Fancy a walk along the beach before we eat?'

'Great idea,' Amy said.

'You and Chelsea go ahead. I'll go and tell them we're here – make sure they keep the table – and catch you up.'

As they made their way down to the waterline, Amy glanced at Chelsea. 'You okay? Your dad turning up must have been a shock.'

'Just a bit,' Chelsea said but didn't volunteer any information.

Amy waited a couple of seconds but when it was clear that Chelsea wasn't going to say anything, she changed the subject of the conversation.

'Being nosey here, but what kind of business is your dad in? He seems very successful.'

Chelsea shrugged. 'All sorts. Since Mum died, he's become even more of a wheeler dealer.'

Amy laughed. 'That makes him sound like Del Boy from that old TV show.' She hesitated before continuing, 'I only ask because I've got this feeling I've met him before somewhere and I have no idea where it would have been.'

'I know he took Mum to Monaco a couple of times. Birthdays and anniversary treats.' Chelsea said. 'Why don't you ask him?'

'Ask me what?' Simon said, joining them.

'Amy thinks she's met you before.' Chelsea said. 'I'm going to run to that rock over there, okay? See you back at the restaurant,' and she sped off across the cove, leaving an embarrassed Amy looking at Simon.

'It's probably just a silly feeling. Maybe you remind me of someone. Do you feel we've met before?' she said, breaking the silence.

Simon shrugged. 'Maybe.'

His 'maybe' confused Amy and she was quiet for several moments as they walked, trying to work out what he'd meant.

'Have you ever been an angel?' she said, stopping suddenly to look at him. 'Perhaps that's it.'

Simon laughed. 'An angel? Me?'

'Somebody who puts up money for a show, play or ballet is known in the entertainment industry as an angel,' Amy explained. 'I thought perhaps we could have met if you backed one of my ex-husband's shows.'

'Believe me, Amy, I'm no angel in any sense of the word,' Simon said. 'Come on. Let's go eat.'

To Amy's surprise, there was a bottle of pink champagne nestling in an ice bucket when they were shown to their table.

'What are we celebrating?' she asked.

'There has to be a reason to drink champagne?' Simon said, feigning surprise, as the waiter opened the bottle and poured them each a glass. 'I didn't realise.'

'Usually, yes,' Amy said. 'It's a drink for special occasions.'

'In that case, let me think. I know – let's celebrate the special occasion of being alive and meeting this morning,' Simon said, handing her a glass. 'Personally, I'm also celebrating the fact that I'm about to have lunch in a glorious location with my daughter and a beautiful woman – who I may, or may not, know already.' Simon's gaze held Amy's for several seconds and she felt the heat rising in her face. How could she feel so attracted to this man whom she'd only met a mere few hours ago?

'Thank you,' she said, tapping her glass of champagne against the one he held out towards her. 'Here's to being alive in a glorious location then. Ah, here comes Chelsea.'

With delicious food, good company, lots of laughter, lunch flew past. Amy loved the connection between Simon and Chelsea. Their father-daughter relationship was a robust one, no doubt strengthened by the tragedy in their lives and the need to be strong for each other.

It wasn't until they'd returned to Belle Vue that Amy realised Simon and Chelsea had failed to talk about anything important.

Chelsea leapt out of the car as Simon parked. 'I'm going

for a swim and then I'm going to read for a bit and top up the tan before I start prepping dinner.'

'Sounds like a plan. I think I'll join you. How about you?' Simon said, turning to Amy. 'Fancy a swim?'

Amy put a restraining hand on Simon's arm as he went to follow his daughter. 'I'm sorry you didn't get to talk to Chelsea this lunchtime.'

'It's not a problem. I can talk to her now down by the pool, no worries.'

'There's something I feel I ought to tell you,' Amy hesitated. 'You do realise that Chelsea blames herself for her mum's death? The guilt is eating her up.'

Simon stared at her. 'That's nonsense. She's never mentioned it to me.'

Amy faltered. Had she upset Simon? But he needed to know how his daughter was still grieving for her mother. She took a deep breath.

'I know, that's why I feel I ought to tell you. Her reason for that is she's scared to tell you. She's afraid it will drive a wedge between the two of you once you know the truth and she can't bear the thought of that. She loves you too much.'

'Did she tell you why she feels guilty?'

'Because she was ten minutes late meeting her mum. She believes if she'd been on time, they wouldn't have been in that particular lane on the motorway and the accident wouldn't have involved them.'

Simon closed his eyes and took a deep breath. 'I need to tell her the truth. It most definitely was not her fault. If anyone should feel guilty it's me. Thank you for telling me how she feels. Time to straighten things out.' And he turned and followed Chelsea.

Amy muttered 'good luck' under her breath, hoping that

Simon would be able to convince Chelsea to forgive herself, before making her way indoors.

Pierre had collected the post from the box at the bottom of the drive and placed it on the kitchen table. Amy glanced through it. Telephone bill, some junk mail and an envelope with 'Mathieu, Lefevre – Notaire' franked across it. Amy stared at it apprehensively for a few seconds before reaching for a small knife and carefully slitting open the envelope.

Taking out the letter, she scanned it quickly, before smiling. The notaire wanted yet more official English papers translated into French, but the good news was that under French law, Kevin had no claim to Belle Vue Villa. Tasha's inheritance was safe.

23

Matilda saved the email she'd written to Josh in draft and closed down her iPad. She'd send it later when she could send some pictures with it. Time to get ready to go down to Cannes.

At two o'clock, Matilda made her way through the garden and was waiting outside the gates when the taxi she'd ordered arrived. Ten minutes later, the taxi had dropped her by the Palais des Festivals and she was making her way to see Troy and tell him her good news about finding her dream villa. Of course, it was bad news for him and it took time to convince him to take her name off his mailing list. In the end, though, he accepted she was unlikely to want to move again in the near future, but, yes, she'd bear him in mind if she ever did need to sell.

Leaving the estate agents with Troy's 'Bon chance dans votre nouvelle maison' ringing in her ears, Matilda took her time to wander up through the narrow streets to Rue d'Antibes. To think in a few months' time this would be her home town.

Matilda smothered an inward sigh as the daunting thought of all the organising she had to do before she moved floated into her mind. William had been at her side the last time and they'd packed up the house and solved any problem that arose together. This time, on her own, she'd have to deal with not only selling up but moving countries as well, and knowing the French, there would be a lot of bureaucracy to get through. She'd need to be super organised.

Matilda straightened her shoulders. She'd cope, come what may. A new life in a wonderful villa was within her grasp and she was determined to give it her best shot.

Passing a couple of street musicians enthusiastically performing with a violin and a saxophone, Matilda dropped a few euros into the hat on the pavement and paused to enjoy the lively music for a few moments. The town had such a vibrant air about it today. She loved the way the streets and ancient alleyways nestled together in a seemingly never ending route around the town with its enticing shops and restaurants – soon all this would become a familiar, daily sight for her. Familiar maybe, but Matilda promised herself she'd never take any of it for granted when it became her home ground.

Despite the crowds all jostling for space on the pavements and the afternoon heat, Matilda was enjoying her walk, but when she saw the entrance to the shopping arcade, she slipped inside. Fewer people and cooler with its marble floors, the mall would give her a brief respite from the heat outside. A beautiful painting of a cottage in a Provençal lavender field in the window of the art shop had her fantasising about hanging one like it on a wall in the villa. It was, of course, far too soon to start buying pictures and, anyway, a quick glance at the discreet label on the frame told her, with all those noughts, she wouldn't be buying that particular painting. But once she was settled in, she'd look for a similar evocative painting for the sitting room wall.

Matilda walked past the next two shops with barely a glance. One she registered as a wine merchants and the other was clearly aimed at tourists and holidaymakers with souvenirs and crudely made ornaments. The boutique further along was busy changing its display and had placed a large orange 'Promotion – 50 per cent' label in the window. Matilda stopped in her tracks as she suddenly realised she was in the mall where she'd seen the coveted blue leather jacket.

Without stopping to think, Matilda pushed open the boutique door. She recognised the sales assistant who greeted her with a smile.

'Bonjour. Puis je vous aider?'

Matilda shook her head. 'Puis-je regarder, s'il vous plait?' She wanted to ask about the jacket, but structuring the sentence in understandable French defeated her. Something else to put on the to-do list for when she lived here – French lessons. She made her way across to a rail where she could see various jackets hanging under a large 'Promo' sign, but the blue leather one wasn't there. *Think, Matilda, think, what's the French for blue leather jacket?* Blue was easy – bleu and leather she remembered was cuir, but jacket?

'You look for this vest, peut-être?'

Matilda turned to see the sales assistant holding out the blue jacket.

'You still have it. Oui. Merci,' and Matilda slipped her arms into the jacket, instinctively knowing that this time it was going to be hers when she left the boutique. A birthday present to herself. What had Chelsea said when she'd shown the jacket to her? Something about wearing it all the time and it becoming her signature South of France look.

'Promo?' she said, pointing to the sign and then at the jacket.

'The woman frowned. 'It is not included in the promo. Mais peut-être I can give you a little – 20 per cent discount, d'accord?'

'30 per cent would be better,' Matilda said bravely, smiling hopefully at the woman. William had always maintained, if you don't ask, you don't get, but she'd always held back before. Today the 'moving to France on her own' woman was in charge and she dared to ask.

The assistant pursed her lips before saying a definite, 'Non, 25 per cent is the best I do.'

'Merci beaucoup,' Matilda said, delighted. Tempted to keep the jacket on, she reluctantly took it off and the assistant wrapped it carefully in tissue paper and placed it in a posh carrier bag.

'Voila. La vest – ça vous va, madame,' she said as she handed it over. 'It suits you.'

Matilda smiled her thanks. She'd wear the jacket tomorrow night for the last dinner of the holiday – and her birthday. Although, of course, nobody was aware of it being her birthday. Should she tell them? She didn't want anyone to feel obliged to buy her a present, but she would like to celebrate the day and the end of a wonderful holiday with her new friends. Perhaps a bottle or two of champagne secreted in the fridge and produced with tomorrow night's dinner was the answer? Leaving the boutique, she re-traced her steps to the wine merchants.

Matilda took her time walking back towards the Hotel de Ville where she knew she could pick up a taxi, the bag with the jacket in it swinging from one hand, two bottles of champagne, boxed and in a bag, held tight in the other. As she walked, she found herself thinking about the others, hoping they were all enjoying spending the day doing their own thing. Waiting for the pedestrian lights to change on the crossroads near the market, she thought she caught a glimpse of Vicky and her husband, but they were quickly swallowed up in the crowd and disappeared from her view. Never mind. She'd meet both Anthony and Chelsea's father later at dinner.

* * *

Chelsea smiled as she climbed out of the pool and saw her father sitting on one of the sunloungers.

'I'm pleased to see you swimming again,' Simon said. 'I was beginning to think you'd never get back into the water and that would have been sad. You used to love swimming so much.'

Chelsea shrugged nonchalantly. 'I thought you were coming in?'

'Later. Bit too soon after that wonderful lunch for me.'

Chelsea picked up her towel, wrapping it around her waist like a sarong, before sitting down on the lounger next to him. 'I don't know what to do about Elsie or the business, Dad. Any ideas?'

'There's nothing you can do about Elsie until she contacts you. And then she might not be ready for your help. As for the business, you do need to think about a couple of things. You and Elsie were equal partners, right? So technically you have to decide whether you want to pursue her for the money she's embezzled, because basically that's what she's done –

not to mention the loss of your earnings because of all the cancellations.'

Chelsea shook her head. Ever since her father had told her the news this morning she'd been thinking about Elsie, wondering how she could help her. 'Nope, can't do that,' Chelsea said. 'Elsie's got enough to deal with, she doesn't need me hounding her for money she clearly hasn't got.'

'Fair enough. Secondly, could you cope on your own with the amount of bookings you need to make the business work, without Elsie sharing the workload?'

'Doubtful,' Chelsea admitted. 'I wouldn't be able to double-book events for the same day. Preparing and making the food isn't a problem, but without Elsie to do front of house for one while I did the other...' Chelsea shrugged. 'I'd need to find someone to take her place and I don't have any money – besides, it wouldn't be the same working with a stranger. It's catch-22 all round really.' Chelsea bit back on her tears as she turned to face her father. 'Oh hell! The business is stuffed, isn't it? There's no way I can survive without Elsie or funds. Next week when I get back, I'll close it down, notify all the creditors, ask for time to pay and get myself a job and start to pay back everyone. Only take me a year or two with luck. Selling the equipment should raise some money too.'

'There's only one person you owe money to,' Simon said quietly. 'And yes, you will need to pay it back, but I'm not setting a timescale.'

'What d'you mean?'

'After I read Elsie's letter, I went to the bank, told them what had happened and paid enough money into the account to pay the part-timers and outstanding bills,' Simon told her. 'If you want to carry on, I'm more than happy to call it an investment to help you get back on your feet.'

'Oh, Dad,' Chelsea said, sighing. 'That's so good of you. I don't mean to sound ungrateful, but can I think about it? Whatever happens I'll pay you back the money you've already laid out.'

'Of course,' Simon said. 'You must do whatever you feel is right for you. I can't tell you how sorry I am how things have ended up after all your hard work. It's unfair, but then we both know life isn't fair or kind at times.'

'It felt strange not being with you yesterday,' Chelsea said quietly. 'I feel guilty I wasn't there to go to the cemetery with you.'

'Please don't,' Simon said. 'It's been five years and life moves on – has to move on.' He glanced across at her. 'I have to ask you about something Amy mentioned to me just now. Why have you never told me you feel guilty over your mum's death?'

Chelsea stilled. 'Amy shouldn't have said anything.'

'I'm glad she did. And I'm telling you now – you have no reason to feel guilty at all.'

'If I hadn't been late, we wouldn't have been on the motorway in the path of that lorry,' Chelsea said, pulling up the corner of her towel to dry the tears on her face. 'Saying it was a tragic accident doesn't change anything. It was still my fault.'

Simon shook his head. 'No, it wasn't your fault. If anybody is to blame, it's me. I was the one who insisted you changed to training at that pool instead of the local one because the coach there was an ex-Olympian swimmer. And I should have been driving you that day.'

'I remember Mum being cross at the last minute change and the late afternoon time of my session. She said she didn't mind the drive, but she'd make sure we didn't have to do it during the rush hour again.'

Simon was silent for several seconds.

'Your mum hated motorway driving, particularly at busy times. I should never have insisted she drove that afternoon. I'd had to ask her to take you because I had a meeting that I didn't want to cancel. I promised her that I would drive you there every day the next week. I should have rearranged my meeting and taken you myself.' Simon closed his eyes momentarily as he placed a hand over his cheeks and mouth and squeezed his jaw in an effort to hold back his emotions.

'But then you'd have died,' Chelsea said softly.

'Not necessarily. Me driving would have created a different scenario of events. Like you told Amy earlier, I drive fast, but I'm a good driver – perhaps I'd have been past the lorry before the tyre burst. Maybe I would have been able to take evasive action.' Simon took hold of Chelsea's hand. 'But that is all hypothetical. The truth is Mum's death *was* a tragic accident that neither of us could have prevented by doing something different that afternoon. But it's taken me a long time to accept that and to stop feeling guilty and responsible. Promise me you'll stop blaming yourself as of now.'

Chelsea sighed. 'I'm not sure I can totally yet, but maybe it will become easier.'

They sat in silence for a few moments before Chelsea looked at Simon.

'There's something else, Dad.'

Simon looked at her warily. 'Yes?'

'How did you find me here? I didn't give anyone the address.'

'Ah. I was hoping you wouldn't realise that. Would you believe I had a tracking device placed in your suitcase before you left?'

Chelsea rolled her eyes. 'As if. The truth please.'

'Can you wait until we're back home?'

Chelsea shook her head. 'No.'

'In that case, I'm going to have to swear you to secrecy. Promise not to mention to anyone, particularly not Amy, what I'm about to tell you.'

'I promise.' Chelsea stared at him, wondering what on earth he was about to say.

'I've stayed at Belle Vue before. Francois, Tasha's husband, was a business associate for several years,' Simon said quietly. 'We became good friends and he and Tasha invited Mum and me to stay here several times. Sadly, when he died, I was in the States and couldn't make it back for his funeral. I didn't know about Tasha's death.'

Chelsea stared at him. 'It doesn't explain how you knew I was here.'

'The photographs you sent me? One taken down here by the pool showing off your new haircut. I recognised the pool and the garden in the background instantly. And then you sent the selfie in the Antibes restaurant with the four of you. I recognised Amy, which confirmed even more that you were staying in Belle Vue.'

'So you have met Amy before?'

Simon nodded. 'Very briefly.'

'Okay, so you put two and two together and came up with Belle Vue, but what I don't understand is why it has to be such a big secret that you've been here in the past. Especially as Amy senses she's met you before and clearly likes you.' Chelsea looked at her father, exasperated.

'You think?' Simon said, smiling, before falling silent for a few seconds. 'I will of course tell her we've met before - and where. I'm just hoping she'll remember the occasion too.' He hesitated for a couple of seconds before continuing.

'You asked me recently if I wanted to meet someone else. After five years, I think I'm finally at the point of being able to move on. This morning when I saw Amy I had a real heart stopping moment – a coup de Coeur, the French would call it.'

Simon glanced at Chelsea. 'I just need time to get to know her.'

24

Lola was sitting on Matilda's lap as Pierre drove her to the villa late that afternoon. As Pierre turned the van into the impasse, Matilda, absently caressing the dog, sighed with happiness.

'I can't believe I'm actually going to buy one of these villas. It's like I'm dreaming,' she said. 'Oh, that villa has a name. Does mine?' She scanned the gatepost as Pierre parked. 'I can't see one.'

'Non, my cousin, he never named the house,' Pierre said. 'Will you?'

'You know, I just might,' Matilda said. 'It deserves to be known by a nice name rather than a bland number eight, don't you think?' As she got out of the van she pointed to the garden opposite. 'I wonder if my front garden will ever be as beautiful as this one.'

'C'est tout possible,' Pierre said. 'Especially if I 'elp you. My cousin, he never bother much with the garden, although I did my best to encourage him and planted things I thought he would like.'

'Well, I'll gratefully accept your help,' Matilda said, smiling at him.

'I brought the key so you can take some photos inside too, if you want,' Pierre said.

'Brilliant. I'll start indoors then and do the garden afterwards.'

'I need to sort the aperitifs,' Pierre said, handing her the key. 'You have a wander around on your own and I'll see you in a bit,' and he turned to pick up a basket from the back of the van.

Matilda felt a thrill of anticipation as she inserted the key in the lock, slowly turning it and opening the front door to let herself into the villa that would be her new home. She stood for a few seconds in the hallway with her eyes closed, soaking up the feel of the house and imagining what it was going to be like living here. The next few months were going to be busy, stressful ones, full of paperwork, no doubt, but living in this wonderful villa with a new life ahead of her would be the reward. She was longing to talk to Josh and share her excitement about the future with him. To know that she had his support in the big step she was taking was essential. Smothering a sigh, Matilda opened her eyes and launched the camera app on her iPad. She could at least send him some photographs.

Ten minutes later, when she went down to the kitchen, Matilda was surprised to find it empty. No evidence of the aperitifs Pierre had said he needed to organise and no sign of either him or Lola. The back garden was empty too. Pierre's van was still parked out front in the impasse, so he and the dog had to be around somewhere.

Matilda took a general view of the garden before wandering around and snapping a couple of the individual borders with their different shrubs and trees. She stopped in front of the white rose that Pierre had told her he'd planted. Like the one in Belle Vue, it was looking spectacular in full bloom and she took a photo of it in all its glory before taking a close-up of a single flower. The perfume was wonderful and Matilda sniffed, wishing she could capture the fragrance on camera too.

'Your favourite rose,' Pierre said, walking down the path towards her, Lola trotting at his side. 'You have enough photos?'

'Far more than I need, really,' Matilda said.

'Bon. We lock up now and leave.'

Matilda looked at him, surprised, as she handed him the key. 'I thought we'd be having aperitifs here.'

Pierre shook his head. 'Non. It is time for you to officially visit the maison of one of your new neighbours. Come on.'

Matilda looked at him, puzzled, before following him out on to the street. When he crossed the road and opened the gate of the villa with the beautiful garden and ushered her in front of him, she looked at him and started to laugh. 'I should have realised you were behind this beautiful garden. This is your villa, isn't it?' She felt unexpectedly pleased at the thought of them being neighbours.

'Oui.'

'Why didn't you tell me before?'

'If you didn't like number eight enough to buy it, there was no point,' Pierre shrugged. 'But now, I thought we could have a glass of champagne with our aperitifs and celebrate the fact you are buying my cousin's villa – and that we are going to be neighbours.'

With its terracotta floor tiles, shabby-chic furniture in the sitting room, a settee with creamy loose covers, a bookcase crammed with books down the length of one wall, long azure blue curtains at the French doors leading to a terrace and a kitchen with its copper pans and a serious stove in the corner, the villa was a delight. For a man who spent most of his time outdoors, Pierre clearly liked his home comforts.

'You have a lovely home,' Matilda said, following Pierre out on to the terrace, where glasses, an ice bucket with a bottle of champagne and a tray of nibbles had been placed on a teak table. 'Have you lived here long?'

'Four years. After my daughter marry, the family home was too big, too empty – I needed to make a change,' Pierre said. 'Have something new in my life. The villa needed some work and the garden too – it was a real jungle.'

'I hope number eight will be the answer to my own life-changing need,' Matilda said quietly. 'And not turn out to be a stupid mistake on my part.'

Pierre twisted the wire off the champagne cork before looking at her. 'D'you feel like you make a mistake?' Carefully he released the cork with a satisfactory 'pop' and poured two glasses.

Matilda shook her head. 'Not really.'

'Peut-ĕtre you took the decision to buy too quickly? You 'aven't signed anything yet. You still ' ave time to change your mind.'

'Deep down I know I'm doing the right thing for me and I can't wait to be here. I'll be better once I'm back in Bristol organising the move – too much time to think and over analyse things at the moment. It's silly, I know, but until I've talked to Josh about my plans and know he's happy, I can't seem to focus properly on anything.' Matilda smiled at Pierre. 'Thank you,' she said, taking the glass Pierre held out. 'Santé. Here's to being neighbours – and hopefully friends.'

'Santé,' Pierre echoed. 'And new friends,' he added, holding her gaze.

As they gently clicked glasses Matilda smiled at him. She

was looking forward to having her friend, Pierre, in her new French life.

* * *

Amy and Simon helped Chelsea prepare dinner that evening. Simon scrubbed new potatoes while Amy washed salad, grated courgette and sliced cucumber. Chelsea, busy filling profiteroles with cream and building a pyramid with them, tried to banish the thought that it was the last time she'd be working in Belle Vue's kitchen.

Amy glanced across at her. 'You're quiet tonight.'

'I've really enjoyed cooking the evening meals and as much as I love barbecues, I almost wish we weren't having one tomorrow night,' Chelsea said. 'How's Olivia? Will she be back to cook for your next guests?'

'I'm not sure Olivia will be back working here again,' Amy said. 'Pierre said recently that both Hervé, her husband, and the doctor want her to retire. Whether she can be persuaded to stop is another thing.'

'Can you do the cooking if she does?' Simon asked.

Amy laughed. 'No. I'm a bit of a liability in the kitchen apart from the really basic stuff. I wouldn't dare to try and cook the cordon-bleu meals Chelsea and Olivia both produce so effortlessly. I've got a friend in Antibes who finds catering staff for the luxury yachts, so I'll have a word with her next week, see if she can come up with somebody for me.'

Vicky was full of apologies when she appeared in the kitchen just as Chelsea was organising the drinks tray for the terrace. 'I'm so sorry. I completely lost track of the time. Am I too late to help?' Vicky said, looking at the prepared food on the work surface.

'No worries,' Chelsea said. 'Dad and Amy have been great. They're out on the terrace now, chatting.'

'Before Amy comes back in,' Vicky lowered her voice, 'I've bought her present, so breakfast coffee tomorrow morning up in the summer house, okay? We can all sign the card then. I'm sorry I didn't run it past you or Matilda, but I just know you'll agree it's a perfect memento.'

'What did you get her?' Chelsea asked curiously.

'A... a candle holder for her new terrace,' Vicky said in her normal voice as Amy walked back in. 'Almost bought one for myself, I like it so much. Is Matilda joining us for dinner tonight?'

'Yes,' Amy said. 'Pierre's taken her to the villa to take some photographs. We'll have to be careful not to mention tomorrow's party when she gets back.'

'I think she's very brave planning to move here on her own,' Vicky said. 'I hope it all works out for her.'

'She knows I'm always here if she needs help,' Amy said. 'Pierre too, and she'll soon make friends. How's Anthony?' she added, looking at Vicky questioningly. 'And how are you?'

'Seems okay. Says he has plans for the future which we'll maybe talk about tomorrow when we go to Monaco,' Vicky said, pulling a face. 'I haven't told him yet that I have plans of my own. How he's going to react will be interesting.'

'Where is he at the moment?'

'Checking emails and then going for a quick swim. I told him he had half an hour before pre-dinner drinks on the terrace.'

'Which are ready now,' Chelsea said, picking up the tray with its glasses and nibbles and making her way outside.

Simon, standing on the terrace, clearly lost in his own thoughts, gazing at the view, visibly jumped as Vicky walked over to him with a plate of nibbles and apologised for dashing off that morning, before saying, 'Your daughter is a wonderful cook. So sorry to hear about her partner running off and leaving her in debt.'

'Thanks. She put so much work into making the business a success, it's hard for her, but I think she's more worried for Elsie than the money.'

Vicky nodded. 'I can understand that. I've only known her for a short time, but it's obvious Chelsea is a caring person.' Vicky glanced at Simon. 'I was thinking of inviting her to London for a weekend. Introduce her to my daughter, Suzie. I'm sure they'd get on. I promise we'd look after her.'

Amy and Anthony appeared on the terrace together at that moment and Simon's reply was limited to 'Good idea' as he turned to greet them both.

If Anthony had been feeling awkward that morning meeting Simon, his rudeness had been banished and his innate good manners had resurfaced and the two men greeted each other with a nod and a friendly smile.

Standing there watching them both laugh at something Vicky had said, Amy became more and more convinced that she'd met Simon somewhere before. She had a sneaky suspicion too, that he knew exactly where but was holding out on her.

A car door slammed and voices drifted up from the driveway before the car could be heard leaving. Minutes later, an excited Matilda appeared. Amy quickly introduced her to the two men before glancing at the iPad in Matilda's hand.

'Did you get lots of photos?'

'I did – both indoors and of the garden. Scroll through if you want,' and Matilda handed the tablet over to Amy. 'You didn't tell me Pierre was going to be my neighbour.'

'Didn't he tell you?'

'Not until this evening when we had aperitifs in his villa.'

Vicky, looking over Amy's shoulder at the photographs, said, 'I love that round arch leading into your sitting room. Oh, your terrace is amazing too. I wish there was time for us to come and see it.'

'Maybe tomorrow?' Matilda said. 'Pierre has lent me the spare key, so I can go back again before we leave.'

Vicky shook her head. 'Anthony and I are going to Monaco for the day tomorrow. Maybe we'll come to France in the future and can pop in and see you.'

Chelsea came out of the kitchen just then, carrying the tray with their starters. 'I'd love to go with you and see it, Tilly,' she said, placing the food on the table.

'After your swim tomorrow morning,' Matilda said. 'About ten o'clock? I can't keep bothering Pierre to drive us, so we'll walk down – it's really not that far. I'll bring my stick, not that I think I'll need it, my ankle is so much better.'

As everybody made their way to the table and Amy disappeared indoors for a jug of water, Vicky caught hold of Matilda's arm. 'I've bought Amy's thank-you present and a card for us all to sign. Breakfast coffee in the summer house tomorrow okay?'

Matilda nodded. 'I can't believe tomorrow is our last full day. The holiday has gone so quickly. And if anyone had told me when I arrived I'd be going home having found and decided to buy my dream villa – well, I wouldn't have thought it possible.' She picked up her glass and raised it in Amy's direction as she reappeared. 'I think Amy deserves a toast for giving the three of us such a wonderful holiday. Amy.'

'I'm curious as to why you'd want to give three strangers a holiday,' Anthony said. 'It's a wonderfully generous thing to have done, but I can't help thinking, why?'

Amy smiled at him. 'Because I'm lucky to have inherited this villa. And because I love the ethos behind the film

Enchanted April. I just thought some modern day women would relish the chance to escape their routines for a while. And because I know Aunt Tasha would have approved.'

'I liked that film too,' Simon said, helping himself to some garlic bread. 'Some wonderful acting in it. Joan Plowright at her brilliant best.'

Amy stilled. Held her breath, not trusting herself to speak as she looked at him. Simon, feeling the intensity of her gaze on him, looked at her and smiled. Tremulously, Amy smiled back. She had met Simon before. And now she finally remembered the exact occasion.

DAY TEN OF THE HOLIDAY – JUNE 16

25

Up in the summer house early the next morning, Vicky, Matilda and Chelsea were all rather bleary-eyed. Long after dinner had finished and the table had been cleared last night, they'd stayed on the terrace chatting companionably together, enjoying the warm and jasmine scented evening air. As the bats had dived and swooped around, candles had been lit, friendships cemented and nightcaps drunk. It was almost midnight, when the owls were calling to each other from the tall trees at the bottom of the garden, before they all reluctantly wished each other 'Bonne nuit' and made for their own rooms.

Vicky had been the first to arrive this morning and she'd opened the summer house door, placed the book in its bag and the card on the table before taking three chairs outside. Chelsea and Matilda had walked up together, Chelsea carefully carrying a tray with three mugs of coffee and a plate of croissants.

The three of them sat in companionable silence, sipping

their coffees and slowly coming to as the caffeine and the croissants jolted their systems awake.

'I hope you like Amy's present,' Vicky said. 'When I saw it, I couldn't resist it, but if either of you two don't agree, I'm happy to keep it for myself and we can find something else. We don't have much time though.' She opened the bag and took the boxed book out.

Matilda picked it up and smiled as she saw the title. 'It's perfect. Amy will love it.'

'Gosh, that is amazing. How lucky to find something so... so just right.' Chelsea added her delight.

Vicky sighed with relief as she took a pen out of her pocket. 'We can all sign the card and I'll wrap it up with the book later.'

As Matilda wrote her message and signed her name inside the card, Chelsea said, 'You did both mean it last night about keeping in touch when we leave?'

'Definitely,' Vicky said. 'I was thinking you might like to come to London for a weekend sometime? Suzie could take you to all the in places.'

'Sounds good. And when your book is published, we'll all come to the launch and cheer.'

'If it ever happens,' Vicky said. 'We'll have had several meet-ups before then.'

'I hope you'll both come and visit me in my new home,' Matilda said.

'I'll be a regular visitor, Tilly, you'll probably get fed up with me,' Chelsea smiled. 'I'm the only one who can't invite either of you to stay. I only have a tiny flat and I'm not even sure how long I'll be able to afford that now.'

'In a few years, we'll both be celebrating with you when you're a famous chef with your own TV series,' Vicky said.

Chelsea sighed. 'You know, I'm not sure I want to be

famous. I just like feeding people with good food. Maybe I'll find a house by the seaside and run a B & B. A retreat like this would be wonderful but...' she shrugged. 'I don't have that kind of money. I know Dad would help, but I'd rather do it independently.'

'Keep dreaming and working towards that,' Matilda said. 'Life's upsets often have unexpected consequences.'

Vicky stood up and picked up the book and card. 'Talking of life and its upsets, I have one right now to sort out. Anthony and I are off to spend the day in Monaco and hopefully to talk rationally about the future. Wish me luck. Enjoy your last day here. I'll see you both tonight.'

Matilda and Chelsea watched her go before they stood up and prepared to follow her along the path.

'I need to check something in the kitchen for tonight's barbecue and then I'd like to have a quick swim before we walk down to your new villa,' Chelsea said. 'Is that okay?'

'I can't wait to show it to you.' Matilda smiled at her. 'I'm so excited.'

* * *

Back in her room, showering and getting ready to meet Chelsea, Matilda thought about the day ahead – her sixty-second birthday.

Her sixtieth birthday had been the last time she'd really celebrated the day. William had been alive then and he'd treated her to dinner and an evening performance of *A Midsummer Night's Dream* at The Theatre Royal. Matilda loved that theatre in the heart of old Bristol and it had been a wonderful evening. It turned out to be their last theatre outing together – five short weeks later William was dead. Matilda hadn't been near the theatre since.

Josh made sure he was home for her birthday last year and had taken her out for dinner to a new restaurant, one that didn't hold any memories for her, and did his best to make the occasion a happy one. And she'd tried, really she had, to accept that this was the way birthdays would be from now on, just the two of them, but it had been hard. Although she'd enjoyed Josh's company, he'd realised the evening was proving to be a difficult one for her and they'd returned to the flat early.

A year on though and things were different. She was definitely in a better place for this birthday – both mentally and physically. She was in France, with three new friends who didn't even know it was her birthday, and Josh was away working for Sea Shepherd somewhere off the coast of Greenland. The most she could expect was a phone call from him later today and a celebratory get-together when he returned home. Something she decided she was fine with. Like her, he had his own life to lead.

Life without William at her side had taken some getting used to during the lonely, despairing months after his death, but she knew deep inside that her new future in France would be one worth celebrating. Hopefully, Josh would be happy about her selling up in England and moving to France. The photos she'd taken of number eight were still sitting on her iPad along with the draft email she'd written to him. She'd been too tired last night to sort through the photos and choose the best ones to send. Instead, she'd decided she'd wait until she was home at the weekend and could go through everything carefully before sending.

Thinking about home reminded her. She'd also have to break the news to Sheila that she was leaving. She wouldn't be about to start a new life in France if Sheila hadn't entered her name in Amy's generous competition and won her the holiday. It had literally been a life-changing event. Once she was settled in at number eight, she'd insist Sheila came for a holiday. It was the only way she could repay her for being so kind and thoughtful.

After she'd dressed, Matilda applied the small amount of make-up she wore these days – foundation, eyeliner and a soft pink lipstick – before reaching into the wardrobe and pulling out her new leather jacket. Today would be a good day to wear it for the first time. Slipping it on, she smiled. She loved everything about this jacket – the colour, the soft leather, the styling, even the smell. 'Happy Birthday to me,' she whispered. 'The beginning of a new year. The rest of my life starts now.'

Stepping out of the French doors onto the terrace ready to walk down to meet Chelsea, she saw a man coming along the path towards her. Matilda blinked. If she didn't know better she could have sworn that it was her son walking towards her, but that was impossible. Wasn't it?

'Mum, there you are. Amy said I'd find you here,' Josh said, before he engulfed her in a bearlike hug.

'Josh! What a wonderful surprise. What are you doing here?

'What d'you think? It's your birthday. I managed to organise some time off. So, Happy Birthday. Where are you off to looking so smart?' he said, stepping back and looking at her. 'New jacket?'

'Chelsea and I are walking down to see a villa and, yes, the jacket is new,' Matilda answered. 'Anyway, never mind that. Where are you staying? How much leave have you got?'

'Amy has very kindly given me a room for tonight,' Josh said. 'Just a week. Planning on spending a few days with you back home. Who's Chelsea and where's the villa you were going to see?'

'Chelsea's a fellow guest here and the villa... well, I'll tell you all about the villa as we walk there. First, let's go and find Chelsea. I suspect she'll still be in the pool. She's a real water baby.'

* * *

After leaving the summer house, Chelsea went in search of Amy.

She found her in the kitchen, having breakfast with Simon.

'Morning, Sunshine,' Simon said. 'Come to join us for breakfast?'

Chelsea shook her head. 'I've had breakfast up in the summer house. I'll have another coffee, though.' Sipping her coffee thoughtfully, she looked at her dad and Amy speculatively, remembering what Simon had told her. In her eyes, they already looked like a couple, they were so relaxed with each other. She couldn't help but be pleased for her dad, he deserved to be happy again and Amy was lovely. She'd be good for him. Fingers crossed it would work out. As long as their relationship didn't stop Amy giving her the answer she was hoping to a certain question Chelsea had intended to ask her this morning. She wouldn't, she decided, ask the question now though. She'd wait until she found Amy on her own later today.

'I just wanted to check the meat for the barbecue was out of the freezer?' she asked.

Amy nodded. 'It is. And your dad here has just offered to be main chef tonight. He tells me he's a whiz with barbecues.' She smiled at Simon as Chelsea agreed.

'Oh, he is. He's well past the burnt offering stage these days.'

'D'you have plans for today?' Simon asked. 'Only—'

'I'm going for a swim first,' Chelsea interrupted. 'And then Tilly is taking me to see her new villa. So relax, Dad – you're free to do whatever you've got planned without me. Don't forget to light the barbie in time though.' Chelsea put her cup in the dishwasher. 'Right, I'm off. I'll see you both later. Have fun.' The gate buzzer went as Chelsea turned to leave the kitchen. 'D'you want me to get that?'

Amy shook her head. 'I'll answer it.'

Back in her room, Chelsea quickly pulled on her swimsuit, realising as she did so that she would have to cut her swim short if she was to be on time for Tilly. Twenty instead of thirty lengths would have to do this morning. Placing her towel on a nearby lounger, Chelsea dived into the pool and powered into a fast front crawl.

Fifteen minutes later, as she climbed out of the pool, she found Tilly and a youngish man waiting for her. Chelsea gulped. She might be off men at the moment, but this one was seriously fit. Tall, broad shouldered, fair hair, dimple in his cheek as he smiled at her and a look in his eyes as he watched her climb out of the pool that made her blush. Grabbing her towel, Chelsea wrapped it around herself and looked at Tilly.

'Chelsea, I'd like you to meet my son, Josh.'

This was Tilly's son? For some reason, she'd pictured him as being in his forties, but Josh looked younger than that, closer to her own age. Probably late twenties, she decided.

'Hi, Josh.'

'Nice to meet you,' Josh said, holding out his hand and taking Chelsea's hand in a firm clasp that lasted longer than strictly necessary and shot her arm through with pins and needles. No, that had to be the result of those fast laps and absolutely nothing to do with him.

'Nice to meet you too,' Chelsea managed to say before taking a steadying breath. 'Any reason for the surprise visit?' Chelsea asked mischievously, looking at Matilda.

There was a pause before Matilda spoke. 'It's my birthday. I was planning on telling you all tonight at the barbecue.'

'Happy Birthday, Tilly,' Chelsea said. 'I'd give you a birthday hug, but I'm a bit damp – later, I promise. I'm glad you treated yourself to the jacket in the end. It looks lovely on you.'

'Thanks.'

'I'm guessing you are dying to show Josh the villa?'

'Yes,' Matilda said. 'So hurry up and change and we can walk down together.'

Chelsea shook her head. 'You must have lots to talk about, so I think it's better for the two of you to go together without me hanging on. I'll catch you both later. Enjoy your day.'

And before Matilda could protest, Chelsea turned and began to walk towards her room. It didn't seem right to intrude on mother and son time, especially today of all days.

26

Vicky decided her new coat of many colours was worthy of an outing to Monaco and took it off its hanger as she and Anthony prepared to leave for Cannes to catch the train to Monaco. As she slipped it on, she wondered whether Anthony would remember her long ago Amazing Technicolour Dreamcoat.

'I couldn't resist this when I saw it in Antibes market,' she said, looking at him. 'What d'you think?'

'I think it makes you look eighteen again. You were wearing a coat like this when we met.' Anthony took her in his arms. 'We've had a good life together so far, haven't we?'

Vicky smiled and nodded. 'We have. I wouldn't have missed it for anything.'

'Neither would I. Whatever the future brings, together we can face it.' Anthony pulled her close and gave her a gentle kiss. 'Come on, the taxi will be here any minute.'

Now, sitting opposite Anthony as the TGV swished along the coast towards Monaco, Vicky realised she didn't want to wait until they were home before starting the discussion regarding their future. At home, it would be all too easy to slip back into her old habit of allowing Anthony to take the lead in all the major decisions without any real input from her. Whereas here in France, she felt more positive and alive, more in control – and more inclined to push her own point of view in telling him what she would like from life from now on. As they exited the train in Monaco and joined the crowds on the moving walkway that would take them from the station into town, Vicky hoped Anthony would be in the mood to listen.

But it wasn't until they were seated in a restaurant with a view out over the harbour having lunch a couple of hours later that Vicky started, in a roundabout fashion, to lead their conversation to plans for the future.

'So, how d'you like Monaco?' she asked. 'I think I've shown you all the important bits – the palace, the cathedral, the casino. It's a shame we don't have time to visit the Oceanographic Museum or the Car Museum, but maybe we can do those another time.'

'It's very hilly and spread out, isn't it? Been a long time since I've done so much walking,' Anthony said. 'But yes, next time for the museums. It is a fascinating place. Those boats,' he gestured in the direction of the luxury yachts, 'are something else.'

'Maybe we can come for the Grand Prix next year,' Vicky said. 'If you're not working.' Her last words stalled the conversation for several seconds before Anthony answered.

'If I'm not working, we won't have the money for trips like that.'

'True.' Vicky picked up her wine glass and took a sip.

'Not that we'll be broke exactly, but holidays in exotic locations will have to be postponed,' Anthony said, looking at her. 'Until we're – I'm back on my feet again.'

Vicky watched and saw him bite his bottom lip, a sure sign that he was nervous. Did he already have something in mind? She raised her eyebrows at him, 'So, these vague ideas you mentioned? Want to tell me about them? The one about selling up and running away to sea like you suggested the other day is, I guess, one of them?'

'Well, that would be my favourite course of action, I have to admit,' Anthony said. He looked at her and took a deep breath before adding, 'I'm actually wondering about working for myself. Setting up a freelance consultancy. What d'you think?'

'Depends.' Vicky said, trying not to show her surprise.

'On what?'

'Lots of things. What sort of consultancy you have in mind. Start-up costs. Where you'd base yourself.'

'I was thinking of something to do with the environment. Green issues. Sustainability. Helping to make the world a greener place. Businessmen, even when they want to help, in the main, have little or no idea of where to begin.'

'Sounds interesting. Do you know enough about it all though?'

'Of course I do. And I have the contacts. I haven't been involved with all those green and climate change government subcommittees for years without learning a lot.'

'Start-up costs?'

'Minimal. Office space. Upgrade the computer maybe.' Anthony topped up both their wine glasses. 'Now the children have left home, we could downsize if we wanted, move out of London even, release some funds to keep us through the first year. You could join me – keep me organised, do the books.' He looked at her hopefully.

Vicky shook her head. 'Sorry, no. Well, not officially anyway. You know I'll back you and help with whatever you decide to do, but I have my own plans for a change of career – or rather, being a late starter and getting an actual career.' Vicky took a thoughtful drink of her wine. 'I agree we could downsize though. Well, not necessarily downsize because the children must always have somewhere to come, but we could definitely move somewhere cheaper, but not too far from London. A little cushion of money in the bank would be good,' she took a deep breath. 'While I'm studying for my MA.'

Anthony looked startled. 'You want to go back and do another degree?'

'Yes, in Creative Writing. I feel if I don't do it now...' Vicky shrugged. 'I've written almost fifteen thousand words this week and when I get home, I fully intend to write for a couple of hours every day.' She looked at him. 'It's what I really want to do and I feel it's now or never, but I hadn't anticipated you giving up politics. As for starting a consultancy,' Vicky sighed. 'It seems we both want to change direction in our lives.'

'Only in our working lives, I hope,' Anthony said, reaching out and taking her by the hand. 'I'm sorry I've been a bit distant over the last few months, trying to keep things to myself and not worry you.' He squeezed her hand. 'You and me – we're still okay though, aren't we? We can work through things together.'

Vicky smiled at him. 'Of course we can. With the children leaving home, it'll be like we were in the beginning. I remember we hated being apart even for a few hours. We talked non-stop then about our plans and dreams for the future.' She squeezed his hand in return. 'Some of those plans worked out, others were forgotten as family life took on its own momentum. As for the dreams we had back then, perhaps some were unattainable, foolish even, and maybe there are a couple still there under the surface but they've also been joined by different dreams. Dreams that are rooted in the reality of our life now.'

'Things are going to take time to sort out,' Anthony said. 'But after I stop being an MP and before we both get started on our new ventures we'll make time for a holiday – a second honeymoon.'

Vicky nodded. 'Already looking forward to it.' She smiled happily at Anthony. They were back on track with each other. Their lives would change over the next few months, but at least they were talking and planning together. All was not as lost as she'd begun to fear, after all.

After Amy had welcomed Josh in and shown him to his room, apologising as she did so for it being on the small side, she went back down to the kitchen and found Simon clearing away their breakfast things.

'You don't have to do that, but thank you. Were you expecting to spend the day with Chelsea?' she asked.

'I was hoping to spend the day with you, if you're not too busy?'

Amy smiled at him. 'Nothing that can't wait. The barbecue for this evening is easily organised later this afternoon.'

'Fancy a trip across to St Marguerite and a picnic on the beach?'

'Sounds great. I haven't been to the islands for so long and I usually visit St Honorat when I do go. I'll organise some food, shall I?' Amy moved towards the fridge, but Simon stopped her.

'I'll do it. You go and change into beach gear, not forgetting a blanket if you have one – oh, and grab a jacket. It'll probably be breezy out on the water going over.'

Amy looked at him. 'Anyone ever told you that you're incredibly bossy?'

'Chelsea, frequently, now scoot.' Simon pulled his phone out of his pocket and waved her away with a smile. 'Just got to make a phone call. We've half an hour to catch the ferry.'

They made the booking office for the ferry out to the islands with five minutes to spare. Amy waited near the pontoon and watched while Simon had a quick conversation with the woman in the booth who, after he'd paid for two tickets, reached down and handed over a cold box with a quick 'Have a good day' and a smile as Simon handed her a twenty euro note as he thanked her.

They stepped on board the crowded ferry seconds before the boat's engines revved and it started to ease away from the pontoon. Staying out on deck, they found two seats together near the bow for the fifteen minute journey out to the islands. Amy took off her straw sun hat as the wind threatened to blow it away and faced the salty breeze spray with her eyes closed for several seconds, enjoying her hair being tugged at by the wind.

Without opening her eyes, she said, 'I have to ask – who did you bribe for the picnic box? I'm sure it's not a service they normally provide.'

'I have a friend who runs a delicatessen and upmarket food delivery service. I rang him last night and had him on standby for confirmation this morning. That phone call I made earlier?'

Amy opened her eyes. 'But you hadn't even invited me for the picnic last night. How did you know I'd accept? I might have been busy.'

'I didn't, I just hoped. And you weren't because you're here.'

Amy smiled. It was difficult to chat with the noise of the engines and the wind whipping past blowing away any words, so the two of them sat in companionable silence enjoying the sensation of the boat ploughing through the water.

Fifteen minutes later, they stepped off the boat onto the landing slipway and began to make their way along the path that edged above the shoreline, in the opposite direction to nearly all the other passengers, who were keen to visit the fortress where the Man in the Iron Mask had been held captive. Amy was glad they were going to the far end of the island. She'd found the atmosphere surrounding the fortress and the museum housed within its walls rather spooky, giving her the shivers before she'd even seen the infamous cell.

'It's a bit of a hike to my favourite cove,' Simon said. 'Most people make for the nearest ones, but I like the walk and the solitude when I get there. I hope you like it too.' There was a pause before he continued, 'Did you know you can go on retreat at the monastery over on St Honorat?'

'Yes. I've never been, but I'm told it's a wonderful experience. Tasha went a couple of times after Francois died and before she became ill,' Amy said.

'I really struggled after my wife died and a friend suggested I booked myself a stay there. A year after Naomi died, I finally took his advice and stayed there for a week,' Simon said quietly. 'Turned out to be a real lifesaver. A week of nothing but silence and my thoughts. Trying to make sense of things.'

Amy touched his arm gently, hoping to convey her sympathy rather than utter mundane words.

'It's amazing just how much solitude and silence at the right time can help put things into perspective,' Simon said.

'Belle Vue was my refuge and helped me to heal when I moved in after Tasha died and I left my husband,' Amy confessed. 'That was one of the reasons I wanted to turn the villa into more than a simple auberge.'

'I can understand that,' Simon answered. 'Right, we're here. Shall we sit by those rocks over there?'

Sitting on the blanket with her back against a sunkissed rock, Amy took in the view out over the bay. A cloudless blue sky, blue water dotted with yachts of all descriptions, water-skiers being towed along fast or falling into the water, depending on their expertise, windsurfers and kitesurfers both exploiting the off-shore breeze and the choppy waves with their bouncing white crests.

'It's so idyllic here. Hard to believe that that coastline in the distance is the real world as we know it. Cannes with all its people, traffic and noise is such a short distance away.' She watched as Simon opened the picnic box and pulled out a bottle of rosé and two glasses.

Unscrewing the cap, he poured some wine and handed her a glass. 'Here's to new friends,' he said.

Amy took a sip of the delicious cold wine before saying quietly, 'You were friends with Aunt Tasha and Francois. Was she the one who recommended the Abbey retreat?'

Simon shook his head. 'No. It was another friend. A pilot actually.' There was a broad smile on his face as he looked at Amy. 'You've finally remembered where we met. I saw a certain look in your eyes last night and hoped you had.'

'Monaco open-air cinema watching *Enchanted April*. Tasha introduced us very briefly just before the film began. I don't remember meeting your wife, though.'

'Naomi was sitting with some other friends,' Simon said.

'I was on my way to join her when I bumped into you with Francois and Tasha.' He hesitated before continuing. 'Now you've remembered when and where we met, I have another confession to make. I stayed at Belle Vue Villa with Tasha and Francois several times. It's how I knew where Chelsea was staying. She hadn't told me the address of the villa, merely that it was in the South of France. I recognised the pool and you in the photos she sent me.'

'You recognised me?' Amy said. 'From such a brief meeting?'

Simon nodded. 'Plus, Tasha had shown us some photos on one of our visits. Your parents were here at the time too. They'd brought photos of your wedding,' he added quietly. 'Tasha didn't take to Kevin, did she? In fact I'd say she actively disliked him.'

'Both she and my mum tried to talk me out of marrying him, that's for sure,' Amy said. 'Sadly I was too pig-headed to listen.'

'Tasha told Naomi once she was worried about you and the way Kevin was towards you. Controlling, she said.'

Amy nodded. 'He was. And I think that's why Tasha left me Belle Vue.' She stopped, remembering that last hospital visit with her aunt. 'She told me that, should an escape route present itself, I was not to hesitate but to take it and run away. So I did, having wasted five years of my life believing I was married to a man who cared for me. Wrong. So wrong.' Amy picked up a flat pebble and threw it forcibly towards the sea.

Before Simon could say anything, she stood up. She needed to get her emotions under control. Self-pitying tears were welling up too close to the surface. If she wasn't careful, she'd be blubbing all over Simon in a moment and she was determined that wasn't going to happen.

'I fancy a paddle. Coming?' and she ran down to the water's edge.

'I'm a very good listener,' Simon said, joining her and catching her by the hand and gently pulling her to his side. 'If you want to talk about what happened.'

So much of her wanted to take him up on his offer. After all, he was starting to open up to her, telling her about the retreat and knowing Tasha and Francois. But was it too soon to start talking about the skeletons in her own closet? Wouldn't it be better to get to know each other a little bit more?

'Thanks,' she said. 'I will tell you the whole sordid Kevin story at some point – but let's not spoil such a beautiful day.'

Simon sighed as he looked at her. 'Promise? Don't judge all men by Kevin. Some of us are completely trustworthy,' he squeezed Amy's hand gently. 'Just so you know, okay?'

27

'This villa you're taking me to see,' Josh said as he and Matilda walked along. 'Who owns it? A friend of yours?'

'No, I've never met the owner – he's a cousin of Pierre the gardener, who has become a friend.' Matilda took a deep breath. 'The thing is, I've decided to move to France and I've agreed to buy this villa. I was going to send you an email – I've half written it – to tell you and show you some photographs of the villa when I got home. But now you're here, you can see it for yourself. We're almost there.' She realised from the silence that greeted her words that Josh was stunned. 'It's something that your dad and I always dreamed of doing when he retired, well, I'm doing it for him – but also mainly for me.'

Matilda glanced at her son, willing him to speak, to say he was happy for her, that it was a good idea, but it wasn't until she pointed to and turned onto the garden path of number eight a few moments later that he spoke.

'This is the villa you're buying?' Surprise registered on his face. 'It's not too big for you?'

Matilda shook her head. 'No. It's a perfect size. I fell in love with it the moment I saw it, and then there was a rainbow, and William's favourite rose is already in the garden. Both signs telling me I was doing the right thing.' Sensing she was gabbling away, nervous of Josh's reaction, she stopped. 'Come on, let me show you inside.'

'You've got the key already?'

'Luckily, Pierre let me have it for today. He knew I wanted to have a look around again. I'll give it back this evening.'

Matilda inserted the key and opened the front door. Whether Josh approved or not, the very act of opening the door of the villa and ushering him inside made her feel it was already her home.

She showed him the kitchen, the sitting room, threw open the French doors leading to the terrace and told him to go and have a look around upstairs. 'Choose which room you'd like as yours,' Matilda said. 'I'm going to have a wander around the garden.'

She was standing by the white roses deep in thought and trying to quell her nervousness over Josh's reaction when he reappeared.

'Well? What d'you think?'

Josh smiled at her. 'I definitely think Dad would have loved the villa, but are you sure about moving here by yourself? It's a huge undertaking.'

'In a way, that's the whole point. It's something that will make me face up to life again. Force me to get on with things without your dad,' Matilda said quietly. 'This holiday has been a step in the right direction. Made me realise I'm still capable of doing anything I want to do. In other words, it's shaken me out of the rut I'd slipped into after William died. I've had time to reassess things in a neutral place without any memories crowding in on me, colouring my thoughts with negative responses.' She gestured at the villa and the garden. 'I love this place. It's exactly the kind of villa Dad and I dreamt of buying together. But I promise you, I'm not looking at it through rose-tinted glasses. I know packing up the Bristol flat will be hard. I know there will be times after I've moved to France that I'll wonder if I've done the right thing but...' Matilda took a deep breath, she needed Josh to understand and accept why she wanted to live here. 'I've still got a lot of life left in front of me and I want to grab at it with both hands and I want to do it here in France. Living in this wonderful place.'

Josh was silent for some seconds before he enveloped Matilda in a hug. 'Okay, Mum. I just want you to be happy and you've convinced me moving here is the right thing for you. I'll even help you move, so long as you promise me that if – and I'm not saying it will – but if it does go wrong and you find you've made a mistake, you won't let pride stop you from admitting it and selling up.'

'I promise, but this time next year you'll see that you were worried over nothing!' Matilda said, returning his hug. 'Next year, I'm going to host a garden party here for my birthday, so save the date!'

'Seeing Chelsea didn't know it was your birthday today – I'm guessing nobody else at Belle Vue knows it's your birthday,' Josh said.

Matilda shook her head. She was beginning to regret she hadn't shared the news before about it being her birthday. 'Now you're here, though, shall we go out for a special meal? Just the two of us.'

'No, you can't disappear on your last night here,' Josh said. 'You must spend it with your new friends. Besides, isn't there a barbecue planned? You know I love a good barbecue.'

'We'll go somewhere good for lunch then, just the two of

us. I'll lock up and we can walk down to the village and find a restaurant. You haven't told me any of your news yet.'

'Nothing to tell really. My contract has been renewed for another three months, by which time I'll be ready for a change. Might even come and join you here in France for a bit,' Josh said, smiling at her clear delight at his words.

As Matilda made sure all the doors were secure and they prepared to leave, Pierre, driving away from his villa, gave them a toot and a wave. Matilda smiled and waved back, disappointed he didn't stop, but he was clearly in a hurry.

'That's Pierre, the friend who told me about the villa. Shame he couldn't stop. I hope you'll get to meet him before we leave.'

The walk into the village didn't take long and Matilda sighed happily as she pointed out the small daily market to Josh. 'I'm looking forward to becoming a regular here. Just look at those shiny aubergines – and those strawberries. Let's have a wander down the main street and see if we can find a nice restaurant. If not, we can always go to Cannes, it's not far.'

It was Josh who spotted Le Restaurant des Olives in a small square off to the right of the main road.

'Looks perfect,' Matilda said happily when he pointed it out.

Greeted with a smile, they were seated at a table near the shade of the largest olive tree either of them had ever seen, nibbles and a bread basket were placed on the table and red leather covered menus handed to them. Josh's order of champagne was taken with a nod and another beaming smile.

'It's lovely here,' Matilda said, looking around. 'I think it may well become my favourite local restaurant.'

'So, tell me about your new friend, Chelsea,' Josh said,

looked at his mother expectantly as he pulled a bread roll apart.

'Chelsea? She's lovely. So sad about her mother.' Quickly Matilda told Josh a little about Chelsea's life. 'She and Simon, her dad, are quite close – you'll meet him later. He turned up unexpectedly. A problem with Chelsea's business. Her partner has done a runner.'

The waiter returned at that moment with a half bottle of champagne nestling in an ice bucket and proceeded to carefully twist the cork out with a satisfactory discreet pop and poured them both a glass.

'C'est un celebration?'

'Oui, my mother's birthday,' Josh said.

'Bon Anniversaire, Madame,' the waiter said, handing Matilda a glass.

Matilda smiled. 'Merci.'

As the waiter turned away to attend to another table, Josh asked, 'Chelsea has her own business?'

Matilda nodded. 'Yes. Well, she did. Catering for functions – parties and business lunches. Not sure what she's going to do now. She's a marvellous cook. She lives in Bristol too – Kingswood – so it should be easy to keep in touch, until I move here, of course, but I'm hoping she'll visit once I'm settled.'

Matilda glanced at Josh. She knew better than to ask him whether he was currently seeing anyone. For the last few years, he'd been too busy travelling with his job to start a long distance relationship with anyone, but he always told her she'd be the first to know when he met that special person. If only he realised how much she wanted to see him with the right girl, settle down, start a family. Chelsea would make a lovely daughter-in-law.

'Happy Birthday, Mum,' Josh said now, raising his glass.

From the look on his face, Matilda guessed that he knew exactly what she was thinking regarding Chelsea, but there was no way he'd let the conversation go down that road. What would be would be, but she was allowed one wish on her birthday, wasn't she? Shame there wasn't a cake with candles to blow out, but she'd make the wish anyway. Josh and Chelsea. There. Together the two names had gone out into the cosmos. Que sera sera.

28

Standing under the powerful shower being pummelled by the hot water, Chelsea tried to marshal her thoughts and make new plans for her day. The last day of the holiday. Tomorrow she'd be back to the reality of facing up to re-organising her life without either her business or Elsie.

Elsie. She couldn't help but feel guilty for not noticing how her business partner was struggling and needed help. They were best friends, for goodness' sake. Why hadn't Elsie confided in her? Actually, she knew the answer to that one – Kit. She'd been too wrapped up in herself to notice that Elsie had a problem. She'd tried to ring and text her several times since Simon had given her the news, but nothing had got through. Sunday morning, she resolved to go to Stokes Croft and see Elsie's parents in the hope they could give her some news, at the very least reassure her that Elsie was all right. Offer to help in any way she could.

Rinsing the conditioner off her hair, Chelsea smiled to herself. Stokes Croft and Clifton were both on the same side of town, so she could casually drop in and see Tilly, make sure she was okay after the journey back.

As she stepped out of the shower thinking about Tilly, Chelsea remembered she hadn't bought her a birthday present yet. Right, that was something she definitely needed to do this morning. She'd take a last walk down to the village, have a wander around and see what she could find. If nothing inspirational jumped out at her, she'd buy a big box of artisan chocolates from the posh chocolatier near the hairdresser. She remembered seeing a mouth watering display in the refrigerated display cabinet in the window.

It felt strange to be alone in the villa, with nobody around to call out goodbye to, or ask if anyone wanted anything brought back from the village – they were all out doing their own thing. Chelsea pushed the 'I'm Billy no-mates' feeling away. Vicky was with her husband, Tilly was with her son. Both completely natural occurrences. Her dad had said she was welcome to join him and Amy on whatever he had planned. Yeah, like she wanted to play gooseberry.

Pierre had just turned into the driveway off the road and the electric gates were beginning to close behind his car as Chelsea ran down. She gave him a wave as she took the opportunity to slip through before the gates silently slotted together again. Ten minutes later, she was walking through the village making for the newsagents to buy a birthday card for Tilly.

After leaving the newsagents, Chelsea walked on down the main road. Past the shop selling beach paraphernalia, the bank, a pet food shop, a butchers and a jewellers. The next shop had a window display full of bright crockery, table-cloths, candles and other things for the home. Chelsea was hopeful as she pushed open the door; surely she'd find something for Tilly in here? Quarter of an hour later, she left disappointed. She'd found several things she personally liked but nothing that she thought would appeal to Tilly – other than a lavender candle, which might prove to be her last resort instead of chocolates.

Chelsea crossed the road, intending to walk back in the direction of the market, but seeing a small street, more of a lane really, between the boulangerie and the pharmacy that she'd not noticed before, she decided to explore. After all, she had all day with nothing to do. She passed a small flower shop with galvanised buckets of roses and lilies standing on the pavement, their fragrance perfuming the air. Further on, a pair of closed wrought-iron gates separated the front garden of what had clearly been a large villa, once upon a time, from the road. Now subdivided into apartments, a panel of door buzzers and names was attached to a side wall. A terrace with a curious mixture of tall narrow houses and shops came next. Intrigued by the contents on display in the window of 'Être Zen' Chelsea stopped to take a closer look and smiled to herself in delight. She'd stumbled upon a French 'new-age' shop. Without stopping to think, she pushed the door open and walked in.

Inside was a glorious mixture of bookshop, clothes shop and ethnic goods from around the world. Crystals, joss sticks, packs of tarot cards, books on the supernatural, self-help books, jewellery, candles, wind chimes and ethnic clothes all jostled each other for space.

There was no sign of a sales assistant. Behind a small counter, a bead curtain hung in front of an opening which presumably led to somewhere private. Tentatively, Chelsea called out, 'Bonjour' and waited, but no one answered. Oh well, if she found something to buy, she'd shout a bit louder and hope someone would hear. She was examining a shelf of reiki friendship bracelets when she heard the bead curtain rattle and she turned to see a grey haired man watching her. A man who looked as though he'd be more at home in a bank than this shop, he was dressed so formally in a suit and tie.

'Bonjour, mademoiselle,' he said, followed by a sentence spoken so fast she could only stare at him aghast, not understanding a word he'd uttered.

'Uum,' Chelsea mumbled as she looked at him.

'Ah, you no speak French. Can I 'elp you?'

Chelsea smiled at him in relief. 'Please.' She pointed to the bracelets. 'I'd like the aquamarine one and...' she hesitated. 'And the rose quartz and moonstone one.' The aquamarine one would match Tilly's new jacket and be perfect for her. And she couldn't resist buying the rose quartz one for herself as a memento of the holiday. 'D'you have a box for this one?' she asked as she held the aquamarine bracelet out to the man. 'It is a present. The other one is for me and I'll just put it on.'

The man nodded as he carefully placed Tilly's bracelet in a box. 'These aquamarines will give your friend courage and protection.'

Chelsea looked at him in surprise. 'Oh. I knew the stones all had different powers according to reiki, but that is just what she'll need – courage and protection.'

'And you, mademoiselle,' he said as he fastened the other bracelet around Chelsea's wrist. 'Your rose quartz will bring you good luck, love and help your new beginning.'

Chelsea stared at him as he looked at her seriously before telling her how many euros she needed to pay. Wordlessly, she handed him her credit card.

'Au revoir, mademoiselle. Bonne journée.'

'Merci beaucoup,' Chelsea managed to stutter as she left

the shop. Well, that had been a bit of a strange experience, but at least she'd found a present for Tilly.

Walking back to the main street, she looked at the new bracelet on her wrist thoughtfully. If she believed that Tilly's gift would give her courage and protection, then she had to believe her own bracelet would do like the man said and bring her good luck. One thing was for sure, she wasn't going to chance taking it off in a hurry, she could do with all the luck she could get for the future.

Chelsea took her time strolling back to Belle Vue, planning to have lunch and then to sunbathe down by the pool before having a swim. She needed to check on the cake too, make sure the icing decorations had stuck.

When she got back, everybody was still out and Chelsea helped herself to a cheese salad, some garlic bread and a large glass of rosé, all of which she placed on a tray and carried down to eat sitting on the terrace by the pool.

Afterwards, lying on a sunbed under the shade of a parasol, Chelsea closed her eyes and allowed her thoughts to drift. Winning the holiday and coming to France had certainly helped her to get over Kit and his lies, but tomorrow she was returning home with a much bigger problem to sort out. Ten days ago, when she'd thought her broken heart was the biggest of her worries, she and Elsie still had the business. Now, having realised Kit had bruised her ego more than really damaging her heart, she knew the loss of her business was far more devastating and likely to have a bigger and longer lasting impact on her life. Elsie's disappearance was another worry. A guilt laden thought flashed again into Chelsea's mind.

She'd been so wrapped up in herself, she'd totally failed to register Elsie's drinking problem. Simon could tell her as often as he liked that it wasn't her fault, she couldn't stop feeling that she should have noticed and done something to help. Maybe she'd left it too late, but once home she was definitely going to try and find Elsie and offer to help in any way possible. Chelsea sighed. Lending her money would be out though, because currently she herself was broke, in debt to her father and jobless. What a scenario to be returning home to. Still, she had the rest of the day here in Belle Vue to enjoy and the barbecue for Tilly's surprise party this evening. With that happier thought, Chelsea found herself drifting off to sleep.

The sound of a car engine, followed by doors slamming and voices, woke her an hour later. Sounded like her dad and Amy were back. She'd have a quick swim – ten laps, no more – to wake herself up a bit and then go in search of Amy. She needed to find her alone and ask her the question she'd held back on earlier.

She was swimming her last lap when Josh appeared.

'Mum tells me you're a real water baby?' he said, as she climbed out of the pool.

'Yes, I am – well, in another life I was. Today I needed to cool off. I fell asleep in the sun,' Chelsea confessed, wrapping her towel around herself, aware that Josh was watching her. 'Did you like the villa? It looked wonderful in the photographs.'

'I did and I can actually see Mum living there.'

'Does she suspect about the party tonight?'

'No. She did suggest we both went out to dinner this evening, but I told her I refused to drag her away from her new friends on her last evening.'

'Well done.'

'Mum's having a nap right now,' Josh said. 'So I thought I'd grab my chance to have a swim Too bad you've had yours -

unless I can persuade you to keep me company?' Josh said, looking at her hopefully.

Chelsea shook her head, inwardly regretting having to decline. 'Sorry. I need to shower and then go find Amy. I think she and my dad are back?'

'Not sure where your dad is, but Amy's in the kitchen on her own.'

'Thanks. My shower can wait then. Enjoy your swim.' And Chelsea made for the kitchen.

As they arrived back at the villa, Simon's mobile pinged several times with incoming text messages. Glancing at the first, he cursed under his breath and turned to Amy. 'Sorry, looks like a spot of bother back home. All right if I make myself scarce for a bit? Make a few phone calls.'

'Of course,' Amy said. 'I need to do some things in the kitchen for this evening. Simon?' she looked at him. 'Thank you. I really enjoyed our day. It's been a long time since I enjoyed a day so much.' She wouldn't tell him just how long it had been.

'It's not over yet, but I hope it's the first of many we will spend together,' Simon answered as he disappeared in the direction of his room.

In the kitchen, humming happily to herself as she began to check on the food for the barbecue, Amy wondered about the day being the first of many they would spend together. Was that just a throwaway line or was Simon serious. She couldn't stop herself from hoping that he was serious. The meat, sausages, kebabs, steaks and burgers were all in the main fridge nicely thawed. The wine fridge had bottles of rosé, white wine and five bottles of champagne. Amy frowned, she'd only put three bottles in ready for this evening. Perhaps Josh had brought them for his mother.

Chelsea had said she'd do the salads, garlic bread was wrapped in tin foil ready to go at the back of the grill and the birthday cake hidden away in the small fridge in the utility room was looking good. With Simon taking charge of the cooking this evening, all Amy had to now was find the 'Happy Birthday' bunting and remember to hang it up between the trees by the pool at the last minute.

'Please can I have a word?' Chelsea, standing in the doorway clutching a towel to her and looking anxious, made her jump.

'Something wrong?' Amy asked anxiously.

'No, nothing wrong.' She paused. 'You jokingly offered me a job earlier in the week – cooking for your guests. Did you mean it? Or is Olivia coming back?'

'No, Olivia is definitely retiring.' Amy answered the last question first, trying to marshal her thoughts. 'And no, I wasn't joking.'

'Well, as I seem to be unexpectedly at a loose end for the rest of the summer, I was wondering whether the offer was still there? Or have you organised a temporary chef with the agency? I have to go home tomorrow and start to sort things out, but I could be back in time for your next guests.' Chelsea hesitated. 'I have to ask about pay, though. I have a few bills to start paying back, mainly Dad, but I do need to pay him. And I'd need to find somewhere to live.'

'I'd love to have you here as my chef. We'll work something out that suits us both if you're serious,' Amy said, smiling at her, and sensed Chelsea relax in relief at her words.

'Thank you. I can't tell you how much I appreciate the

job. Please don't tell Dad yet though, will you? I want to surprise him.'

The gate buzzer sounded at that moment.

'Shall I get that?' Chelsea asked, moving to the intercom and not waiting for Amy's answer. 'Hello?'

'This is Kevin. I need to talk to my wife, so I would be grateful if you would open the gate.'

'I'm not sure she wants to talk to you,' Chelsea said, looking across at Amy.

'Just tell her I simply want to talk to her.'

Amy crossed to the intercom. 'I'm busy. If I let you in, you've got five minutes to say whatever it is you've come to say this time and then you leave. Got it?'

'Yes.'

Amy pressed the button to operate the gate.

'You sure about seeing him?' Chelsea asked.

Amy nodded. 'This will be the last time.'

'D'you want me to stay?'

'No. I'll keep my phone in my hand and if there's a problem I'll press the set number for the local gendarmes.'

'Okay, if you're sure.' Chelsea gave her a worried look and left.

After leaving Amy and intending to go straight to her room for her delayed shower, Chelsea changed her mind. She didn't know where her dad was, but Josh should still be down at the pool and she'd get him to go and check on Amy and Kevin while she went in search of her dad.

To her relief, she found them both in conversation down at the pool. 'Dad, I'm worried for Amy. She's just let Kevin in because he says he wants to talk and she says it will be all right. She's got her phone ready to call the gendarmes if she needs to but—'

'Kitchen?' Simon was on his feet before she'd finished speaking and running up the path.

'Yes.'

Josh looked at her. 'Shall I go as well? Quite happy to lend support.'

Chelsea shook her head. 'No. Dad should be able to deal with it.'

'Who's Kevin anyway?'

'Amy's horrid, estranged, soon to be ex, husband.' Not wanting to gossip about Amy, Chelsea changed the subject quickly. 'When Tilly told us she had a son, I imagined you'd be much older.'

'And when Mum told me about this other guest called Chelsea, I imagined a sophisticated career woman in at least her late thirties,' Josh quipped back. 'Although calling you a real water baby should have warned me you were younger.'

'Not really a water baby any more,' Chelsea said. 'That was a whole different life. Now I just swim for pleasure, not competitively.' Seeing Josh look at her speculatively, she added, 'I swam for both the county and the national teams and at one stage I was even being considered for the Olympic team.'

'Mum told me your mum died in an accident – is that when you stopped?' Josh asked gently.

Chelsea nodded. 'Swimming stopped being all important.'

'I'm sorry about your mum,' Josh said.

'Thanks. It's five years ago now, but I still miss her.' She glanced at Josh. 'Tilly still misses your dad – I expect you do too. It's hard, isn't it?'

Josh nodded. 'I feel bad about working away so much now that Mum is on her own but...' he shrugged. 'I'm glad she's starting to make new friends,' he added, smiling at her.

Chelsea took a deep breath. 'Right, I'd better go and have a shower and start thinking about getting ready for the party. I'll see you later.'

'Ciao,' Josh said.

'Ciao,' Chelsea echoed.

As she walked back to her room, she couldn't help but wonder what else Tilly had told Josh about her?

29

Amy, waiting in the kitchen for Kevin to appear, wished a) she hadn't been so quick to agree to see him – what was the point after all? – and b) that she'd asked Chelsea to stay for moral support. Briefly, she wondered too, if Pierre was around and had seen Kevin arrive this time.

She instinctively clenched her hand around her phone as the door opened and Kevin appeared. For several seconds, they regarded each other silently. It was Amy who broke the silence.

'What do you want to talk about?'

'Us. The future.'

'You seem to have forgotten, there is no us any more,' Amy said. 'We don't have a future.'

'We could have. We were good together once. We could be again.'

'You want me to let you back in my life?' Amy let out a bitter laugh. 'After everything that happened between us? No way is that going to happen. Our divorce will soon be in its final stages and I hope never to have to see you again after that.'

Kevin's face grew hard as he stared at her. 'Placed on the market, this villa must be worth a few million euros. I could build a good future on that. If we don't get back together, I'd quite like my share.'

'Your share? Are you serious?'

Kevin nodded. 'Oh yes. Of course, you could always keep the villa and just buy me out. Maybe Aunt Tasha left you some capital? I'd settle for... oh, let's say a million euros would come in handy right now. Get me back on my feet.' Kevin threw her a look of spite and his voice hardened. 'After all, we're still married and I reckon you owe me now you own this place.'

'I owe you?' Amy almost chocked on the words. 'You're in financial trouble, aren't you? You really are a despicable piece of work, Kevin, d'you know that? To think I was once stupid enough to believe you were worth my love. You used and lied to me from the first day I met you.' Amy took a deep breath. 'Even if I had the kind of money you want, I wouldn't give it to you. But I don't. Belle Vue is not for sale and there is absolutely no way you are entitled to a share of it.'

'Not what my lawyer says.'

'He should talk to my notaire.' Amy stared at him before saying slowly. 'Under French law, inherited funds, either before or during your marriage, are your sole and separate property and are not subject to any claim by your spouse. And as we've been separated anyway for five years...' Amy allowed the sentence to die away before adding quietly, 'I'd like you to leave now before I phone the gendarmes and have you arrested for harassment.'

'What if I don't want to go?' Kevin said belligerently, taking a step towards her. 'You going to make me?'

'No, but I will,' and Simon walked into the kitchen from the terrace, stood next to Amy and put his arm around her shoulders. 'I suggest you do as Amy asks and leave now before I make you wish you'd never seen me.'

'Who the hell are you?' Kevin demanded, stepping back.

'Doesn't matter who I am. Get off the property now. Or we'll call the gendarmes.'

'All right. I'm going.'

As Kevin turned to leave, Simon gave Amy's shoulder a brief squeeze before following Kevin out of the villa and onto the drive.

Amy had collapsed shaking onto a chair at the kitchen table when Simon returned less than twenty seconds later.

'Pierre's frogmarching him down the drive,' he said. 'Are you all right? Want a hug?'

Amy nodded and slid off the chair into Simon's arms. 'I'm okay. Just can't believe he feels that he has a right to a share of Belle Vue. Or that I owe him anything after the way he treated me.'

'Do you want to talk about it? Like I said earlier, I'm a good listener.'

Amy hesitated for a second. Could she tell Simon about the biggest mistake of her life? Did she want to? Some things were still too hurtful, too painful to even think about without crying tears for the future life she'd lost. She knew instinctively though, that Simon wouldn't judge her, that he would feel her pain – maybe even help her come to terms with it.

'Yes. I think I would. But not here. Somewhere we can be a bit more private.'

Five minutes later, they were sitting up in the summer house, a bottle of water and two glasses on the table before them.

'Thank you for coming to my rescue back there,' Amy said. 'How did you know I needed help?'

'Chelsea told me Kevin was here and I jumped to the right conclusion.'

'I love your daughter,' Amy said. 'I always wanted a daughter – one like Chelsea would have been perfect.'

'She likes you too,' Simon said.

'After Chelsea, did you and Naomi want more children?'

'Yes, but complications with Chelsea's birth scared Naomi so much. I was frightened for her too, so we didn't push it,' Simon shrugged. 'We adored Chelsea and by the time she was at school, life had morphed into a comfortable routine, so we settled for being a one child family. I know Chelsea wishes she had a sister.'

There was a short silence before Simon spoke again.

'You were going to tell me your tale of woe.'

Amy suppressed a smile. A perfect description of her story.

'I'm not sure where to begin,' she said, pouring them both some water.

'You accused Kevin of lying to you,' Simon said quietly. 'Maybe start with that.'

'Kevin lied to me from day one. It turned out our whole relationship was based on a major lie. Promise me, if we are to be,' she hesitated, 'friends, you will never, ever lie to me?'

Simon took hold of her hand. 'I promise I'll never hurt you or lie to you, okay?'

Amy smiled gratefully at him.

'Kevin first came into my life when I was in the corps de ballet and he was the choreographer. I was twenty-four years old and flattered by his attention. Of course, he should never have got involved with me, it was against all the company rules, so for a couple of years he convinced me to keep our affair a secret.'

Amy took a sip of water and tried to curb the nausea that was threatening to overtake her as she remembered Kevin's actions.

'Then he was offered a job with a famous ballet company as head choreographer. He suggested I went with him as his PA and his wife.'

'Not as a dancer?'

Amy shook her head. 'No. He told me bluntly that I wasn't good enough to make principal dancer, I would always be the understudy, so I might as well marry him and give it up. And I was foolish enough to believe him.' She bit her lip. 'I was in my late twenties by then and dancers retire notoriously early – bit like footballers are past their prime at thirty! So I gave it up to marry Kevin and start the next phase of my life – having a family. Three months after we married, I learnt the real reason I'd never made principal dancer with the company was because Kevin had vetoed it. I had been good enough after all. But it was too late to turn the clock back for me.'

'Did you confront him about it?'

'I did try, but he shrugged it off, telling me I was paranoid and shouldn't listen to gossip. Anyway, I'd hoped to fall pregnant quickly and when I hadn't after two years, I started to worry. The gynaecologist I consulted arranged for some tests.' Amy was silent for a moment, remembering back to those stressful days, the fear of never being able to have a child, the large number of tests she willingly endured, only to be told there was nothing wrong with her and to 'just give it time'.

'Did Kevin go for tests?' Simon asked.

'No. He let me go for all sorts of tests but typically refused to go for any himself. He took the stance of it's always the woman's fault. The phrase "low sperm count" was uttered several times by my doctor, but Kevin insisted there was nothing wrong with him.' Amy took a long drink of water. 'And technically he was right.'

Simon was still holding her hand and he gave it a sympathetic squeeze while she regained some of her composure and tried to keep the tears at bay.

'I've always wanted children, a family to look after. Lie number one was when Kevin assured me, before we got married, that was what he wanted too. The truth, though, was the opposite. He had no desire at all to have children. In fact, he'd taken a deliberate step to ensure he never had any.' Amy took a deep steadying breath. 'Six months before we married, he had a vasectomy. An operation he elected not to mention to me.'

Shock registered on Simon's face and Amy caught the muttered word 'bastard'.

'Funny how the word vasectomy never entered our discussions until the night he got so drunk and told me in a blind rage that he didn't want kids ever, so I could just get used to it.' Amy gave Simon a wry smile. 'I think me giving him some leaflets about IVF may have sent him into meltdown.'

'But you must have been devastated,' Simon said.

Amy nodded. 'I was. If I'd known the truth, I wouldn't have married him. Might even have become a famous ballerina.' She shrugged her shoulders before continuing. 'He managed to shatter two of my dreams with his actions. No career and no family.'

'What did you do once you knew the truth?'

'I left him the next day. Went home to my parents and tried to regroup, as they say. Inheriting this place when Aunt

Tasha died some months later was my saviour. Thankfully, Aunt Tasha never knew the awful truth about Kevin. She was quite ill by then and Mum and I decided she didn't need to know anything other than I'd left him. She was happy about that.'

'Why did you take so long to file for divorce?'

Amy sighed. 'I was in a bit of a mess the first few months after I left him - couldn't seem to think straight over anything. Then Tasha died and I ran away to this place and life became all about making it work. But it's all in hand now. A few more months and it will be over. I'll be a divorced woman.' Relief flooded through her body at the thought. A new chapter in her life could begin. She glanced at her watch and stood up. 'Come on, we've got a surprise birthday barbecue to organise.'

'Just one more question – what will you do if he comes back again?'

'I don't think he will now that he knows he can't touch the villa, but if he does, I'll get a restraining order.'

As they started to walk back down to the villa, Simon carried the glasses and water bottle in one hand and held her hand tightly with his other one.

'Thank you,' Amy said quietly. 'It was good to talk. And you're right – you are a good listener. I'm glad you know the sordid details of my past life now.'

'I must admit, I don't like to think about you being alone here,' Simon said.

'I'm not alone often. Pierre is around a lot and...' Amy hesitated, about to say Chelsea would be here for the summer before remembering Chelsea had sworn her to secrecy. 'I've got guests coming throughout the summer, and my parents will be here in about a fortnight.' She glanced across at him. 'Maybe you'll visit again too,' she said, a questioning note in her voice.

'No "maybe" about it. I was going to ask you if it was possible to reserve the Ernest Hemingway room for me for the rest of summer,' Simon said. 'Be good to know I have a room waiting.' He grinned at her as she stopped in surprise.

'I'm not sure I can do that. I'm going to have to employ a live-in cook this summer and that would be the room I use for that.' Amy smiled at him. 'But I'm sure one of the other rooms will be available.' The thought of Simon being a regular visitor over the summer was a surprisingly happy one.

30

Early evening and Chelsea and Matilda were sitting by the pool watching Simon and Josh carrying food down to the summer kitchen before setting up the barbecue. Well, Matilda was watching them, Chelsea was lying on her tummy giving her back a last burst of sun.

'I feel I should be helping them,' Matilda said.

'No way. You know how possessive men can get over barbecues,' Chelsea said. 'Best leave them to it.'

Once Chelsea had organised the salads, Amy had charged her with keeping Matilda away from the kitchen and the evening preparations in case she should find out about the surprise party. Chelsea glanced at her watch. Ten more minutes and she'd suggest they both went for showers and start to get ready for the evening. That should give everyone enough time to get the balloons inflated and put up the Happy Birthday bunting and anything else that still needed doing.

Matilda watched as Josh helped Simon erect a trestle table alongside the large barbecue, ready to take all the accompanying side dishes for the cooked meat, as well as plates, cutlery, glasses and wine. Matilda smiled to herself, Josh turning up unexpectedly for her birthday was such a wonderful surprise. Had quite made her day.

'Chelsea, my dear, I'm going to need your help later on.'

Chelsea rolled over on to her back before sitting up and looking at Matilda. 'Go on.'

'There are a couple of bottles of champagne hidden in the fridge. Will you fetch them for me later when everyone has eaten and get Josh to pour everyone a drink?'

'Of course I will,' Chelsea answered. 'But I'm cross with you. You should have told everyone it was your birthday. We could have had a proper party, with balloons and presents and things.'

Matilda shrugged. 'I didn't want to make a fuss,' she said quietly.

'Oh, Tilly, that was just plain silly of you. Come on. Time to go and glam ourselves up for our last evening at Belle Vue.'

As the two of them stood up, Chelsea called out to her dad. 'We'd offer to help, but we're *both* off to shower and get ready,' she emphasised 'both' knowing that he'd get the message.

'See you later,' Simon called out, giving her a thumbs up before turning to Josh and mouthing, 'It's balloon and bunting time.'

Vicky and Anthony returned from Monaco not long after. Anthony went straight to help Josh and Simon, while Vicky went to find Amy and see if there was anything she could do.

Amy, busy in the kitchen packing ice around several bottles of rosé and champagne she'd placed in a large oval ice bucket, smiled. 'Think we're all done, thanks.'

'I'm so sorry we were late getting back. Unbelievable how crowded the train was. And then the traffic through Cannes. I feel guilty for not being here to help, but I promise I will do my fair share of clearing up after the party.'

'No worries. How was Monaco?' Amy asked.

'Good. We talked properly about what we both want for the next few years. Lots of decisions to be taken when we get home but...' and Vicky held up her hands with her fingers crossed. 'I think – hope – we'll weather the storm together.' She glanced at Amy. 'And your day?'

'Lovely. Simon and I went across to St Marguerite for a few hours. Afterwards, back here wasn't so good for a while – Kevin turned up again. Luckily, Simon came to my rescue and I think the message finally got through to Kevin that he's not welcome here.'

'Well done, Simon. So we'll both enjoy the party this evening,' Vicky said, smiling.

'Talking of which – grab a handle and help me carry this monstrosity out and we can get the party started,' and Amy emptied the last of the ice around the already condensed bottles in the tub before picking up the opposite handle to Vicky.

When they got down to the pool area, it was transformed with bunches of balloons, the Happy Birthday bunting strung across the front of the summer kitchen and Michael Bublé crooning out of the speakers Josh had set up. Pierre was there, busy lighting the citronella candles in jars that were dotted around. Simon and Anthony were diligently keeping an eye on the array of meat sizzling on the barbecue.

'This lot should be ready soon,' Simon said, carefully turning first a row of sausages and then one of burgers. 'The steaks will be next. Ah, here come the others with the birthday girl.'

Amy quickly started to pour champagne into eight glasses ready to hand them around.

'Oh, my goodness,' Matilda said as she realised it was a surprise birthday party for her. 'I didn't think anyone knew. Did you tell?' she asked, turning to Josh.

'Guilty as charged.'

'Happy Birthday, Matilda,' and everybody raised their glasses in her direction.

'Right, food's ready,' Simon called. 'Grab your plates, ladies, and tuck in.'

Sometime later when the barbecue food had been eaten and dusk had started to fall, Chelsea slipped away to fetch the bottles of champagne Matilda had secreted in the fridge. Bringing them back, she handed them to Josh and whispered, 'Can you do the honours with these, ready for another toast please? I have to fetch the cake.'

When she reappeared with the cake, its sparkler candle fizzing, Simon led the singing of 'Happy Birthday'.

As the last words faded away, Vicky and Anthony called out, 'Speech. Speech.'

Matilda laughed. 'Really? I'm not one for speeches, but here goes.' She took a deep breath. 'Thank you all so much for tonight, the surprise party, the presents, the friendship. Thank you for everything. Here's to you all,' and she raised her glass in acknowledgement to everyone. 'Thank you all for a wonderful birthday. I shall remember it forever.'

Chelsea handed her a kitchen knife. 'Now you can cut the cake.'

Once everyone had a slice of cake, Chelsea tapped on a bottle for their attention. She gave Simon an apologetic look before starting to speak.

'I don't want to take the limelight away from Tilly on her birthday, but I have something to tell you all. I'm Amy's new chef for the summer. I'm coming back next week to take over Olivia's job.'

After everyone had congratulated her, Chelsea made her way over to her dad who was standing with Amy.

'Great cake, Sunshine. And congratulations again on the job.'

'Thanks,' Chelsea hesitated. 'You okay about it? I need to start paying you back, but it won't be quick – unless I win the lottery. I'll start selling off the equipment when I get back, so that might speed things up a bit.'

'I told you, there's no rush. I'm just sorry for you after all the hard work that the business has gone the way it has.'

'No guarantees in life – isn't that what you've always told me?' She glanced at Amy. 'Have to admit I'm looking forward to being an employee again with no paperwork or VAT to do in the evenings.'

'That can always be arranged if you miss it too much,' Amy laughed. 'I hate it too.'

Chelsea shook her head. 'No thanks. I'm going to get another small slice of cake, either of you want some more?'

Both Amy and Simon declined and Chelsea made her way across to the table where the remains of the food were. She helped herself to the smallest slice of cake she could see and had just taken a bite when Josh appeared at her side.

'Thank you for making Mum a cake,' he said quietly. 'She really appreciated you taking the trouble. So you're coming back to work here this summer.' He topped up his wine glass with some water.

Chelsea, her mouth full of cake, could only smile and nod at him while she chewed and quickly swallowed.

'I've promised to help Mum move, which she seems to think will be around October November time. You likely to still be here then?'

'Depends on Amy's bookings, I guess,' Chelsea said. 'Could be back in Bristol by then living with dad. If he isn't living over here,' she added, glancing back to where Simon and Amy, chatting together, were clearly oblivious to everyone around them.

'How d'you feel about that?' Josh asked quietly.

'I thought I'd find it strange if Dad did ever meet someone new after Mum died, but I'm actually very happy for them both. Amy's lovely and Dad, well, Dad deserves to be happy again,' Chelsea said. 'I hope things work out between them. Long distance relationships can be difficult.'

'That's true,' Josh agreed thoughtfully. 'I'll just go and check on Mum. See if she wants anything else.' He walked away before Chelsea could answer.

The rest of the evening passed in a blur of conversation, laughter and friendship for everyone. The solar lights around the pool and garden were glowing and the underwater lights were illuminating the pool as Vicky started to collect plates to return them to the kitchen. Matilda smiled as she saw Pierre making his way over to her as she stood chatting to Josh.

'Thank you for coming this evening,' Matilda said. 'And for the strawberry tree plant for number eight. I can't wait to see where in the garden you've planted it when I return.'

Pierre smiled. 'I am thankful you like.'

'I have so much to be grateful to you for,' Matilda said softly. 'Showing me number eight and encouraging me to start a new life down here on the Cote d'Azur, to name but two.'

'I am looking forward to seeing you 'appy in your new life,' Pierre answered. 'Now, I say au revoir until you return and we become neighbours. Tomorrow will be busy for me.' And to Matilda's surprise, he leant in to kiss her in typical Provençal fashion on both cheeks.

'Au revoir, Pierre. See you soon,' Matilda responded,

watching as he shook Josh by the hand before turning and leaving.

As Pierre walked away, Matilda noticed Josh looking at her quizzically.

'What?'

Josh shook his head. 'Nothing. He seems a nice man.'

'He is. And very kind. I hope the two of you are going to get on.'

'Is it important for me to like and get on with him?' Josh asked, with a strange look on his face.

'Of course it is,' Matilda said. 'We're going to be neighbours.'

She suspected the real question Josh wanted to ask was did she really like him? A question she didn't yet fully know the answer to herself. All she knew currently was that she was looking forward to getting to know Pierre better when she moved to France and they became neighbours.

Amy, standing by the edge of the pool watching everyone slowly drift away at the end of the evening, instinctively leant against Simon when he tentatively put his arm around her shoulders. What a day this had turned out to be.

'You okay?' he asked.

'Tired. Been a long day.'

'You'll be able to relax tomorrow when everyone is gone,' Simon said.

'Mmm,' Amy said thoughtfully, not bothering to mention all the bed changing she needed to do before the next guests arrived. Still, she could take her time with that.

'Before I forget, Chelsea told me to tell you – the three of them would like you to join them for breakfast in the kitchen tomorrow morning. About 8 o'clock, for one last breakfast together.'

'Hope I'm awake in time,' Amy said, smothering a yawn.

THE MORNING OF
DEPARTURE

31

Chelsea made her way to the kitchen early the next morning, pleased to see Pierre had already been and left the usual bag from the boulangerie on the kitchen table. She switched the coffee machine on, placed the croissants and pains au chocolat in the basket and put plates and cups ready on the table. She smiled happily to herself. This kitchen was going to be her domain for the summer – she couldn't wait.

Sitting there waiting for the others to arrive, her thoughts drifted to what was likely to happen when she got home. So much stuff to sort out. Stuff she wasn't looking forward to dealing with, but it had to be faced. The only consolation was she'd be back here soon, ready to stay and work for the rest of the summer. Chelsea was mentally writing a to-do list when Matilda appeared. 'Morning, Tilly, how's the birthday girl the morning after?' she said, pouring a coffee and handing it to her.

'Last evening was such a lovely surprise,' Matilda said. 'I'm still in shock, to be honest. Everybody was so kind, spoiling me with presents.' She shook her head. 'I love my friendship bracelet, it's so pretty,' she said, looking at Chelsea. 'It will remind me of you every day.'

'Morning, you two, this is all very intriguing,' Amy said, coming into the kitchen and helping herself to a cup of coffee but declining a croissant when Chelsea pushed the plate towards her.

'Vicky will explain when she gets here,' Chelsea said. 'Ah, here she is.'

'That coffee smells good. Just what I need this morning,' Vicky said as Chelsea poured her a cup. She placed a gift wrapped package on the table and an envelope with Amy's name written across it alongside it.

Amy looked at it and then at the three of them questioningly. 'You've bought me a gift?'

'Belle Vue is a such a special place and we wanted to say thank you for giving all of us a wonderful holiday here. I think it's safe to say, your generosity has proved to be something of a life changer for the three of us,' Vicky said quietly. 'I found this in the brocante market in Cannes and as a thank you present we all agreed it fits the bill perfectly. We hope you like it,' and she gently nudged the package across the table in Amy's direction.

Amy pulled the wrapping open carefully and gasped with delight as she saw the book and realised what it was. 'I don't know what to say other than thank you all so much. I've always thought Belle Vue to be a special place, a little bit of paradise, and I'm happy that you've found it to be special too. I truly wasn't expecting anything, but this is wonderful. It will have pride of place in Belle Vue Villa. Thank you.'

* * *

An hour later, Amy was on the terrace, preparing to say

goodbye to everyone. Seeing the two cars being loaded with luggage, Amy felt strangely deflated and close to tears. Over the course of a year at Belle Vue, she welcomed so many guests that saying goodbye to people she had become fond of was a common occurrence and something she'd learned to deal with as part of the business, but these three women had turned out to be special. She was going to miss them so much. Chelsea at least would be back soon. And Matilda, of course, would be moving to France within the next few months.

First to leave were Vicky and Anthony. Pierre was driving them to Nice airport for the midday flight to London. As Anthony and Pierre put their luggage in the car, Vicky hugged Amy.

'Thank you again for a wonderful holiday. Belle Vue will always be my favourite writing retreat. It seems I'm the only one not coming back to France in the near future, but you and I will keep in touch, won't we?'

'Definitely,' Amy said, hugging her back. 'You're welcome at Belle Vue any time you want to come. And you get that novel written, so I've an excuse to come to London for a book launch.'

'Will do,' Vicky said, getting into the car.

Everybody waved as Pierre drove off and watched as the car disappeared in the direction of the A8 autoroute.

Matilda and Josh had accepted Simon's offer of a flight home to Bristol with him and Chelsea, instead of taking the budget airline they'd planned. Matilda had confided in Chelsea how excited she was. She'd never flown in such a small plane. Now, as Josh loaded Matilda's luggage into Simon's 4 x 4 ready for the short drive to Mandelieu-la-Napoule Airport, Matilda held out the walking cane she'd had to use when she first arrived, to Amy.

'May I leave this with you please? I don't need it now.'

'Of course. I'll keep it for when you return,' Amy said and gave Matilda a hug. 'I'm so looking forward to you moving over. Anything I can do to help, just ask.'

Matilda returned her hug. 'Thank you. With luck, I should see you in about three months.' A kiss on the cheek and she walked over to the car and got in.

Chelsea threw her arms exuberantly around Amy and hugged her tight. 'I can't wait to come back. I promise to be a model employee for you. I think Dad will have something to say if I'm not, won't he?' and then she was gone, sliding onto the back seat of the car to sit next to Josh.

'My turn, I think,' Simon said, putting his hands on Amy's shoulders and giving her a gentle squeeze. He brushed her forehead with a light kiss before he whispered, 'I wish I didn't have to leave right now, but I'll be back soon. This is just a very brief au revoir.'

EPILOGUE

Vicky sniffed appreciatively at the perfume from the red roses bath oil she'd poured into the water before she stepped into the bath and sank into the hot water. Bliss. The bathroom up in the converted eaves of her new home was nowhere as luxurious as the bathroom at Belle Vue, but nevertheless it had been a deciding factor in buying this cottage.

After talking everything over with Tom and Suzie, they'd decided that, yes, they would sell and move out of London. Where to go had been an easy decision to make when Vicky had applied for and been accepted on an MA at Bath Spa University. She and Anthony had had a fun month or two scouring the property pages and viewing houses and when their old London house had sold quickly and for a better price than anticipated, they'd taken the decision to buy this thatched cottage tucked away down a quiet lane on the outskirts of Bath. Three weeks ago, they'd moved into Owl Cottage and Vicky and Anthony had lain in bed that first night listening to the cottage's namesake tu-whitting and towhooing in the tall trees at the bottom of the garden, instead of the incessant drum of London traffic.

With Christmas fast approaching, there was a lot to do for the first family Christmas of their new life, but Vicky was looking forward to adding new traditions to the ones they'd created down the years. She stretched out and turned the hot water tap on for a few moments as she thought about everything she needed to do before Tom and Suzie arrived for the holiday. Their bedrooms were as ready as they could be for this first visit – the beds were made and the wardrobes were in situ. Neither of them had actually seen Owl Cottage yet other than on estate agent's photos and Vicky was looking forward to showing them both the cottage and exploring Bath for last minute shopping with Suzie.

Anthony was still an MP and routinely travelled to London, which wasn't a problem with Bath's good rail links, and he'd rented a flat in his constituency for the days he needed to stay in town and also as a base for Tom and Suzie. There was more and more talk of a general election early in the New Year when he would finally be free to concentrate on his new consultancy business. There had been very little time for Vicky to do much writing, but that too would change in the New Year when the conversion of the small box room into her office overlooking the countryside at the back of the cottage would be complete.

Vicky stretched out her leg and nudged the hot water tap on with her foot. She was so much happier than she'd been at the beginning of the year and she knew Anthony was too. They were back to enjoying each other's company and working together at this new start to their lives. This time last year, she could never have imagined how different her life would be twelve months later, thanks to the generosity of a stranger. A stranger who was now a good friend and planning to fly over soon for a girls' get together. Vicky smiled to herself, thinking about how Amy's life too had changed since she'd invited three complete strangers for a holiday.

The holiday in France, which seemed such a long time ago now, had turned out to be much more than a vacation. Vicky knew she would be forever grateful to Amy and Belle Vue Villa for helping to get her life back on track.

* * *

As the instruction to 'Fasten your seat belts please, ladies and gentlemen' came over the aircraft PA system, Chelsea closed her book and did as instructed. Five more minutes and she'd be back on French soil. She couldn't wait.

After spending the summer cooking for Amy's guests, Chelsea had gone back to Bristol in October to finish the final sorting out of her life there. Her dad had insisted, while she was in Bristol, his apartment was her family home and she was to use it as such. Something she'd been extremely grateful for. She'd terminated the lease on her own flat during that brief visit home after her holiday and moved her stuff into the apartment then, before returning to Belle Vue for the summer.

During the last two months in the UK, Chelsea had officially closed the business and sold the equipment, which had made a sizable dent in the money she'd owed her father. She'd signed on with an agency and had temped at various restaurants around the city, earning some much-needed cash. Despite her sadness over the reason that had made this necessary she'd quite enjoyed moving from kitchen to kitchen. December, being the time of office Christmas parties, had been a fun and hectic month.

There had been a rather fraught visit to Elsie's parents,

who had been unable to tell her anything about Elsie's current condition or even her whereabouts. Chelsea, promising to keep in touch and giving them her mobile number, asked them to let her know when, or if, they heard from Elsie. And to contact her if they felt she could help in any way.

Right now though, Chelsea was generally loving life and looking forward to Christmas and New Year at Belle Vue. In her luggage today, packed in carefully with all the presents, there was a large traditional pudding she'd made a couple of weeks ago on Stir Up Sunday, the traditional day for making Christmas puddings, a couple of jars of mincemeat and a posh box of Christmas crackers. Amy had already asked her to be in charge of Christmas dinner at Belle Vue. Everybody would help she'd said, but there needed to be someone in charge who knew what they were doing. Her dad and Amy's parents were spending the festive season at Belle Vue, and Tilly, Josh, Pierre and Sheila, Tilly's friend, were joining them for lunch on Christmas Day. Cooking for nine people in the kitchen she'd become so familiar with in the summer held no fears for Chelsea and she was looking forward to the first proper Christmas since her mum had died.

Tilly had told her Josh would only be there for a few days as he had a new job starting January the second and still had to get various things organised. Fleetingly, Chelsea wondered whether Tilly had told him about her moving into number eight with her in the New Year for a couple of months. Amy had introduced her to the friend who ran the catering agency in Antibes and she was going to do some freelance catering until Easter when she'd be back at Bell Vue full time cooking for the retreat guests. After the disasters of recent years, when her life had fallen apart in every direction, she finally had hope for the future. Not that she had any intention of taking anything for granted ever again. She was well aware that life could change without prior notice.

Grabbing her suitcase off the conveyor belt, Chelsea followed the crowd towards customs. Walking out into the Arrivals Hall, she smiled as she saw her dad holding out his arms to her. As he engulfed her in a tight hug, she sighed happily. Life was good.

* * *

There was a chilly wind blowing around the market square and Matilda was glad of her jacket, but the sky was blue and the sun was shining as she made her way from stall to stall early on the morning of the day Sheila was due to arrive. The festive season was in evidence everywhere: Father Christmases hung from building facades and chimney pots, festive decorations stretched across the street swung in the breeze, the branches of the village Christmas tree, daubed with false snow, waved and rustled, and carols drifted out on the air from the nearby coffee shop.

Matilda had only been a regular customer for just over a month now, but already the stallholders recognised her and greeted her with a smile. The move, delayed until November, had turned out to be very symbolic: two years to the day of William's death. When she'd realised that was the date her solicitor had earmarked for completion on the Bristol flat, she'd panicked and wanted to change it, but apparently she was the top of the chain and changing the date would affect a lot of people. In the end, she'd managed to take it as a good sign, that William would have loved the idea of her move happening on that day and it had gone ahead smoothly.

She'd flown down to Nice, Amy had met her and taken her back to Belle Vue for the two days it took for the pantechnicon with all her worldly goods to make the journey south. Amy had come to the notaire's with her too, for the signing and handing over of number eight's keys. And then taken her to the Carlton for a celebratory lunch.

From that day over a month ago, life had become a blur as Matilda had unpacked and settled into her new life. With Christmas on the horizon, she was hoping her new home was straight enough for her to relax and enjoy not only Josh's company but also Sheila's.

Sheila had taken some persuading to come for Christmas, but Matilda had insisted. She wanted to say a proper thank you to Sheila for winning her the holiday and was determined to spoil her for the ten days she was staying. Josh wouldn't arrive until Christmas Eve and then only for five days. Still, it was long enough for him and Chelsea to get to know each other better. She still nursed secret hopes for that relationship, although she had said nothing to anyone about it. She was so looking forward to spending Christmas Day with everyone at Belle Vue. She'd been thrilled to see how close Amy and Simon had become over the last few months.

She was hosting Boxing Day tea at number eight for everyone and hoped it would be a small 'thank you' to Simon, Amy and Pierre for all the help they'd given her.

A smile touched her lips at the thought of Pierre. He was rapidly becoming an indispensable part of her French life.

Turning to leave the market and walk home, Matilda couldn't help feeling that this Christmas, which was actually the third since William had died, would mark another important turning point for her. She was at the beginning of a new life in a new country, all made possible by Amy's generosity.

* * *

After Simon had left to collect Chelsea, Amy wandered into the sitting room, where the smaller of the two Christmas trees she'd bought in the market yesterday was waiting in its pot to be decorated. Something she hoped that the three of them could do this evening after supper.

The tall six foot pine in the hallway was already festooned with decorations and lights. Amy suppressed a grin. She and Simon had had such fun last night decorating and pinning the holly and mistletoe around. Simon had wanted to do the other tree as well, but when Amy had suggested they leave it for when Chelsea had arrived and the three of them could do it together, en famille, he'd readily agreed.

He'd wanted her to go with him to meet Chelsea off the plane, but a delivery due sometime during the day had made that impossible. Besides, Amy secretly thought it better that he went alone and they had some father-daughter time together before the house filled up with people.

Turning to go into the kitchen to make herself a cup of tea, her glance took in the bookcase with the boxed book of *Enchanted April* the girls had given her, with the beautiful card they'd all signed propped up against it. Whoever would have guessed giving three strangers a free holiday as a way of saying thank you for her own good fortune would change her life so dramatically?

The three women were all so different, each had their own problems and yet they'd all got on. Had melded together harmoniously. Amy couldn't help thinking that somehow serendipity had played its part in arranging for those partic-ular three women to meet up at Belle Vue this past summer. Matilda had found the courage to start living again without the husband she'd clearly adored. Vicky too, had dug deep inside herself to challenge Anthony and to do something she longed to do. And Chelsea? Well, Chelsea was a lot happier these days than she'd been at the beginning of summer.

A sobering thought occurred to Amy: what if she hadn't impulsively posted the competition on Facebook – and what if Chelsea hadn't been one of the winners. Without that scenario, she and Simon might never have met again. And as she couldn't imagine her life without him in it now, that simply didn't bear thinking about. Amy smiled to herself.

Scarcely a week had passed before he'd returned after that brief 'au revoir' and for the rest of the summer Simon had been a frequent visitor. He'd been at Amy's side when she opened the official letter containing her Decree Nisi. It was then he'd taken her in his arms and surprised her by admitting how he truly felt and asked about her feelings for him. The smile on his face when she told she felt the same had reflected the one on her own and from that day on their lives had started to become more and more entwined. She was so looking forward to this, their first Christmas together, and what the New Year would bring.

As the kettle boiled, Amy opened a packet of wafer biscuits that had recently become her favourite snack, although right at that moment what she really fancied was a mince pie. Hopefully Chelsea had remembered her promise to pack a large jar of mincemeat and would make some for Christmas. If she had forgotten, there was still time to ring Fleur and ask her to bring some on Christmas Eve.

Her parents had been delighted, ecstatic even, to meet Simon again during their July visit and to realise that something good was happening between their daughter and him. Fleur had asked, as the competition was such a success in more ways than one, would she do it again?

Would she? Amy had shrugged her shoulders at her mother's question. Inheriting Belle Vue Villa had given her the courage to change her own life. Winning the competition had helped Vicky, Chelsea and Matilda change their lives. Deep down, Amy knew that, yes, she would like to do it again. Maybe not this coming year, but certainly sometime in the future, she'd definitely think about it.

Because quite simply, as a random act of kindness, it had been life changing.

ACKNOWLEDGMENTS

Thanks as always go to Team Boldwood for their encouragement and expertise, especially my editor Caroline Ridding.

This time too I must thank Dale Franklyn, computer expert, for rescuing me and my computers from total melt down and preventing everything connected to A Riviera Retreat from disappearing. Thanks, Dale.

Thanks also to all my readers who read and say they enjoy my books – it's you who keep me writing. Hearing from readers who like my stories is a real morale booster., so please don't hesitate to contact me.

MORE FROM JENNIFER BOHNET

We hope you enjoyed reading *A Riviera Retreat*. If you did, please leave a review.

If you'd like to gift a copy, this book is also available as a ebook, digital audio download and audiobook CD.

Sign up to Jennifer Bohnet's mailing list for news, competitions and updates on future books.

http://bit.ly/JenniferBohnetNewsletter

Villa of Sun and Secrets, another gloriously escapist read from Jennifer Bohnet, is available to buy now.

ABOUT THE AUTHOR

Jennifer Bohnet is the bestselling author of over 10 women's fiction novels, including *Villa of Sun and Secrets* and *The Little Kiosk By The Sea*. She is originally from the West Country but now lives in the wilds of rural Brittany, France.

Visit Jennifer's website: http://www.jenniferbohnet.com/

Follow Jennifer on social media:

facebook.com/Jennifer-Bohnet-170217789709356

twitter.com/jenniewriter

instagram.com/jenniebohnet

bookbub.com/authors/jennifer-bohnet

ABOUT BOLDWOOD BOOKS

Boldwood Books is a fiction publishing company seeking out the best stories from around the world.

Find out more at www.boldwoodbooks.com

Sign up to the Book and Tonic newsletter for news, offers and competitions from Boldwood Books!

http://www.bit.ly/bookandtonic

We'd love to hear from you, follow us on social media:

facebook.com/BookandTonic

twitter.com/BoldwoodBooks

instagram.com/BookandTonic

Printed in Great Britain
by Amazon

35897443R00193